D0284514

Dead End Girls

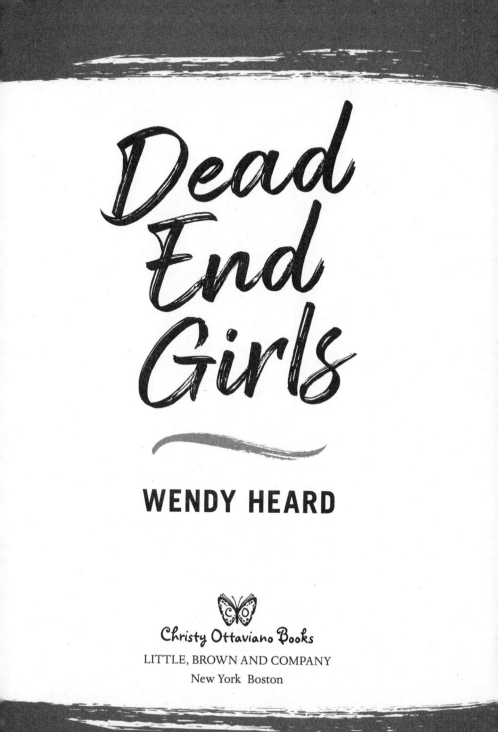

Dead End Girls

WENDY HEARD

Christy Ottaviano Books

LITTLE, BROWN AND COMPANY

New York Boston

399 7410

Christy Ottaviano Books
Hachette Book Group
1290 Avenue of the Americas, New York, NY 10104
Visit us at LBYR.com

First Edition: May 2022

Christy Ottaviano Books is an imprint of Little, Brown and Company. The Christy Ottaviano Books name and logo are trademarks of Hachette Book Group, Inc.

The publisher is not responsible for websites (or their content) that are not owned by the publisher.

Library of Congress Cataloging-in-Publication Data
Names: Heard, Wendy, author.
Title: Dead end girls / Wendy Heard.
Description: First edition. | New York ; Boston : Little, Brown and Company, 2022. | Audience: Ages 14–18. | Summary: Desperate to escape suffocating expectations and menacing families, seventeen-year-old Maude and her step-cousin Frankie fake their own deaths while on a family vacation in Hawaii, with deadly consequences.
Identifiers: LCCN 2021032557 | ISBN 9780316310413 (hardcover) | ISBN 9780316417884 (ebook)
Subjects: CYAC: Death—Fiction. | Deception—Fiction. | Lesbians—Fiction. | Gender identity—Fiction. | Stepfamilies—Fiction. | Family life—Fiction. | LCGFT: Novels. | Thrillers (Fiction)
Classification: LCC PZ7.1.H4314 De 2022 | DDC [Fic]—dc23
LC record available at https://lccn.loc.gov/2021032557

ISBNs: 978-0-316-31041-3 (hardcover), 978-0-316-41788-4 (ebook)

Printed in the United States of America

LSC-C

Printing 1, 2022

They tried to be too clever—
and that was their undoing.

—Agatha Christie, *The Mysterious Affair at Styles*

One

I RING THE DOORBELL. IT LIGHTS UP BLUE, AND A FAINT CHIME echoes inside the house.

I wait on the porch with my suitcase, scanning the dark suburban neighborhood with tired eyes. It's been a long day.

The faux-Mediterranean houses are almost identical. It's like that here: every tree the same height, probably planted on the same day, watered on synchronized timers, any misbehaving too-big or too-small trees torn up by the roots. The night air smells like jasmine, but I don't see flowers anywhere. The city of Irvine probably has air fresheners hidden in the hedges.

The door opens. My chest tightens.

She looks tired. Her long auburn hair is a little tangled, her makeup faded.

"Hey, Mom," I say.

She backs up to let me in. "It's late."

"Academic Decathlon." I bump my suitcase up over the threshold.

She wrinkles her nose at it. "Would you put that in your room?"

My room. I laugh bitterly under my breath and cross the white-tiled foyer to the carpeted stairs. As I climb, the twins come thundering down. "Maude!" yells Caden, who's in the lead.

"Maude!" echoes Andrew, chasing Caden down the stairs, through the foyer, and around the corner to the kitchen.

I shake my head at the miscreants and resume my trudging up the stairs. The heavy suitcase *thunk-thunk-thunks* behind me.

On the landing, I am confronted with Todd. My stomach sinks. He's six feet away, but I can smell his cologne. He's broad-shouldered and polo-shirted, his light brown hair parted on the side, a walking advertisement for tennis rackets.

He forces a smile. Here we go. We're having an interaction.

"Maude," he says.

"Todd," I reply. It rhymes. He grins. It's tight, almost a grimace. My skin crawls with discomfort. "I'm excited about next week," I say, just to say something. "It was nice of your family to invite me again."

This makes him beam with self-satisfaction. They're

so charitable, the Maxwells, willing to bestow their riches upon us lowly plebes. "Aw, that's fine, Maude! Glad you're coming along."

Mm-hmm. "Well, I'm gonna get cleaned up." I point to the guest room.

He steps aside. "Go to it, kid!" He trots down the stairs jauntily. What a guy.

I rush along the hall with my rolling suitcase, let myself into the bedroom, and breathe out in a huge *whoosh*. I shut the door behind me and stand there in the dark, relishing the silence and privacy.

I wasn't lying; I am excited about next week. I'm exhausted and stressed, with so many details crowding my brain it's like living inside an ant farm, but...

Wow. Next week. Is this real? Am I finally here?

I flip on the light.

It's like a hotel room. They bought this house when my mom was pregnant with the twins, and the decor is completely impersonal to me, picked out by the interior designer so as to double as a guest room when I'm not here.

This house has four bedrooms. You'd think the twins could share, leaving me with my own room, but my mom and Todd feel it's unhealthy for them not to have their individuality. I haven't unpacked since I was eleven, but no one wonders whether it's healthy for me to have all my possessions in this suitcase.

Speaking of which, I roll it to its usual spot by the dresser, squat beside it, and flip it open. I dig out my pajamas and bathroom bag, and then I reach into an almost-invisible slit in the lining and pull out a manila envelope. I open it and make sure everything is still inside. It's become a nervous compulsion to check on it daily.

Usually I'm at my mom's for seven days. On day seven, I do exactly one load of laundry, repack my suitcase, go to my dad's house (which is twenty minutes away), and repeat the whole thing. When my parents got divorced, they split everything neatly in half, including me.

But this week is different. When I left my dad's house this morning, I was doing it for the last time. We fly to Hawaii on Saturday, and a few days later I'll be dead. It will be a tragic accident.

I seriously cannot wait.

I make sure everyone is in bed before I venture downstairs for something to eat. I rummage around in the fridge, annoyed that there's kid food, stuff to make kale smoothies, and nothing else. What am I supposed to eat?

"Caden has a fever."

I jump out of my skin and whip around. My mom's behind me, looking tired, a bottle of children's Tylenol in her hand.

"Oh," I say, not sure how I'm supposed to respond. I wasn't mentally prepared for a conversation.

"Can I get the ice pack out of the freezer?" she asks, annoyed.

"*Oh*," I repeat, understanding now. I'm in her way. I step aside. The fridge is one of those stainless-steel-with-glass-doors things. It brings back memories of the ancient honker of a fridge we had when I was a kid in our old apartment in Santa Ana. I remember her and my dad moving it up the outdoor stairs on a dolly because they couldn't afford movers. I try to imagine Todd, whom I sometimes call Todd-bercrombie, attempting to move a refrigerator up a rickety concrete staircase and smile faintly.

She gets the ice pack and goes to a drawer for a hand towel. I return to searching for something to eat.

"Make a smoothie," she recommends, about to leave the kitchen.

Her smoothie comment feels passive-aggressive. As always.

My eyes flick down to her hip, where her pajama tank leaves a couple of inches of flat stomach bare. "I can still see the cherries," I say meanly, for revenge.

She whips around, trying to see the back of her hip, where two red cherries are half-blurred out. "I have five more laser treatments," she replies, defensive. "They'll come off."

"Is it going to be mom-kinis on the cruise again so Morticia doesn't see your tat?" I'm referring to her mother-in-law, the matriarch of Todd's family and a woman my mom is terrified of. Morticia inherited her husband's commercial real estate development business when he died, and apparently she runs it ten times better than he ever did. Todd has some job in her office dealing with clients, which pays suspiciously well.

Mom breathes at me for a second, clutching the towel. "Don't call her that."

"Worried she'll hear?" I look up at the ceiling. "Think she has cameras in here? You could be right. She has to keep an eye on her baby boy."

Mom shoots me a last glare and storms silently from the room. All this mental energy just to measure up to a family that builds tract housing.

I watch her go, vengefully satisfied. The slightly trashy tattoo is a remnant from her youth, when she was poor and lived in crappy apartments with my dad and me, back in the days when they were working toward the college degrees that would ultimately buy them a better life while I was going to Head Start preschool. She was curvier then, when she and I were both young, before she knew how to count every calorie and shove hours of Pilates into a jam-packed schedule. She looked a lot like me, actually, when she was my age, but from her attitude you'd think she'd been born a size 2.

Fuck your smoothie, I think, and decide to eat the boys' chicken nuggets.

As the dino nuggies warm up in the microwave, I picture my mom's face when I go missing. Will she be frantic? Will she be distracted by the need to shelter her smaller children from what's happened? I hope not. I hope she really feels it.

I eat the chicken without tasting it. I usually have dinner at one of my secret part-time jobs, but tonight I was in LA arranging a secret bank account, which is why I didn't get here till nine; the 5 freeway between Orange County and LA is no joke. I should have eaten in LA, though. I could have had tacos, and no one would have noticed my big ass while I ate except people who appreciated it.

School is a distraction. It has to be done, though. Like social media and texting with friends and taking selfies while doing stupid, mundane things that never needed to be documented—it's all part of the game.

Lucas meets me at my car, and as always I feel pangs of guilt. He's exactly what I needed: sweet, a little shy, a bit nerdy, but with a solid family and a loyal group of friends.

"Hey, Maudie." He trots toward me, backpack bouncing, and envelops me in a soft hoodie-and-aftershave hug. I return the embrace, aware we're being watched by a group that includes Deanna, a girl I made out with at fat camp (disguised as basketball camp) last summer.

"Hey, Lukie." I kiss him, which is soft and warm but not my thing. At all.

We make our way through the bright, shimmering Irvine morning. Irvine High School is something out of *Mean Girls*. The mascot is a vaquero, which is...not representative.

As Lucas and I walk to class, he tells me about a video

game thing I can't quite understand. I'm distracted. All the time I was planning, I hadn't considered how difficult this last week would be. It's crunch time now and crucial for me to act completely normal. Not one thing can go wrong. All it would take is Lucas telling the cops, "She seemed distracted, like something was eating at her," to get them looking where I don't want them looking. With this in mind, I pay careful attention to his story, laughing in the right places. At the door of his first-period class, I kiss him on the cheek and tell him I'll see him at lunch.

I exhale heavily as I walk toward my own class. Lucas is kind, and he doesn't deserve to be used like this. *Compartmentalize*, I command myself.

Deanna is in my first period, AP Government, and I can feel her eyes on me as I take my seat a few rows in front of her. I don't meet her eyes. I can't change the fact that she exists, that in dark, whispered moments with our shirts off, I confessed my total and complete gayness to her, that she is someone who could poke all kinds of holes in my veneer of perfection with Lucas. I'm riding on the hope that she won't do that to a dead girl.

I make sure every upcoming test is entered into my calendar. I take copious notes in Google Docs on my MacBook. I spend all day planning for the week after spring break, which is midterms, groaning with classmates about how I'll have to study on my trip, kissing Lucas at lunch in front of his friends, posting selfies and videos. I do these things because I am a funnel spider, and I am building my web.

Two

LAX IS A HOT MESS, AS ALWAYS, A TANGLE OF CONSTRUCTION AND crowds. Having made the harrowing journey at six a.m. despite the twins' best efforts, we finally reach the security line, carry-on bags in hand. Todd and my mom are as coiffed as always, but they're strained and exhausted; the twins are whining, and I'm not as helpful as I usually am. I'm busy second-guessing each step of my plan and mentally cataloging every item in my suitcase.

A TSA agent is examining the security line critically. She looks Todd and my mom up and down. Her eyes travel to the boys, who are trying desperately to escape, and then to me. I attempt to appear calm. What does calm look like? Suddenly I don't know. A rictus grin is stretching across my face. That's not right. That's not how normal people smile at the crack of dawn.

"Good morning, Maude," a quiet, singsong voice says behind me.

I whip around. It's Frankie, Todd's niece—my step-cousin. She's my age, and we've run into each other over the years at family events. The last time I saw her was at Christmas dinner. She has wavy, dark hair in a shaggy, collar-length cut I could never pull off. She's always wearing baggy, nondescript clothes, which is interesting; she's the oldest grandchild in this family, heir to the throne, and she slouches around, face averted, looking like she's hoping to bum a cigarette. I was honestly shocked the first time I met her, having expected a cheerleader or a Harvard-bound vale-dictorian, someone buttoned up and Pelotoned. It's not that she isn't pretty. She's got huge dark eyes, smooth, tanned skin, and almost-black hair she inherited from her mother, who my mom says used to be an Italian fashion model. It's just that she's so different from the rest of her family.

Over Frankie's shoulder, I see her dad, Todd's brother Chris, arrive with his arm around a woman I don't recognize. The adults spot each other, and a flurry of loud "Hey, mans" and "Nice to see yous" ensues.

"Does your dad have a new girlfriend?" I ask Frankie.

"New wife. Leah." She has a low, husky voice.

"I didn't know he got married. Was there a wedding?"

"Nope. An elopement." Her mouth tweaks into a little smile. "Grandma freaked out. Calls her the 'little gold dig-ger.' Won't even say her name."

"Oh, wow. That's amazing." I give the woman—Leah—another once-over. She's a good deal younger than Frankie's dad, who looks exactly like Todd but two inches shorter. She has black hair that cascades down her back and an olive complexion that's been helped along by spray tanning. With glee, I imagine my mom's discomfort; this woman is thinner and fitter than she is, not to mention younger.

"Do we hate her?" I ask Frankie. "Or do we love how much she pisses off your grandma?"

She grins, mischievous, and a dimple appears in her left cheek. "We love it. She's nice, actually."

"Get in line," the TSA agent yells at the Todds. "You need to be in line or step away."

My mom shoots her an angry-Karen look as she and Leah step sideways to continue their conversation within the confines of the line. I retreat into a nervous silence.

We inch forward, and I sneak looks at Frankie, who is quiet behind me. Stepfamilies are weird. Your parent remarries, and you're supposed to feel instantly close with this group of complete strangers. And everyone keeps up the farce; no one ever calls bullshit. Why does the fact that my mom made empty promises to Todd mean I should develop some sort of immediate, mushy connection to his golf-douche brother?

The line starts moving faster. I gnaw on the inside of my lip, repacking my suitcase over and over again in my head, reminding myself that there's no reason for TSA to search it.

They'll send it through the X-ray and be done. It's going to be fine.

"What's your deal?" Frankie murmurs, snapping me out of it. "You seem stressed."

I stare at her blankly, shocked. If she can tell I'm nervous, so will the security personnel. I scramble for a response. "I'm frustrated with my mom," I reply. She cocks her head like she's considering that. I need to get my act together.

At last we're approaching the TSA ticket agent, who looks at our IDs. Beyond him loom the shining X-ray machines and conveyor belts. My stomach is twisting around inside me, my heart pounding like I'm running a marathon.

Todd gets called up, leaving my mom to deal with the boys. Then Chris goes through, and Leah, and then my mom with the twins—she shoots me dirty looks for not helping her, even though I don't think I'm legally allowed to escort them through security—and at last it's my turn.

I take a breath to steady myself. I roll my suitcase toward the TSA agent, handing over my driver's license. As I place my boarding pass under his little scanning machine, he examines my ID. "Maude? How old are you?"

"Seventeen."

He looks at his computer monitor. "Hawaii! Nice!" He grins at me. "Lucky girl. Have fun."

The smile I give him is weak as I take my ID back and get in line for the conveyor belts. I can barely hear the din of the airport over the pounding of blood in my head. I slip out of my sneakers, set them inside a gray bin, and lift my carry-on bag onto the rolling metal casters.

Frankie appears beside me and flings down her black duffel bag. She hops around, unlacing her high-top Vans. I offer my arm, and she grips it, saying, "I always wear the wrong shoes to the airport."

Her socks become visible. One has kittens on it, and the other has sugar skulls. She shoves her shoes into a bin and catches me studying her socks. She lifts a foot to wiggle the toes at me. "You like?"

"It's a look." I push my belongings onto the belt. It's time now. Pass or fail. I need an antacid.

As I walk toward the human scanner, I try to ignore my carry-on bag. I wait in line behind a family who seem happy to be on vacation together. It's a mom, a dad, and a girl who's maybe five years old. She looks tired, and her mom is quietly stroking her hair.

The mom's gentle fingers sift through the girl's curly locks, and I all at once feel deeply sad and completely alone.

The girl is afraid to walk into the scanner, so the mom goes first, then squats down with open arms, and the daughter walks right into her embrace.

The cloud of grief fills me up. I don't know where it came from. I don't know those people. Why am I—

"Miss?" The TSA agent beckons me impatiently.

Here I go, walking into the scanner. I put my hands on my head and spread my feet apart. It revolves around me, and then I'm done. The agent lets me out, and I step aside to look for my bag.

It's still in the X-ray machine. Two agents are looking at the screen together, pointing to something.

Suddenly beside me, Frankie says, "You didn't pack your shotgun, right?" I don't answer her. I can't breathe. The edges of my vision are going dark.

And then they send my bag through the conveyor, out onto the pickup platform. I suck in huge gulps of air and step forward to grab the bag.

Nothing else stands in my way. The world is wide open in front of me.

Three

THE BIG ISLAND OF HAWAII IS A BEAUTIFUL PLACE. THE SOFT, SALTY air tickles my bare arms, and the resort carries a second set of smells—chlorine from the fake river winding through it; spa lotions from the endlessly massaged and manicured visitors; eucalyptus from the diffusers hidden all over the common areas. We come here every year, and it never fails to amaze me that Morticia spends god knows how much to travel from South Orange County to Hawaii, only to surround herself with the same types of people in the same types of buildings. As long as I live, I don't think I'll ever understand rich people, even after spending so much time around them.

The thought cheers me up because I'm not going to spend the rest of my life dealing with the likes of Morticia and Toddbercrombie. Only a few more days.

We're on the patio of the resort's most upscale restaurant, Morticia at the head of the table, Chris and Todd on either side—her eternal simpering butlers. She's a petite woman, everything about her tight and controlled. Her chin-length, ash-blond hair seems fixed, like you could poke it and discover it was a helmet, and even in this humidity, her blue linen suit is somehow wrinkle-free.

The waitress arrives with cold glasses of white wine for the adults. I study her with interest. She's in her early twenties, a pretty, tanned blond. I wonder if she lives around here.

Frankie and I are at the far end of the table, seated by the twins so the adults can talk. I'm keeping the kids quiet with a steady stream of chips and salsa. As I take a sip of my water, Caden flicks a tortilla chip across the table at Andrew, who prepares to retaliate until Frankie shoots him a look that makes him think twice.

Today she's wearing a pair of loose cutoff shorts and a green tank top. She's got a great tan going; we spent the day at the beach. She read a book on a towel, wearing a bikini I worked hard not to look at—like, we are not related in any way, but I still feel puritanically guilty checking her out— and I chased the twins around until I was exhausted while my mom schmoozed with the Todds under *I'm a tourist* umbrellas.

Frankie has interesting features. Her nose has a petite roundness to it; her thick eyebrows and eyelashes are a deep shade of brown. I never looked closely at her before, probably because she has a queer vibe and I'm afraid of setting off her gaydar. I wonder what it's like for her, growing up in this family. I know her mom abandoned her; my mother wickedly recounted the history to me last Thanksgiving, with cutting little remarks about Frankie's mom returning home to Italy to party with her fancy friends. Truly the worst family.

I keep catching myself staring at people, almost like I'm trying to memorize them. I did it on Friday at school, too. Am I being sentimental? I'm doing it again now, memorizing the way my mom looks against the backdrop of the bright blue ocean, trying to feel something that might make me change my mind.

When I look away from my mother, I realize Frankie is watching me, unruly hair tumbling down over one eye.

"What?" I ask, defensive like I've been busted doing something wrong.

"There's something different about you on this trip." She shoves her dark waves away from her face and leans her elbows on the table. "Are you going through something right now?"

"No. Why?" I look into her brown eyes, willing myself to seem truthful.

"You're still with that boyfriend? Everything's okay at school?"

I have this answer at the ready; it's the same one I've been giving for weeks. "Everything is great. We have big plans for junior prom. We're, you know, in love and stuff." My cheeks feel warm. Selling a hot queer girl this story about being in love with my boyfriend is maybe one of the more humiliating moments in the preparing-for-death routine.

She leans back in her chair and folds her arms across her chest. "I mean, you look good. Put together. Everything *looks* fine. But something's off."

I'm wearing exactly what I should be wearing: a sundress, sandals, my hair in neat auburn waves just like my mom's. None of it is what I would pick out. All of it is meant to support the story after I die: Maude was so happy, the very image of a successful, upwardly mobile teenager. I've been creating this Maude persona for so long, I don't know what it will feel like when I can just...be. I don't know what I will pick out when I'm shopping for me and not the appearance of me.

"Francesca," Morticia calls imperiously. "Come here."

Frankie groans almost inaudibly, gets up, and walks around the table to the head, where Morticia pulls her to her side and wraps an arm around her waist. Her dad has to scoot his chair over a little to make room, which squishes Leah. They hiss at each other.

"Tell us about school," Morticia says.

Frankie looks uncomfortable. "It's fine."

"Are you doing any extracurriculars?"

"Not really." Frankie is directing her words to the fork sitting on Morticia's plate. Her shoulders are slumped inward, and her right hand is gripping her left wrist. Leah leans over to murmur something in Chris's ear, a frown

18

on her face. I wonder if she's trying to get his mom to leave Frankie alone.

Morticia continues. "You should be doing as many extracurriculars as possible! It's very important for college applications that you show yourself to be well rounded. Chris, why isn't she in any sports, any clubs? This is your responsibility."

He stammers about having thought she was in some clubs, which is clearly bullshit, and then he makes his usual "I'm on my own, Mom—it isn't easy" comment, referring to his martyrdom as a single father. That is also bullshit, since I get the impression that Frankie was raised by nannies and he's never worked a full day in his life.

My mom leans over and whispers to me, "Tell her about Academic Decathlon."

"Why?" I ask.

"Just tell her!" She makes an encouraging hand gesture.

I realize she wants me to compete with Frankie and come out on top. "You're pathetic sometimes. It's sad, Mom."

She looks wounded. The words are mean and I know it. But I want to leave her with something to remember me by.

Four

I HAVE ONLY TWO DAYS LEFT TO LIVE, BUT I THINK I'M GOING TO LOSE my freaking mind. These kids are driving me nuts. "Stop jumping on the bed!" I scream at them. The small room, which is part of a suite shared with my mom and Todd, has two full beds and a couch that folds out into a sleeper sofa. My suitcase, with its precious cargo, is tucked against the side of the bed I've claimed.

They scream louder, jumping higher and higher.

"Mom!" I yell.

Nothing. The door between our rooms is closed. She's done parenting for the night.

I grab my room key and phone and slam out into the hall. It smells like stale fries and sunscreen. I sink down onto the carpet and close my eyes. I breathe deeply. Through the wall, I hear the boys jumping and shrieking.

I pull up a chess game on my phone and start playing. I love chess. I almost joined the chess club at school, but I thought that might be a little dorky for Maude's image. Plus, I had secret jobs to work, money to earn. So I play against the computer.

A thump—something hits the wall behind me, and the boys screech with delight.

I lean over and pound on the door. "Stop throwing things!"

I text my mom. **I'm not dealing with them anymore. Go discipline your own kids.**

Across the hall, Frankie's door opens and she pokes her head out. "What's going on?"

I gesture to the closed door behind me. "They're terrible little heathens and I hate them."

She smiles faintly. "Yeah, they're pretty awful." She hesitates. "Do you want to . . . hang out in my room? I'm watching *Pirates of the Caribbean.*" She says it like she's sure I'll say no.

Keira Knightley's corset immediately springs to mind. I get to my feet, collecting my phone and room key. "You may never get rid of me," I warn her. I text my mom: **Hanging out in Frankie's room. If they kill and eat each other, so be it.**

At last she answers. **Get back in there and tell your brothers to go to bed.**

Nope, I reply. **You chose to reproduce. Not me.**

Frankie steps aside to let me into her room, and I groan with envy. "You have two queen beds all to yourself. It's not fair." I plop onto the bed closest to the door. The other is rumpled and surrounded by her various possessions, including a journal she plucks off the nightstand and hides under her pillow when she thinks I'm not looking. I couldn't care less about her secret diary; I'm thinking about my own suitcase. I know there's no reason for my mom or the boys to go through it, but still, I hate to leave it unsupervised.

She flops down, grabs the remote, and jabs at it until the movie resumes. I settle back onto the bed, hands behind my head.

I wonder how Frankie will feel when I die. I hope she isn't traumatized by it. She barely knows me. If anything, maybe she'll enjoy the excitement of the police investigation. I feel bad about ruining her vacation, but she'd probably rather watch the police investigate my death than spend another week with Morticia grilling her about private school. And she'll be able to help my brothers while my mom is distracted. As annoying as they are, I'm sure they'll be upset.

On-screen, Orlando Bloom is sword fighting. I blink hard, trying to clear the tears that are suddenly burning my eyes. Why now? I guess it's the thought of my brothers' confusion and sadness. *They'll get over it*, I tell myself. *They're well on their way toward narcissistic personality disorder.*

The movie pauses. Frankie is cross-legged on her bed, and now she points the remote at me. "Okay, something is clearly wrong. Can I help? Did you break up with your boyfriend or something? Are you pregnant?"

I stare at her, struck mute. She can't think something's wrong. That could be the end of everything.

My brain races around, searching for the right thing to say.

"Sorry," I say at last. "I'm PMSing, and my mom makes me babysit my brothers constantly. I just get frustrated, you know?"

Her eyes narrow. "But why is this bothering you now? It's been like this forever."

She is way too perceptive. "It's always bothered me," I say with a forced amount of indignation. "Just because you never noticed doesn't mean it didn't."

She looks chastened. "I'm sorry."

Wow. I am such a jerk. I'm also a great manipulator, apparently. I get up. "I'll leave you alone."

"No. Stay here. I have an extra bed. Why should you have to cram yourself in with those monsters?"

I debate this. I can't see how this might work out badly for me in the view of anyone after I'm dead. A brief fantasy flashes through my head—us making out in our pj's—but I squash it flat. Absolutely not.

I find myself smiling. "Okay. Cool. Thank you."

I cross the hall to get my things, and when I beep myself into my room, the boys are gone, the door to my mom's room ajar. I tiptoe to peek through it, and my mom, Todd, and the twins are snuggled up in their king-size bed, watching TV. The kids are falling asleep. My mom makes an angry, pinched-lip face at me, and I close the door on them.

I can't sleep.

I roll onto my side and check on Frankie. She's passed out, one arm flung above her head, lips parted slightly.

I lean over and peer down at my suitcase, which is tucked between my bed and the wall. I touch it with my fingertips. I compulsively want to check on my things. I want to pull all the documents out and confirm they're in order. I want to turn on the secret burner phone and make sure it has service.

I should actually do that last one. I haven't tested it since we've been in Hawaii, and I need to make sure it works.

Stealthy, I slip out of bed, unzip one corner of my suitcase, and slide my hand inside. I know exactly where to look, in the side pocket near my underwear, and I pull the little black Android phone out along with its charger.

I do a quick check of my papers by feel, pulling them out and shuffling through them, counting them. I return the documents to the suitcase and close it.

I keep an eye on Frankie's motionless silhouette as I tiptoe to the bathroom and pull the door shut behind me. I leave the light off, sit on the closed toilet lid, and power on the phone.

Blue light glows. I plug the charger in by the mirror and connect it. The phone buzzes in my hand, an unfamiliar logo flashes, and then I'm at the home screen. I open the browser and practice Googling something. The results load slowly, but then it works.

Okay. This is great. I'm in business.

I pull up Google Maps and make sure the directions work. I spend a few minutes confirming that the maps I need are downloaded, and I check on my plane reservations. I have an island-hopper flight booked to Honolulu out of Kona, and then I'm joining a cruise that's passing through Hawaii en route to Bali. I figured if anyone suspected me of running away, they'd search flights, not old-people cruises. I check the charge on the phone; it's at 98 percent. I have two portable batteries anyway. I'm ready.

I power off the phone, roll up the charger cable, and push open the door.

Frankie's bedside light is on. She's leaning against the wall next to the bathroom, examining something in her hands.

I gasp, jumping out of my skin. "Jesus Christ," I breathe. I press a hand to my chest. "You startled me. Sorry, did you need to use the bathroom? Go ahead."

She looks up from the thing in her hands. "Candace White? Did you make that name up, or did they give it to you?"

My heart plummets.

The words feel like they echo, like she's saying them over and over again. *Candace White. Candace White.* That's my fake identity, the one I'm using to get to Bali.

I drop the phone. It lands soundlessly on the carpet.

I'm a statue. My head feels hollow.

And now I see what she's holding, the thing I've been hiding and cherishing and checking on every day. It's Candace's passport, the metallic United States icon shimmering in the faint light from under the hallway door.

She flips it aside, and I see she has my British passport as well.

Oh my god.

She says, "Your British name is Elizabeth Lewis? That feels very Victorian." She flips to the third thing in her hands. "And a Hawaii driver's license for Candace. Interesting. Is this a wig you're wearing in all these pictures? What's the plan? You're going to leave Hawaii as Candace and, like, start a new life in England as Elizabeth?"

It's over. I'm caught.

"You went through my stuff?" I say at last. I sound so small, like a child who's been betrayed.

"How long have you been planning this?" she asks. "How are you going to get away?"

"But why did you go through my suitcase? How did you find those in the first place?"

She lifts one eyebrow. "I saw you shitting yourself when your bag was going through security. And you've been trying to hide it, but something is clearly wrong. I've been worried about you. I thought you had a weapon in there or something; I thought you might be planning to hurt yourself, make some dramatic gesture to get back at your mom,

26

and damn, I guess I was kind of right. You're running away? This is awesome."

It's done.

The sheer size and weight of the blow is making me actually dizzy.

Two years of planning, thankless jobs, all my hopes... gone.

I sink down onto the floor. I stare at the burner phone, discarded on the carpet. I don't need it now. I may as well throw it into the ocean. A small, desperate voice in my head tries to bargain: I could bribe Frankie, beg her to keep this a secret....

But no. If she knows what I'm doing, eventually she'll tell someone. That's always been my rule with this: If even one person figures out my plan, I have to be willing to walk away. I can't leave behind anyone who knows I'm still alive.

Working toward this plan has given my life meaning and purpose. How am I supposed to go on? Do I return to Irvine and go back to faking a relationship with Lucas? The thought makes my stomach turn over with nausea.

Frankie squats down beside me. "Hey, don't freak out. I'm not going to rat you out." A moment of silence hangs between us, and then she says, "I want in. Take me with you."

Five

I STARE UP AT HER. THE INITIAL SHOCK AND SADNESS ARE WEARING off, and anger is setting in. "You want in? You want to *come*?"

She sits down on the carpet. "You don't understand. I need this."

"*I* don't understand?" I laugh, the sound dry and bitter. It's the most ridiculous thing anyone's ever said to me. My entire life has been a secret for the last two years. The amount of detail involved in this plan—*I* don't understand?

I need to remain calm. I need to think.

"You can't come with me," I tell her. "I can't just conjure you a fake passport. And now that you know about this, I can't go, either."

She protests. "We can steal a passport. We're in a resort."

"You can't just—" It's such a ludicrous suggestion, that

we can simply steal a passport and expect it not to get traced, like there aren't computers and tracking systems.

She says, "I know you can figure it out. You're smart. Like, *smart.*"

"You don't—know—me," I say between clenched teeth, so quietly intense that she winces. Ignoring this, I demand, "Why do you want to come with me? Why would you even want that?"

She looks down at her hands. "I have some problems," she replies quietly.

"Problems," I repeat. I'm so angry, I can't think straight, and then the comedy of it overwhelms me, and I release that dry, choked laugh again. "Your life must be really hard. How many bedrooms does your mansion have?"

Her dark eyes flash. I haven't seen her angry before. "Last I checked, you weren't exactly destitute yourself."

I jump to my feet and march to her bed. I throw her pillow aside and grab the journal out from underneath it. "Let's find out why you're so *unhappy*," I say.

She's already on me, clawing for the journal. "Give that back!"

I shove her off. "You go through my stuff, I go through yours. Doesn't feel good, does it? Now, let's see." I flip to a place at random, where her messy scrawl, barely legible, fills the page.

She attacks me from behind, grabs the journal, and snatches it away. She chucks it across the room and says, "You think I care if you hate me? You think I'm not used to it?" Her voice is rough but controlled. "Either you figure out a way to bring me along, or I'm going to take your fake passports to our parents and tell everyone what you've been planning."

My whole body is my heartbeat, furious and hurt.

I can't give her what she's asking for. The only place I know how to get a good fake passport is in Los Angeles, where I got mine.

Something occurs to me: You don't need a passport to travel from Hawaii to the mainland. You just need a driver's license.

I remember the waitress. Hmm.

"You have an idea," she says. "I can see it on your face."

I sit on the edge of the bed and stare at the wall, considering. "I can see one way. Maybe."

"Tell me."

"If we go back to LA, we can get you a passport from the same place I went to. We just need to find you a driver's license for the flight to California." Warming up to my subject, I turn toward her. "Here's what you don't understand. It's not just about getting out of the country. You need a real identity, one you can use to apply for jobs, for school loans."

"But you have one."

"Mine took weeks."

"But you know where to get it."

"Yeah, but..." I sigh. "I mean, I guess we could go back to my guy in LA. But it's expensive, Frankie. And what would we do while we waited for weeks?"

Her eyes are alight with hope. "We'll figure it out."

I hate that statement. It implies a level of carelessness, a lack of planning, that I'm not comfortable with. I am a spider. Spiders build webs.

She says, "So we go back to LA. We get me a passport. And then what? England?"

I meet her eyes. "You can go wherever you want. But you don't come with me. And you don't get caught. If you're found out, they'll know we're both alive. You'll ruin everything."

Her eyes are gleaming. "Okay. Yes. That's fine."

"You're serious about this? You know how hard it will be to start all over? You won't be rich anymore. You'll have to support yourself working in—"

She waves that off. "I don't care. I'm in."

"Think about it, Frankie. Your dad, your grandma, your mom in Italy—are you ready for everyone you've ever known to think you're dead?"

"Yes. I'm ready."

I let myself fall back onto the bedspread and look up at the ceiling without seeing it. We're silent for a handful of minutes. I consider my situation. She's only asking me to delay my plan by a few weeks. I'd rather wait a few weeks to get what I want than give it up altogether.

She lies back next to me and cradles her head in her hands. "I always thought you were super shallow. Just another type A, overachieving future executive. Instead, you're this, like, criminal mastermind. It's amazing how little any of us actually knows the people in our lives."

I swell with pride. That impression she got was the result of years of careful curation. "I don't know what I thought of you," I reply honestly. "You're always quiet. But you definitely weren't what I expected. I thought you'd be, like, a mini-Morticia. Maybe a cheerleader, or maybe academic, but not..."

She snorts. "Not what?"

I shake my head. "I don't know."

"Neither do I." She rolls onto her side and rests her head in her hand, studying me. "You didn't answer my question. How are you going to get away?"

"I'm going to fake a boating accident. They'll think I'm dead."

She lifts her eyebrows. "Very nice. There will be no body because you washed out to sea."

"That's the plan."

"And then you'll use this Candace ID to get back to... Well, why do you have an American and a British passport? And what's with the different hair in each one?"

"I needed an interim identity to get me off Hawaii, and then I was going to switch IDs in Bali to get to London. I didn't want the same person to show up in the security cameras in different airports; hence the hair. Frankie, this is not some makeshift plan. There's so much to consider. Are you sure you want this? How could you possibly have had time to think this through?"

She smiles at me, and her eyes glisten like she's going to

cry. "You don't understand. This is, like, divine intervention. I'm in. I'll do whatever it takes."

Her tone is so intense, it makes me feel uncertain all over again. For the first time in as long as I can remember, I don't know if I'm doing the right thing. Should I just pull the plug?

I can't bring myself to do it. If there's a way to move forward, I want to try.

I sit up. "All right. We need to get organized. I was going to fake my death tomorrow morning, but I think we'll want one extra day to prepare. That's okay, though, since I'm not bound by the cruise I was going to take..." My voice trails off.

It hits me. All the chest-filling excitement and dreams of vaulting off into the bright blue Pacific, to great adventures in the wide-open world, come crashing down on me. We're going back to LA. Treacherous, smog-filled LA.

Six

FRANKIE AND I SIT SIDE BY SIDE AT THE LARGE TABLE ON THE PATIO of one of the resort restaurants. It overlooks the fake, chlorine-scented river that makes a circuit through the Mediterranean-style hotel buildings. Below, families cruise the Listerine-turquoise water in boats that look like something from a Disneyland ride. I try to imagine how pristine and glorious this island must have been before all this. We're a scourge.

I return to my crepes. I'm trying to eat them at a normal speed, not wanting to betray my nervousness. Frankie is quiet beside me, powering through a plate of bacon and eggs like she's being forced to eat it at gunpoint. Across the table, the twins are getting rowdy. Morticia shoots Todd a steely look. This isn't the peaceful brunch she'd hoped for, apparently.

Todd leans over the boys, his face dark. "Knock it off," he growls, and they shut right up, eyes wide. That's his default parenting move: intimidation. Morticia nods approvingly. I feel a twinge of guilt at leaving my brothers here with the Todds. But then, these are their people. This is where they belong.

Frankie's dad is in quiet conversation with Leah, who has a mimosa clutched in delicate, manicured fingertips. Morticia shoots a disapproving look her way, and I stuff a large bite of Nutella crepe into my mouth, eliciting a similar glare from my mom. She looks haggard after a single night of parenting, and I picture the coming days with glee. As I think this, Caden screeches wildly and flings a strawberry at Morticia. The whole table gasps as the berry connects with her pale yellow sweater, leaving a pink splotch and tumbling to the carpet.

Silence.

Frankie's face is frozen in an expression of pure, rapt delight.

My mom has gone completely white. She looks like she's witnessed a murder.

I wipe my mouth with my linen napkin, set it on the table, and push my chair back. "I think I'm going to leave you guys to it. Frankie, want to get out of here?"

"Yep." She sets her napkin beside her plate and stands up.

My mom's eyes snap to me. "Where do you think you're going?"

Standing, I look down at the whole dysfunctional lot of

them. Whatever I say now will be repeated to the police, to the newspapers.

"This is a mess," I say, gesturing to the twins, to Morticia's stained shirt. "Good luck. We're going exploring."

I turn to leave, and as I go, I hear Morticia digging into them. I smile, satisfied.

Frankie walks jauntily by my side. "That was awesome," she says.

Resentment boils inside me. I don't want to chat like we're friends. I hate that she's here with me at all. But there's work to be done, and the task ahead needs my full attention, so I put the lid on my anger and try to focus.

In Frankie's room, I obsessively check and recheck the belongings we're taking with us. We'll both carry our usual purses, and I'll have a large beach bag for everything that will come into death with us. We can't bring much: a few outfits, my fake passports and driver's license, a small toiletries bag, and a travel-size umbrella. We'll have to buy new clothes, new devices, new everything. I have money saved for that, of course, but I'll need to stretch it twice as far to pay for Frankie's stuff, too.

"You're already wearing your bathing suit, right?" I ask Frankie.

She lifts her T-shirt to show me her bikini top, something I didn't need to see. I hold a hand up to stop her. "A 'Yes, Maude' would have been fine."

She notices the two snorkels laid out next to my bag,

alongside two inflatable life vests, and asks, "Where did you get those?"

"I stole them this morning."

"Where?"

"From a little surf shop next to the corner market. I did it when I went for a walk."

She picks up a snorkel and turns it over in her hands. "How did you steal them?"

I tell her the truth. "I've been practicing shoplifting. I figured it was a skill I might eventually need."

She raises her eyebrows. "You think of everything."

I take the snorkel from her and stuff it into my bag. "You promise you're a strong swimmer?"

"Sure. I took lessons."

I study her. I'm waiting for some sign that she's going to screw this up. At last I nod. "All right. Let's do this." I take one last look around the room, my eyes landing on the kitty-printed suitcase. I feel a twinge of remorse. That suitcase has been my traveling home. I'll never see it again.

We leave the room, the large beach bag bumping my side. The resort is huge; the idea is that you can stay here and never have to experience the inconveniences of a real place. I watch a pair of housekeepers wheel a cart full of cleaning supplies down the hallway, and I wonder where they live.

It's beautiful out in the sunshine, the air moist and

warm. I lead Frankie out of the resort, onto the coastal highway, and turn left, heading for a popular beach frequented by many tourists from neighboring hotels. We walk silently, cars *whoosh*ing beside us, past hotels and restaurants and surf rental shops. We're walking parallel to the beach, and I trace the shoreline in my mind, comparing this route to the map I have memorized.

Ten minutes later I steer Frankie onto a small street that's crowded with parked cars and tourists with beach gear piled into bags and baskets. After two blocks, we come to a walkway between resorts that leads to the sand. With the beach in view, I pull her aside.

"You see how this is a cove?" I ask, pointing to the rocky formations to the left and right of the softly rolling water filled with kids and families.

"Yeah," she replies, eyes invisible behind her sunglasses.

I point to the left. "We're going kayaking in the next cove over. It will look like we got lost at sea, but we'll actually just swim underwater here, to the next cove. We need to find a place to hide our stuff so we can get it afterward."

She grins. "After we're dead."

"Exactly."

We hunt around; it's a challenge, with so many people and so little privacy. We end up choosing a spot off the walkway, behind a waist-high retaining wall, under a decorative hedge. I hate—*hate*—leaving the bag here. I stuff it under the hedge and stand there, shifting my weight from foot to foot, worried.

"What's wrong?" Frankie asks.

"If someone steals this, we're screwed."

"No one will steal it."

"You don't know that." I step back, looking at the spot from various angles.

"No one can see it," she reassures me.

"Okay. Let's do it."

Taking our Maude and Frankie purses with us, we head back to the sidewalk, sweating our way past sunburned tourists, and turn right on the coastal highway. I lead Frankie into a water-sport rental place called Island Aquatics.

Inside, it's cool and shady. The walls are full of hanging surfboards, kayaks, and scuba gear. A pair of guys our age is organizing paddleboards against the far wall. A golden retriever watches them, head tilted to the side like it's critiquing their progress.

The one nearest me calls, "You here to rent some gear?"

"Yes, I have a reservation. My mom called it in."

He takes us to a counter and looks me up in the computer. Frankie and I give him our real driver's licenses, and he makes a forgettable comment about California. He asks for our paperwork; we had to bring forms signed by our parents. I forged them, of course, badly on purpose; it will all be part of the investigation. We're a couple of teenagers misbehaving, and it will cost us our lives. Maybe this will even draw criticism of my mom; she was always forcing me to be the grown-up, never caring for me the way a mother should.

I doubt it. She'll be all white-lady fragility in the interviews. The media will eat it up.

The kayaks weigh a thousand pounds, and we have to carry them in the sweltering sun down the street, to the beach, and onto the scorching sand. This beach is even more packed than the one where our bag is hidden; I picked it because of its popularity. It's wall-to-wall families with paddleboards and boogie boards. Purses slung across our shoulders, paddles dangling over our arms, we heave the kayaks awkwardly onto the sand, where we stop and slouch over them, gasping for breath.

"This kayak weighs more than I do," Frankie wheezes.

"I know. I can't believe they expect us to carry these." My hands are like claws from gripping the edge.

"Where do you want to go?"

"Over there." I point to the right, at the north end of the cove. "We're going to get caught on those rocks."

We heft the kayaks and drag them for what feels like forever, and then we drop them side by side on a vacant patch of sand. Frankie crawls around to sit beside me, and we look out at the turquoise water.

"You know faking a death is called pseudocide," I tell her.

"I didn't know there was a word for it."

"It's not technically illegal in itself. But we're going to commit a lot of crimes in the process. Using a fake ID, theft, leaving the country under false identities."

She nods.

I pinch the side of her sunglasses and push them up onto her head so I can see her eyes. I search their dark brown depths for answers. "Why do you want to do this, honestly? How do I know you aren't going to panic and chicken out?"

"I won't."

"Maybe not today. But what about a year from now? Ten years from now? Imagine—you grow up, you get married. You can't even tell your life partner the truth about your childhood. Are you *sure*?"

She leans back on her kayak and puts her head in her arms. "I'm sure."

I sigh heavily. I wrap my arms around my knees and look out at the ocean. This is my last chance to call the whole thing off. After this, there will be no going back.

It feels reckless to move forward. I'm breaking my own rule. Frankie will always be a liability. Anytime, anywhere, she could make a single phone call and destroy me.

"Hey. Maude." Frankie puts a hand on my arm.

"What?" I don't look at her.

"If you could see into my life, if you could see what's waiting for me if I go home, you wouldn't be worried at all. You'd know I have no other choices. I know you don't care, but you're saving me."

She's right; I don't care. I want to save myself. But her words ring with truth. I feel my resolve solidify.

So it's moving forward, then, even though it's the wrong thing to do.

Seven

FRANKIE GETS HER KAYAK INTO THE WATER EASILY, WAITING FOR A break in the waves and gliding it into the shallows. Mine keeps tugging away from me, and I curse and inhale salt water. At last my kayak is floating in calm swells that reach my waist.

"You okay?" Frankie asks, unruffled, tanned and natural-looking in her bikini. I try not to feel self-conscious; I don't love having to spend so much time in my bathing suit in front of her.

"I'm fine," I reply, gritting my teeth. "Let's get in."

A pair of boys our age splashes past us, tossing us flirtatious grins as they throw a football between them. I wait for them to go away so they don't witness my clumsiness, and then I squirm into the kayak in the most unathletic, uncoordinated way possible. Frankie puts one hand on each side of the seat, lifts her legs up like she's a freaking Olympian, and settles herself in easily. She grabs the paddle. "Let's do it."

I tell her, "We should paddle around a little so people see us."

"Roger that." She moves forward with powerful strokes, and I follow her grumpily with much weaker ones.

We pass families and kids playing, paddleboarders drifting around in the translucent water, and, as we get farther out, the occasional kayaker. Soon we're alone in deeper water, headed for the north point of the cove. The current is calm out here. The people on the beach are specks now, all the boogie boarders and inner tubers tiny little ants. It's scary being this far out. I feel like it's possible we may come to the exact death we're faking. Wouldn't that be poetic justice?

Frankie paddles as close to me as she can. "Should we go for it?"

"I think so." My heart is pounding hard.

I pull two inflatable life vests out from beneath my knees and hand her one. "Don't blow it up all the way; we need to be invisible from the shore, so we have to stay mostly underwater."

We inflate them halfway and put them on; they're small, just enough to keep someone from drowning, not the big, ugly kind we left behind with our bags and towels. They'll find those when they find our stuff, which will support the narrative: Two teenagers cared more about looking good than being safe and came to an unfortunate end.

I hand Frankie her mask and snorkel, and we pull the masks on over our noses. "How do I look?" she jokes, nose and eyes insectile behind the clear plastic.

"Amazing." My voice is nasal and unrecognizable.

She grins. It's ridiculous in the mask.

We're near the north end of the cove now. From here I can see the next cove, our destination. It's almost identical to the one we came from, separated by a rocky outcropping the guys in the surf shop had warned us to avoid. "And don't go out to sea," they'd said, laughing.

I swing a leg out of the kayak, then the other. It tips, plopping me on my face in the water, and I struggle to right myself. When I get my head out and spit salt water from my mouth, Frankie is giggling a few feet away. She's treading water effortlessly. Her hair isn't even wet.

"You okay there?" she asks.

"Shut it." I fix my snorkel. "It's important that no one see us swim away from the kayaks. We need our heads to be underwater. Hence the snorkels."

"Do you even know how to swim, though?" She's still teasing.

"Shut *up*." I laugh despite myself. "Let's go."

I bite down on the snorkel and go under. With the mask on, I can see the whole huge ocean beneath us, and my heart races even faster. It's deep and clear, and suddenly we're passing over a coral forest I hadn't known was there. In the depths, fish and turtles weave slowly through the coral's pale fingers.

As we approach the other cove, the rocks get closer and

closer, and I realize the outcropping extends much farther than it seems to from the shore. I want to stop Frankie and ask her if she thinks we should swim out to sea more, but I don't want to put my head above water and be seen entering the cove. I decide to stay the course. Even if we have to swim right above the rocks, it's fine. We're going slowly, and we'll be careful.

Kelp reaches up to brush my legs with its slimy, cold little tentacles. A turtle floats by, totally unconcerned with our presence. We're basically in the kelp now, and my breath is coming in scared little pants, metallic through the snorkel. We have to keep going. We're almost there. I focus on the beauty of the schools of fish below me, the magic of the turtles.

The fish and turtles change direction, scattering away. We must have scared them. They hadn't seemed to notice us, but maybe—

Something dark swims below, in the depths. Something big. It undulates languidly, body like a snake, graceful and liquid.

Shark. A big one. At least ten feet long.

My heart knocks madly against my ribs.

I pull my head out of the water, as if not seeing the creature will save me somehow. Frankie surfaces beside me. She pulls the snorkel out of her mouth. "What—"

Doggy-paddling hard against the pull of the current, I open my mouth to ask Frankie if we should go back. My foot kicks against something sharp. I cry out into my snorkel.

"What's wrong?" she asks.

"Shark! Down there! Big. I think I hurt my foot." I put my face in the water to look. Sure enough, I cut my foot on a high finger of coral. Dark blood trails off into the water around it. I pull my face back up and say to Frankie, "It's bleeding." I hardly recognize my voice.

"We need to get into shallow water." She's deadly serious, in a hurry.

"Let's go." I bite down on my snorkel and we resume our course, swimming hard. I'm doing a steady crawl now, not trying to stay underwater. Frankie is beside me. The shark is a dark shape slithering through the coral below us. Is it closer to the surface now? I can see striations of color on it that I couldn't before. It's mottled, maybe gray and tan or tan and white. I can see its tail, its fins, the distinctive shape of its head. It's *so big*.

My foot hits something again, and I cry out into the snorkel. I'm injured, for sure, but I keep swimming, blood trailing into the water behind me. Frankie taps my shoulder and indicates that we should turn right a little, heading into shallower waters with the rocks on our right. I follow her, my foot aching and stinging. She's a strong swimmer, and I can't quite keep up, but she glances back every few seconds and adjusts her speed for me. I don't see the shark anymore, but it can't be far away.

I see the sandy bottom underneath Frankie; we're almost to the shore. I keep swimming, my breathing hot and shallow.

It's all a blur of motion, my limbs cold and shaking, my heart pounding violently, breath hot and wet in the snorkel.

But the sand is close, and then we're touching it with our fingertips, and at last we're tumbling out of the soft little waves onto the shore. We rip off our masks and lie on the sand, panting. There aren't many tourists this far down the beach, where the rock-lined water is choppy.

After a minute I say, "We need to go. We can't let people see us here." My voice is shaky.

"Let's look at your foot first."

I sit up and examine it. The top is badly scraped, blood seeping out of the raw wound. There's nothing to be done about it right now.

"Come on," I say, standing up on unsteady legs. "Let's go. Take off your life vest."

She obeys and I follow suit. I roll the vests up and tuck them under my arm.

My foot throbs and burns all the way through the sand, and we duck our heads, hurrying past tourists. I pray silently that they don't notice us, don't remember us later. The hot sand burns like fire on my wounded foot. I clench my teeth to keep from screaming.

We reach the walkway, and I pull her behind the retaining wall. I snatch my bag out from underneath the hedge. First, I settle a cheap blond wig on my head and fit a baseball cap on top of it. The hat saves me the time of pinning it to my hair. Then I hand Frankie a baseball cap. She arranges her hair underneath it, and I give her a baggy navy-blue men's T-shirt and a pair of men's swim trunks. I stole this outfit from the poolside lost and found. She pulls on sneakers while I wiggle into a big, frumpy sundress.

"Shit," I murmur. I've left bloody footprints along the walkway, little crescents where the blood has trailed down to the arch of my foot.

"You should clean your feet before putting shoes on," Frankie says. "Come on, this is a resort. I'm sure there's an outdoor shower by the pool." She gives me a little smile. "We escaped a shark. A *shark*. That is so metal." She holds her hand up for a high five, and I pat my trembling hand against it.

"We're dead," I say. "How does it feel?"

She tugs on her baseball cap, pulling it sideways a bit. "It feels better than living has for a long, long time."

Eight

THE BUS STOP IS JUST UP THE STREET ON THE HIGHWAY, AND WE wait in anxious silence. I wonder if anyone has discovered the kayaks yet. If so, I wonder if they've called the police, or if they'd shrugged them off as tourist carelessness. I imagine it could take anywhere from an hour to a few days for our disappearance to be connected with the abandoned kayaks. It depends on how alarmed people get when they find them floating in the ocean.

By the time the bus arrives, other people are waiting, too. They look like service workers: women in maid uniforms, a man in a stained coverall, and a pair of women in black pants and polo shirts with a resort logo on the breast. I'm surprised. It's a ninety-minute bus ride to the other side of the island. Do people really do this commute to work every day?

We pay with exact change and sit toward the back. No one looks at us. My foot is on fire, and I try to take my mind off it by watching the scenery out the window. We turn away from the coastal road and head inland, on a highway that cuts straight across the island.

I know the basic topography of the Big Island from previous trips here; this resort is a favorite of Morticia's. But I've never driven across the middle, and I'm surprised by the landscape. It's a lot like California, grassy and flat, with green hills in the distance. We pass miles of open fields occasionally populated by cows. At one point, the brown grass turns green, with barbed wire around the tops of the high fences, and Frankie whispers to me that she read there are cannabis farms around here.

I find myself studying her profile, partly obscured by the baseball cap. Everything about her is a liability.

The motel I chose online is a dingy, weathered building a half mile off the bus line in Hilo, in a humble area with run-down houses and chickens pecking along the edges of the streets. It's kind of a relief to see a part of Hawaii that doesn't look like a resort owned by billionaires. While I check in, Frankie heads to a nearby corner store to get first aid supplies for my foot.

At the front desk sits an older man with a gray ponytail and a handlebar mustache. The reservation is under my Candace identity, and the guy barely glances at the photo as he logs me onto the computer. My heart pounds nonetheless. He hands me an old-fashioned door key and tells me my room is around the corner and up the outdoor stairs. I wait outside for Frankie, my mind flitting through all the things that could have happened to her, until she appears, a paper bag clutched in her arms.

The room is what I expected from a cheap motel, based on movies and TV shows. The bedspread and carpet are burnt orange, the old TV duct-taped together. I take a shower in the yellowed stall and wash my foot with soap, getting all the sand out of the wound, which stings like crazy. I wrap a towel around myself and sit on the toilet to coat the gash in the Neosporin Frankie bought. Exhausted, I pull the ugly sundress back on and give my hair a rub with the towel. Good enough.

I check the time. Four o'clock. They could potentially be in search-and-rescue mode by now. I get the burner phone out of my bag, sit on the toilet lid, and Google "teenagers" "missing" "Hawaii." Jackpot: a YouTube video on the KILA news website here in Hawaii. I press Play.

A young woman with a serious expression stands in front of the beach we'd disappeared from. "A search is underway for two teenage girls from Orange County, California. They have been declared missing from a beach near Kona, where they went kayaking this morning. Their kayaks were found floating offshore, and their belongings were located on the beach with their life jackets, suggesting they were not wearing life vests while kayaking. Visitors are cautioned to always wear life vests when enjoying water sports, even if they consider themselves good swimmers."

I stop the video. My foot throbs in time with my heartbeat.

It worked.

Hearing the exact narrative I engineered recounted from the mouth of this newscaster does something to me. I feel bigger, like I'm standing on top of a mountain, looking down on the kingdom I built.

Adrenaline floods my extremities, and my hands go tingly. I forget all about the pain in my foot. I am dead. I'm *dead*! Two years of planning, and I'm dead, dead, dead.

I open the bathroom door. "Frankie," I call. "Come see this."

Frankie appears in the doorway, a little drowsy, like I've woken her from a nap. "What's up?"

"Check this out." I hand her my burner phone.

She watches the video with wide eyes. "It totally worked," she says.

I lay towels down on the sink and floor, and I get the little toiletries bag out of the beach bag. Seeing the few articles of clothing we have reminds me that we need to go shopping.

I'll have to pay for all of Frankie's expenses, not just clothes and luggage. Food, transportation, a burner phone...

She hasn't even mentioned it. People who grow up rich have no concept of other people's money.

"Have you thought about where you want to go after

LA? After you have your ID?" I ask as I pull out a little container of hair dye. I set it on the towel-covered sink along with a small pair of hair scissors and some latex gloves.

"I was thinking Mexico City."

I raise my eyebrows, impressed. "Good choice."

"It seems big enough to disappear into, and it's far away." She sits on the closed toilet and watches me comb out my waist-length hair and segment it neatly into six pieces. Just below my chin, I tie off each segment with a small rubber band. She says, "You're doing the Elizabeth haircut? The bob?"

"Yep. And then I'll put the Candace wig on top. But this way, if someone sees me without my wig, I still don't look like Maude." I make the first snips above one of the rubber bands. The long, slim ponytail detaches, and I set it on the sink. The less mess, the better. I don't want housekeeping to find any traces of this project.

"Are you dyeing it?" she asks, examining the little bottle of hair dye I brought.

"My hair isn't naturally this color. It's dark brown. I've been lightening it for years so I could grow out my natural color in England."

She lifts her left eyebrow. "Diabolical."

"My freckles are fake, too. Every few days, I put them on using a template and a marker. No one's ever noticed."

Her jaw drops. "You're kidding me."

I can't help but smile as I snip off the next little ponytail. It does feel great to be able to brag about all my scheming.

Once I finish cutting, my hair is neck-length and a bit shaggy. "You want some help evening it out?" she asks. "I cut my own hair. I've been doing it for years."

"Sure."

She takes the scissors from me, and I sit on the toilet lid while she works. She's wearing her sports bra and jeans, and I find my eyes drawn to her tanned stomach, to the line of her throat. I wonder vaguely if we could sleep together, just as a convenience. I've only ever made out with one girl—Deanna, at camp—and I can't imagine I'm going to find myself alone with another probably queer girl anytime soon. I've never had sex. I'd been avoiding the topic with Lucas, trying to drag it out as long as possible. Would it count if I had slept with him? I wouldn't have enjoyed it.

While she snips innocently away, I mull over the concept of virginity. I decided long ago that it was fake news. I hate the idea that a virgin is something you can be, like a part of your identity. Sex is something you *do*, not something you *are*.

She steps back to examine me critically, and her own hair flops wavy over her left eye. She pushes it aside impatiently.

I feel sad all of a sudden. I'm still Maude. As long as Frankie's here, Maude can never be dead. I'm just boring, vanilla me, Irvine me, nothing me. It makes me hate Frankie all over again, that she's diminished this moment into just another memory in Maude's vapid life.

"Done," she says, stepping back. I stand and examine myself in the mirror. I'm impressed. It looks professional. I turn my head back and forth. "I love it," I tell her. "I look like a different person."

"It's very sixties," she replies, examining the back. She snips a couple of strays. "What should we do with mine? Chop it really short?"

I consider. The chances of finding her a passport with a corresponding haircut are nil. We'll be going for a vague resemblance, not matching haircuts. And short will make her look the least like Frankie, since Frankie's thick hair is so recognizable. "Yeah. I think short is best if you don't mind," I say.

"I've been dying to cut it, but my dad and grandma would—" She shakes her head. "Just, yes. Cut it all off."

"I don't have clippers, so it's not going to be, like, a perfect cut."

"It's fine. I don't care."

I find a YouTube tutorial and get to work, parting her hair and sectioning it according to the video's instructions. What's my plan, anyway? Look for someone who resembles Frankie and pick her pocket, steal her license from her purse?

I guess, yeah. Not great, but that's the plan.

What if it takes days—weeks—to make that happen? Every additional hour we spend in Hawaii is a giant risk.

"What are you thinking about?" Frankie asks, meeting my eyes in the mirror. "You look stressed."

I pause the video. "I'm worried we won't be able to find you an ID, worried we'll get caught."

"We can do this."

I narrow my eyes at her. How can I resent someone this much when I know her so little? "You don't know that."

"How long have you been planning this whole thing? It must have taken a long time. You found somewhere to buy fake passports that look real. You saved up money."

"Two years."

"We can do this."

Anxiety and anger are snakes in my gut. As they slither and wrestle with each other, I set my mind to planning. I can't let self-doubt slow me down. The bridge has been burned; there's no going back.

Nine

WE LEAVE THE MOTEL AND HEAD FOR THE CENTER OF TOWN, WHERE I hope we'll find bars and restaurants. I've never tried pick-pocketing, but if a place is crowded enough, I can imagine sneaking my hand into a purse and grabbing someone's wallet.

Frankie's dressed in her baseball cap, jeans, and a baggy men's T-shirt; with the short haircut I just gave her, she's serving butch-hot extremely well. It's possible she might pass as a guy from afar, which further helps our disguise. I'm in my blond wig-with-hat, cutoff shorts, a jersey, sneakers, big hoop earrings, and hot-pink lipstick. I even brought a little container of fake-tanning lotion, so I'm now an interesting shade of tan orange. Frankie hooted with laughter when I came out of the bathroom in this getup.

As we walk across the street to the bus stop, I tell Frankie what I'm picturing. "When we find someone, you'll have to distract her. Talk to her. Be funny. Whatever. I'll need to get the wallet out of her purse, quickly find her license, and slip the wallet back in."

"Why not just take the whole wallet?"

"Because I don't want her to notice right away. If I just take the license, she'll think she misplaced it. But the whole wallet—she'll report her license stolen, and it will get flagged at the airport."

"Smart," Frankie replies.

"I know." She snorts, laughing at me a little. I don't care. I know I'm smart. What's the point in false modesty?

Despite our carefully made plans, by nightfall we've been wandering around for hours without luck. We've been through shops, restaurants, cafés, finally ending up at the beach just south of the main drag. My foot hurts so bad, I don't think I can stand it another minute. I'm going to have to buy Advil or something.

I sit down on a concrete bench facing a rocky beach below us. Frankie sits next to me.

I breathe deeply, in and out.

"Your foot?" she asks.

I nod.

The air cooled off when the sun left the sky, and the nighttime ocean is purple charcoal. I try to focus on all the corduroy ripples and take my mind off my burning, throbbing limb.

Frankie says, "Take your shoe off. I'll change the bandage."

I glare at her, but then I concede and pull my sneaker and sock off. She peels the bandage back while I wince. When the fresh air hits the exposed skin, the sting of cold makes me gasp in a breath.

"Hmm..." She's turning my foot this way and that.

"Let me see." I pull the foot away from her and hold it up to the light. The scrape is raw and red, which I expected, but it looks puffy, and the area around the wound looks pink. I'm pretty sure that's bad.

Frankie's already gotten the Neosporin and bandages out of my purse, and she uses hand sanitizer before spreading the ointment onto the wound. "I can do that myself," I protest, feeling weird with my stinky bare foot in her lap.

"I may as well make myself useful." While she unwraps a new bandage, I navigate to Google and search for more news stories about us. A flurry of headlines populates the results.

"We're all over the news," I tell her.

"Really? Let me see." She finishes with my foot, and I pull it out of her lap so she can sit next to me and look over my shoulder.

I click on a video titled "Family Begs for Help from Local Boaters as Search Continues for Missing Teens." In this one, my mom is delivering a tear-filled plea to the camera, asking people to help them find Frankie and me, since the Coast Guard is only deploying a few boats to search for us. They cut to a spokesperson from the Coast Guard, who explains that, given tidal currents and ocean conditions, they're highly unlikely to find us. The newscaster ends with commentary I don't pay attention to. I rewind the video and pause it on my mom's face.

She looks how I imagined: pale. Shattered.

I search myself for the feeling I've been chasing for two years. I examine my mom's face, waiting for it to trigger some chemical reaction.

Frankie's too close. She's intruding on my moment. I can't feel anything except annoyance.

The sky rumbles, and it starts to rain.

I extract the little umbrella from my purse and pull my sock and shoe on. "Let's go back to the motel," I tell Frankie. "I'm calling it for today." The failure weighs heavy on my shoulders as she pops open the umbrella. This island is closing in on us with every passing news cycle. We need that ID, and we need it fast.

Ten

WE'RE A MILE FROM THE MOTEL, WALKING THROUGH A RESIDENTIAL neighborhood, when I hear the faint sounds of dance music ahead. "You hear that?" I ask Frankie.

She nods.

We keep walking, or limping, past low-slung houses set far back from the curb. We're just a few houses from the upcoming busy street when I hear the music again.

"Hang on," I say, putting a hand on Frankie's arm. I listen hard.

It's upbeat: hip-hop, pop, something with a strong bassline.

I follow the sound. It's coming from a house across the street, on the corner of the six-lane thoroughfare, up a long driveway that's packed full of cars. I notice the street's shoulders are full of cars, too, something you wouldn't expect with expensive houses spaced apart like this.

"It's a party," I tell Frankie, excited. A car passes us and heads up the driveway. The driver is a college-age girl with blond hair and a deep tan. She's laughing with the people who are squeezed in with her, and she tosses us a smile as she slows to advance toward the house.

I grin at Frankie. "Time to make some new friends."

She shrugs. "Sure, let's crash a party."

I examine us critically. We're a bit bedraggled from the rain. "Come here," I say, leading Frankie from the driveway and into a bank of trees. I comb through my tangled wig with my fingers. "Take your hat off and straighten out your hair. Let's get some lipstick on. You're wearing a tank top under that shirt?"

She removes the cap. This short haircut suits her. She finger combs her hair to the side while I dig around in my purse for my makeup bag. I hand it to her and pull my jersey off, leaving me in a camisole and shorts, and she applies lipstick using the compact mirror. Finished, she hands me the makeup and takes off her baggy shirt. She's wearing a tight black ribbed tank underneath, and I force my eyes off the shape of her body.

I roll our shirts up along with Frankie's cap and tuck them into my purse. "I'm Candace," I tell Frankie as we start walking up the driveway. "Do you have a preference for names?"

She considers. "Gia."

The music gets louder as we get closer. Houses look different here, lower to the ground and with sharper corners, a type of architecture I've never seen back home. This house is encircled by a deep porch, where a number of surfboards are propped. The front is lined with sliding glass doors, most of which have been left open to accommodate the crowd. The light spilling onto the porch is a soft golden hue, and partygoers are packed inside and scattered across the lawn. Behind us, a pack of guys is headed up the driveway, laughing and talking loudly.

"What do you think this is?" Frankie asks, raising her voice above the music. "Someone's parents out of town?"

"I think they're too old for that. I'd guess a group of people rents this place, and it's a party house."

We're at the sliders now, surrounded by people. Inside, the furniture is worn out, the house messy and disorganized. The smell of weed hangs heavy over the crowd.

"Let's find something to drink," I tell Frankie. "We'll blend in better. Don't get drunk, though. Don't even get tipsy."

"Roger that."

I lead her through the house, sliding sideways between people. The weed smell gets stronger the deeper we go inside, where it mingles with the scents of cologne, beer, and sweat. People are dancing in the living room, girls and guys grinding against each other. It's too loud to talk, so I motion to Frankie that I'm heading toward the kitchen.

Sure enough, there's a keg in the kitchen, where people

are eagerly pouring beer into red cups. We get in line, and I search for girls who look enough like Frankie to fit the bill. The tan skin isn't going to be a problem; in fact, I'm starting to feel optimistic about our chances.

When it's our turn, I realize I don't know how to work the keg. I grab a couple of red cups off the nearby counter and fumble with the little hose and nozzle.

"Need some help?" a nearby girl asks.

I look up gratefully. She's a pretty Asian girl, around twenty years old. "Sure. Thank you."

She takes the nozzle from me and fills my cup, then Frankie's. She's part of a group of friends I noticed in passing when we entered. In their group is a brunette just about Frankie's height. I tell the helpful girl, "To be honest, I hate beer."

She grins. "And the beer at these parties is always the grossest kind, right?"

"Totally." She looks like she might leave, so I say, "I'm Candace. This is Gia."

Frankie grins winningly. "Hey."

"I'm Madison. Nice to meet you."

I tell her, "We came to meet a friend here, but I don't see her anywhere. It's so typical. She probably left with someone and forgot to tell me."

She laughs. "We all have a friend like that."

I roll my eyes, but I'm smiling like I'm remembering our imaginary friend's antics.

She gestures with her beer to her own group. "Come meet my friends. We'll adopt you."

"Hey, thanks!" I give Frankie a smile. She winks at me. We follow Madison to where her friends are gathered around a little counter-height bar table in a corner of the dining room.

"Hey, guys, I made new friends," Madison yells over the music when we approach. They turn their attention to us. "This is Candace and Gia." She points us out as she says the names. "And this is Ivy." Ivy is the brunette. I get a better look at her now, and I decide, yeah, her ID would probably work. She and Frankie are a similar build, similar height, both brunettes with brown eyes. My heart beats faster. Now to figure out how to get inside her purse.

"This is John—he's from San Antonio," Madison goes on, and from the way she looks at him, I guess they're in the very early stages of dating. John is tall and broad-shouldered, clearly a dude who spends time in the gym, wearing a barely-there tank top that provides a lot of information about his armpit hair. John gives me a once-over, and a smile that tells me he has noticed my ass and approves.

Madison doesn't miss the look he gives me; she shoots me a little glare like it's my fault somehow.

"And this is Nathan," Madison continues unhappily. "He's from Santa Barbara."

Nathan is hanging back, obviously shyer than his friends. He's got light brown hair that's a bit shaggy and wears clothes that look performatively thrifted. I would place a thousand-dollar bet that he's a vegan. "Hey," he says, the word lost in the music. His eyes land on Frankie, whose black tank top hugs her in ways that make my eyes wander in her direction, too.

"You want a drink?" John asks me, despite the fact that we're already holding drinks. Madison steps away from me, almost like she's reeling back in anger. Not good.

I look to Frankie for help. She's frowning, clearly picking up on the same things I am.

To John, Frankie says, "I already got my girl a drink." She smiles at me in a weirdly sweet way.

It takes me at least two seconds to catch on. "Right. Well, Madison did," I answer, returning the fake smile.

She kisses my cheek. Her face is warm and soft. "I'll see if I can find something that isn't beer. I know it's not your favorite. Be right back?"

"Okay."

I return my attention to the group, who are giving me a range of looks. Madison and Ivy are recalibrating; the guys are in various stages of not understanding and being vaguely excited.

"What?" I ask, playing dumb.

"Are you...?" Ivy gestures back and forth between where Frankie was standing and me.

"Are we what?"

Madison says, "Are you together?"

"Oh! Yes! I'm sorry. I thought that was clear."

John's eyebrows rise, Madison seems to exhale five breaths of relief, and the group returns to whatever conversation was going on before we arrived. I learn they're all students at the University of Hawaii at Hilo. Madison and Ivy are from Texas and Ohio, respectively. I find it fascinating how far from home they are.

Frankie reappears with two new red cups that she says are rum and Cokes but are actually just Cokes, and we join in the chatter. Madison is our friend again, and Ivy is doing everything she can think of to retain Nathan's attention while he sips his beer in mostly moody silence.

Eventually we all end up on the dance floor, my foot aching and burning with every movement. I'm deep in thought about Ivy's purse. It's a small bag she wears across her body. There's no way I can get inside it without her noticing. I wonder if she's the kind of girl who likes to go to the bathroom in a group and if there's any potential opportunity for thievery in that scenario.

"What are you thinking about?" Frankie yells in my ear, looping an arm around my waist. "You're, like, the worst fake date ever. You're barely even dancing."

"Shut up. My foot hurts." I can't help but laugh. "I'm trying to figure out how to get into Ivy's purse."

"I've been thinking about that, too." She pulls me a little closer and puts her other arm around my waist, too, which is a bit more than I was ready for. I don't know where to put my hands, so I loop my arms around her shoulders lightly. She just dances away like this is no big deal, seeming to enjoy the music. My hands creep together, at last resting lightly on the soft, prickly back of her head. It would be so easy to pull her face toward mine. Could I? It wouldn't have to mean anything. It could just be something to do.

She pauses her dancing. "Sorry. I can tell this is weird for you."

I shrug, stiff. "It's fine." I have to say it into her ear, which brings me in proximity to her neck. My chest feels tight.

She pulls back, examining my face. "You okay?"

I nod, but I must look like something is wrong. I can't put my Maude face back on, and I don't know how to be Candace or Elizabeth yet. This face I'm making must be something else, something raw, something I don't want seen.

She says, "I'm really sorry. I didn't mean to out you. Pretending to be a couple seemed like a good way to keep Madison on our side. And we'll never see these people again, right?"

The words echo inside my head, along with the music. At last, I repeat them. "Out me?"

"I'm so sorry."

She's known this whole time? Somehow she could tell? She knew me as Irvine Maude, girlfriend of Lucas. I did everything I could to keep a lid on this. Am I that gay, where she could tell after meeting me just a few times?

I should be in Bali right now. I shouldn't even *be* Maude anymore.

I feel my face close down into a hard, mean expression.

"You ruin everything. You know that? You fuck everything up, Frankie."

She reels back like I slapped her. My throat aches, my eyes sting, and I wish I could pull the words back into my mouth. But they hit their mark. She steps away from me, and the intimacy between us is broken.

Good. That's what I deserve.

Eleven

"I'M SO DRUNK." I LAUGH, FAKE STUMBLING BEHIND FRANKIE ALONG a cracked sidewalk in the warm rain, away from Nathan's car. Apparently he's the group's designated driver; he's barely been drinking, unlike Ivy, Madison, and John, who are completely wasted. It's a busy street, cars and trucks *whoosh*ing past, splashing rainwater onto the sidewalk. The pain in my foot is like background noise, loud and sharp every time I take a step.

"Shh," Madison warns, but then she starts giggling. She slips and almost has to sit down. Ivy grips her arm, and their laughter is high and wild.

John grabs Madison's house keys, pockets them, and picks her up, tossing her over his shoulder. She and Ivy break into hysterics, and so does Frankie, who's doing a good job at pretending to be wasted. We're carefully avoiding each other's eyes, though, the mood between us tense.

John turns off the sidewalk onto a little walkway that winds between the darkness of close-packed trees and bushes. Beside me, Frankie walks into a spiderweb and sputters as she thrashes away from it.

Ivy and Madison live in a private little cottage tucked behind a larger house, completely surrounded by trees, vines, flowers, and palms, paid for by their work in food service. Spiderwebs glisten all through the greenery. Nathan sneaks up on me as I'm in the shelter of a giant palm, examining a particularly spectacular web at the center of which nestles a fat arachnid.

"Orb weaver," he says in my ear, making me jump.

"Oh," I reply, not sure what to say. He stares at me a beat longer than is comfortable, and I slip away to the cottage with everyone else.

It's a one-bedroom with a hodgepodge of furniture that gives it a homey, bohemian feel. Ivy grabs a couple of towels from the hall closet and tosses them to us, and we remove our shoes and dry off as best we can while giggling drunkenly. Rain taps down on the roof, a cozy, metallic sound.

John produces a pipe and a baggie of weed from his pocket, and Ivy brings a bottle of vodka and one of guava juice from the kitchen. Madison turns on the TV, and everyone pours themselves drinks and starts passing around the pipe. I keep a nervous eye on the screen, worried a news story will come on featuring Frankie and me, but they're streaming a reality show about celebrities on a cable channel, and I reassure myself that there won't be local news. I don't think. I hope.

Frankie and I are sipping just-juice, but we're pretending to be as drunk as everyone else. We fake inhale from the pipe John passes around. Nathan, who didn't drink much at the party, takes long, deep hits, his eyes going bloodshot after the first few.

After a while, John and Madison slip off to the bedroom, leaving us in the living room with Ivy and Nathan. They're too messed up to do anything but stare at the TV, and eventually they fall asleep, Ivy on the couch, Nathan on the recliner. Ivy manages to still look pretty while asleep, but Nathan's mouth is hanging open, head lolling, and he's snoring.

I gesture to Frankie. "This is it," I mouth. "Come on." We get up and tiptoe into the adjacent kitchen.

"Now what?" she whispers.

"Keep an eye on them." I gesture toward the sleeping people in the living room. "I'll find the ID."

I pad silently around the apartment, looking for the girls' purses, filling slowly with dread as I realize they must have stashed them in the bedroom, which is now very much occupied.

I tiptoe across the hall and press my ear to the door. Frankie stands behind me, looking back at the living room.

Silence.

I calculate how long they've been in there. An hour?

I turn the handle, grimacing as it squeaks, and push the door open a few inches. In the dim light of a side lamp, Madison and John are passed out in one of the two small beds, snuggled together under a sheet, clearly naked.

I slip inside and shut the door behind me. There are only a few pieces of furniture amid the mess of clothes on the floor: a small desk without any drawers, two nightstands, and two dressers. I don't see a door for a closet.

Their purses have to be here somewhere. Why couldn't they just toss them on the kitchen table like normal people?

I search the messy floor on my hands and knees. I find clothes, more clothes—god, these girls have a lot of clothes.

I see the purses. They're thrown together on the floor by a nightstand.

I crawl across the tiles. A rustling above me; someone moves under the covers. I freeze, panicked. There's nowhere to hide.

It quiets. The person settles.

I peek up at the bed. It was John, rolling over. His face is six inches from mine.

Mentally, I curse Frankie. This is all her fault.

I lie flat on the floor and open what I think is Ivy's purse, but when I get the wallet out, I find Madison's ID. I chastise myself for misremembering and grab the other one, pull the wallet out with shaking hands, and exhale a sigh of relief when I see it.

Ivy Samantha Balbuena. I say a brief prayer of thanks over the Hawaii driver's license and slip it into my bra. Carefully,

I put the purse back exactly where I found it and army crawl across the floor like I'm in some sort of action movie. I push through the door, stand, and close it gently behind me.

Frankie and Nathan are face-to-face in the kitchen. Nathan has his phone out, and Frankie looks stricken.

They turn toward me in unison. Nathan says, "Hi, Maude."

It's like a gut punch.

He waves his phone at me. "Social media is blowing up about these girls from Orange County, missing in Hawaii. Apparently there's a reward. I just need to find..." He starts clicking through things on his phone.

I see what he's doing. He's looking for the number to call. He's going to turn us in.

I leap across the hall and snatch the phone out of his hands. "Slow him down!" I hiss to Frankie, worried about waking up the others. I bolt for the front door, intent on destroying his phone, aware it only solves the problem for a minute. He'll just borrow one of the others'. I know that, but I sprint outside into the rain. Behind me, I hear a clatter and a man's angry voice. Frankie must have tackled him on the walkway. I emerge onto the sidewalk. Traffic *whooshes* by on the busy street; it's not as late as it feels, only midnight or so. I hear voices behind me. Nathan is closing in, Frankie right behind him, grabbing at his shirt.

A gap in traffic is coming. I run into the street, narrowly missing a scooter, which honks nasally at me. I cross the opposite lane, just a few feet from getting squashed by an

SUV. I hope I've lost Nathan, but then a new gap in traffic opens up, and he sprints out into the road. I run faster, trying to come up with some way to destroy his phone. I could throw it out into the street, hope a car runs it over—

A squeal of brakes, of tires. A *crack*.

I turn. Nathan is nowhere to be seen. An old pickup is angled across the right lane. On the other side of the street, Frankie stands with her hands to her mouth.

The pickup straightens out. The driver guns it, spraying water, and drives away.

Where is Nathan?

I turn toward the street, and then I see him. He's crumpled on the ground between two parked cars.

The truck hit him.

I step off the curb and crouch down beside him, blood roaring in my ears.

He's bent backward unnaturally. His eyes stare up at the sky, raindrops collecting on his cheeks.

He's dead.

I step back, trip over the curb, and land on my butt in a puddle.

His phone is clutched in my hand. My fingerprints and DNA are all over it.

Frankie appears beside me, staring down at Nathan with huge, horrified eyes.

I get up and stand next to her.

"What do we do?" she asks. Her voice is quiet through the rain and road noise.

I feel like I'm frozen, like my brain has short-circuited. I keep thinking of all the things in that apartment that we touched, all the people who saw us, what it will be like to face our family if we get caught.

If the police find Nathan dead, they'll take statements from everyone, ask to see ID. Ivy will notice that her license is missing. And of course she and Madison will tell the cops about the two girls they met tonight.

"Maude?" Frankie shakes my arm. "Do we run? Do we call the police?" She's soaked, her hair plastered to her head.

"We do not call the police," I tell her.

We need time, at least a few days. We need to get off the island before Nathan is found.

Oh god. I know what to do.

"Frankie, listen to me." I turn to her. "I can make this work, but it's bad. How much do you want this? Because we can turn ourselves in now, and they probably won't send us to jail. We can pretend we ran away and changed our minds. Is that what you want to do?"

She shakes her head, lips set in a grim line, raindrops trailing down her forehead. "I can't go back." It's the first time I've seen the same desperation in her that lives in me.

I nod. "Okay, then. We can fix this."

Hilo is small by my Southern California standards. It doesn't take long to leave it behind, even in Nathan's old car that won't go as fast as I want it to.

We're quiet on the drive. Frankie looks straight ahead, out the windshield at the rain and darkness. Even with the heater on, our clothes are sopping wet, and we're both shivering.

Frankie's eyes dart to the rearview mirror every so often. She's worried about getting caught in a routine traffic stop. So am I.

This is the most dangerous thing I've ever done. If we get pulled over on this drive, it will be so much worse for us than if we had left Nathan in the street. It will be the end of everything.

The city falls all the way behind, leaving us on a long two-lane highway that stretches invisibly to a darkened horizon—the side of the island we disappeared from. All around the road, an endless expanse of fields and grass makes me feel lost and very, very small. We're retracing our steps, following the bus route in reverse. Was that today— or technically yesterday? It seems like a year ago.

I glance sideways at Frankie. She's silent, tense. I return my eyes to the darkness of the road and say, "I saw a news story. That's how this started."

She stirs. "What do you mean?"

"I was in eighth grade. The story was about this woman who tried to fake her own death on a cruise ship." I falter, feeling suddenly self-conscious. I never talk like this, not to anyone, not ever. I clench my hands at ten and two on the steering wheel. "Anyway, she was sloppy. She got caught. She didn't think through all the details."

"Like what?"

"Well, for one, she didn't have a good fake ID. She had a stolen passport. For another, she didn't consider the forensics. She tried to make it look like she was murdered, but she messed it up. And she did it in American waters, so our own FBI was brought in to investigate. She did so many things wrong."

"And that's what gave you this idea?"

I nod. "I saw all the things she should have done differently, and I started researching. Anonymously, of course; never in traceable ways, don't worry."

"Oh, I wasn't."

"I looked into the kind of ID that would really work. You can't use a fake one. There are professionals who take over the identities of people who die. I got hooked on the research, and at some point, I was like, I'm really doing this."

After a long moment, she says thoughtfully, "That cruise ship lady had to have a reason, right? You don't just randomly fake your own death."

"I think she was running from an abusive husband. Something like that."

"And what's your reason?"

I'm feeling confessional. Besides, we're in it together now, for real. There's no going back. "Let me tell you what my life is like," I say. "On Sunday night I arrive at my mom's house with my suitcase. No one wants me there." She starts to protest, but I say, "You want the villain origin story or not?"

"Sorry."

My voice doesn't crack, but my throat feels tight. "If my mom could do it all over again, she wouldn't have me. She'd wait for Todd so she could breed little mini-Todds. I make things messy."

We sit in a brief, tense silence.

"The next week, I take my suitcase to my dad's house. He's remarried, too, but he and my stepmom don't have kids. They're almost never home. One time my dad forgot I was coming, and he had a whole houseful of guests. I had to sleep on the floor. When I asked him how he could have forgotten about me, he said, 'Out of sight, out of mind.'" I shrug. "They wish I didn't exist. Now they get their wish. And so do I."

"Maude." Her voice is soft.

I slice a hand through the air. "Don't start. We have a dead body in the trunk; it is not the time to go soft."

We drive on, haunted, buffeted by the wind, checking over and over again out the window for cops. I'm glad for the edge of fear. It's a reminder, like the pain in my injured foot: We're here. We escaped. We're paying the price.

My burner phone *dings* in the console—the navigation. I turn right onto an unpaved lane and kill the headlights. According to the map, this is a wildlife preserve. It seems totally deserted.

After a few minutes of violent bumpiness, I pull off to the side. "I think this is good," I murmur, as though I'm worried about being overheard.

"Okay." Her voice is hushed, too.

"Quick." I pop the trunk.

We jump out of the car. The rain has stopped, and the humid night is alive with the rustling of grass. A warm summer smell rises off the ground.

"Don't touch him," I remind Frankie. "DNA."

"I know."

Using the shirts we stripped off at the party as makeshift gloves, we pull Nathan's feet out of the trunk. I get him by the shoulders and heave, and he drops with a thick crunch onto the gravel. We pull-roll him off the road, into the grass, and then we take turns dragging his feet while the other takes his wrists. Our breathing is the loudest sound in the darkness. My foot is burning and aching, but the pain is overshadowed by horror. Fifty feet from the road, we find a natural dip in the ground, and we roll him into it. We pull grass and weeds out of the ground to cover him. We haven't said a word.

At last we're standing over him, catching our breath. I shine the flashlight from my phone downward, inspecting our work. You can't see him at all.

"This is good, right?" I check with her.

She nods. Her eyes, glinting in the dim light of the moon and stars, are huge. "Let's get out of here."

We walk back to the road, crunching and swishing through dead grass, and then we start running, wild and irrational, away from Nathan and what we just did. As Frankie throws herself into the passenger's seat, I jump into the driver's side, put the car in drive, flip a U-turn, and head back the way we came. We bump onto the highway, returning to Hilo to abandon his car somewhere it won't be noticed for a while.

The darkness whips past. My heart is racing, like my favorite song is playing even though there's nothing but the sound of the wind.

We don't belong on this island. We don't even exist here. We're no one, going nowhere, untraceable, untamable. And now I wonder if we're truly wild, because what we just did isn't what Maude would ever do. It's not even what Elizabeth would do. I'm someone unexpected, with new and dark potential, and I feel...

Alive.

At last.

IN FRONT OF MY BATHROOM MIRROR, I TUCKED THE green polo shirt into the slacks I wasn't supposed to wear and examined my hair with a critical eye. It was getting too long. I smeared some gel on my hands and messed it up until it covered part of my face.

A wave of nausea rushed through me. I put a hand on the sink to steady myself and waited for it to pass. The wave rolled in and then out, leaving little rivulets of stomach cramps behind.

As it receded, I lifted my face and looked at myself in the mirror. I had gone pale, and my eyes were dark and shadowed.

I'd been feeling this way a lot lately, sort of swoony and sick to my stomach. Maybe I had an iron deficiency or a hormone imbalance.

Or perhaps I was experiencing an immaculate conception. The folks at my Catholic school would be delighted.

I straightened up and shook off the anxiety that always came with the stomach problems. I was running late to school. I grabbed my almost-empty glass of chocolate milk from the counter and took a tentative sip. My stomach didn't protest, so I finished the rest. I made a mental note to get a physical soon. Looking at the milk-streaked glass in my hand, I wondered if I'd developed a lactose intolerance. That would suck; chocolate milk had been my signature drink since kindergarten.

I liked routines. They were something to depend on.

I gathered my belongings into my backpack, hunting through the mess on my floor for my phone. As soon as I opened my bedroom door, I heard them.

"Babe? Don't forget your charger again," Leah called from the kitchen, her voice echoing around the foyer. Our house was one of the pretentious Mediterraneans everyone has here, with a big open entry that all the upstairs and downstairs rooms let out into.

"Got it!" he yelled back from their bedroom.

I hurried down the stairs, gripping the wrought-iron banister in case the stomachache returned, and found Leah in the kitchen. She was dressed for her job at a high-end real estate brokerage: a hot-pink blouse and black skirt that hugged every curve of her body. When I entered, she tossed me a smile. "What are the chances that he actually has the charger?"

"Very small." I opened the fridge to get more chocolate milk, and she poured egg whites into a skillet.

My dad came trotting into the kitchen. "Hey, girls," he said, dropping a kiss onto Leah's mouth. Every time he did this, she smiled like he'd awarded her some kind of medal. It was sweet, actually. I was glad he'd found somebody, and the house wasn't so empty since she'd moved in.

I drank my milk quietly while they chatted about their evening plans. They were going to some fundraiser dinner that required them to get dressed up, and Dad needed to remind his assistant to pick up his suit at the dry cleaner's. He worked at Grandma's real estate development company, doing what appeared to be courting potential clients and mostly involved him hanging out on the golf course and schmoozing around country clubs in LA and New York. It seemed like Grandma had tried to make him useful; I got the sense he had been a partyer in high school and college, while his brother Todd had fulfilled all her dreams of a perfect son.

I put my glass in the dishwasher. "You guys will be home late?"

Turning the stove off, Leah said, "Chris, give her money for dinner." He dug his wallet out of his pants, and she winked at me. I returned the smile weakly; everything felt sort of underwater. Dad palmed me a twenty along with a joke about "not spending it in the wrong places," and I scooted for the door, leaving them to their egg whites.

My car, a vintage Mustang I'd gotten for my sixteenth birthday, was waiting for me in the driveway, a puddle underneath it. I'd told Dad the day before that it was leaking fluid, and he'd said he'd have his assistant get it fixed. Clearly, he'd forgotten.

Whatever. I was running late. I patted the hood affectionately, hopped in, and started the engine, relishing the growl it made as it caught. I loved my Mustang. I liked to sing "Mustang Sally" to her when no one was listening.

I was about to back out of the driveway when my stomach lurched and the interior of the car went sideways. I pressed a hand to my mouth, worried my milk was going to come up.

I rested my forehead on the steering wheel. The car spun around me.

After a minute the wave passed, leaving me fuzzy and floaty. Emotionally, I felt great all of a sudden, like the world was a safe and happy place. The feeling of well-being didn't line up with the dizziness, and there was a racing in my heart that didn't make sense with any of it.

School. Right. I'd call the doctor during lunch.

I put the car in reverse. My vision seemed normal. I didn't think driving would be a problem.

Our house sits on a hill in Coto de Caza, in a neighborhood I like to call *La Doucherie*. I drove down the hill toward school, passing McMansions and McBiggerMansions. When I braked at the first stop sign, my car came to a shuddering halt and made a loud squealing sound in protest.

I decided I'd just take Sally to the mechanic myself. There was no point in waiting for my dad to become a responsible parent. If you wanted a plane ticket for a spontaneous trip to Europe, my dad was your guy. If you wanted someone to remember your annual physicals or make sure your car had oil in it, you were better off writing a letter to Santa.

The next part of the drive was a steeper decline, winding down to the lake, where I would turn right. Sally picked up speed, and I braked gently to correct.

It made that same shuddery, squealing noise, and then my foot went straight to the floor. The brake pedal had lost all resistance.

I pressed it again, harder, and again. The car was rolling faster and faster, hurtling toward the upcoming stoplight. I tried again. The brakes did nothing.

I pulled the emergency brake as hard as I could. It made a horrible, dry squeal, and I was rocketing toward traffic now, the lake approaching fast.

I yanked the steering wheel to the left, trying to force a U-turn back up the hill. I was going too fast; I spun out, tires screaming. The driver's side lifted, and the car launched into a roll. The world spun. *Crunch*—glass—my shoulder jammed against the door—the airbag blew open in my face—

Silence.

The first thing I heard was my own breathing. I was panting, wheezing, sounds of pure fear.

My vision was obscured by the pillowing sheet of the airbag. The spinning in my head slowed, and I felt gravity pulling me down to the right. I looked left out the window and saw the sky.

I felt myself start shaking, an earthquake inside me, and then the dizzy nausea was back with a vengeance. This wave was from a deep, dark ocean, and it carried fear and death with it. It was going to wash me away completely.

Thirteen

IT'S THE DEAD OF NIGHT, AND WE'VE PARKED NATHAN'S CAR ON A lonely street on the farthest side of town, near the beach. I'm hoping the cops will think he came here for some early surfing or a swim and got swept away.

I turn the car off and pocket the keys. "Wipe everything down," I instruct Frankie. "We can't leave any fingerprints."

"With our shirts?"

"Yeah."

She grabs them from the back seat, and we use them to wipe in silence. I keep an eye on her progress, but she's doing well, being careful. After a few minutes, we get out, and I wipe down the exterior handles and the trunk. I return the shirts to my purse and straighten my tangled wig.

We make eye contact. "Done?" she asks.

"I think so."

We set off, walking north. My foot is on fire, and I'm limping. The night is soft and quiet around us, but I feel exposed. My heart hasn't stopped pounding since we were in the apartment. We're not just runaways anymore. We're fugitives.

"Are you okay?" Frankie murmurs as we pass through a dark, quiet residential area.

"Are you?"

"Weirdly, I am. I guess it hasn't sunk in yet." She's been calm this whole time, actually. I trace our days together, going back to the resort, and I realize she's just a calm person. Interesting.

It takes us two hours to walk back to the motel. By the time we let ourselves into the room, I could cry with relief to be off my feet. I sit down and remove my shoe, then the sock, revealing the bandage, which is bloody and brown red. I peel it off, whimpering, while Frankie watches. The wound is oozing red-clear from the slashes.

"We'll need to get this looked at first thing tomorrow," she says.

I shake my head. "I can go to a clinic in LA. Not here. Hilo is too small."

I disinfect the wound and leave it to air-dry while I look up flights on my burner phone. We don't mention Nathan. We don't mention anything. It's changed, the vibe between us. What we've done hangs heavy in the room, hovering in the air like an apparition.

While Frankie showers, I find us a flight leaving

tomorrow afternoon from Hilo to Honolulu, followed by a nonstop to LAX. It's expensive because it's last-minute, and I cringe as I use my prepaid Visa to book the flight. It's almost two thousand dollars.

There's no time to think about that. I have to move forward, visualizing what comes next: me in London, living my new life.

Showered and in our pj's, the dark room creaking with nocturnal Hawaii sounds, we lie on our separate sides of the queen bed, each of us silent but awake. At last I break the silence.

"Tell me why you wanted to come with me."

There's a long pause, almost like I didn't say anything, but I wait her out. When she answers, her voice is low and rough. "The same reason you did this whole thing in the first place. I wanted to escape my family."

"There's more to it." I roll onto my side, facing her.

She turns her head to look at me. Her dark eyes shine, sparkling in the faint blue light coming from the neon sign outside the curtained window. "I was going to die if I stayed."

"Why?"

She resumes looking at the ceiling, her hands clasped over her stomach. "Just because."

I sigh heavily, getting my head comfortable on the pillow. "Well, your dad is a narcissist. So I imagine he's emotionally unavailable. Your mom is off in...Italy?"

"I think so. At least, she was the last time I heard from her. Haven't talked to her in a couple of years."

"Why did she go?"

"I think..." She frowns. "My dad was the typical horrible trust-fund kid, partying his family's money away in Europe and stuff. She was this girl he met in a club in Italy, a spoiled kid herself. She was excited to come to America and, you know, do the whole American money thing, but then she got bored of it, and she didn't fit in with Grandma at *all*."

"I'm kind of loving imagining Morticia's face when your dad brought your mom home. Is she really beautiful?"

"Oh, ridiculously. Thick, long black hair, big dark eyes, skin a little darker than mine, like something out of a movie. She's one of those people who are so pretty they don't seem real."

"And European, so I'm picturing her topless on the beach in Newport and stuff."

She laughs. "That's pretty much the vibe. She was miserable, I think. So she went home. And, like, a kid would be dead weight, right?"

"But there's more than that," I persist. "This isn't enough to convince you on a dime to throw your whole life away."

"There's always more," she replies, her voice blurry with sleep.

I prop myself up on my elbow. "You said you'd have died if you stayed. Were you thinking about..." I hesitate. This is touchy. "Were you having... Do you mean you think you were going to hurt yourself if you stayed?"

She opens her eyes and gives me a tired smile. "You cannot let this go, can you?" I glare at her, and she sighs. "I wasn't going to hurt myself," she answers, rolling over so her back is to me.

"So what, then?"

"Good night, Maude."

If I were any less exhausted, I wouldn't let it go. Resigned, I roll over to go to sleep. For a minute, I realize that we're in the same bed, and my fantasies about kissing in our pajamas run rampant around my brain, but then they morph into nightmares and I'm deep into a dark and heavy sleep.

Fourteen

THE HONOLULU AIRPORT IS WARM AND HUMID, NOT AIR-CONDITIONED as aggressively as the ones in California. Everything looks a little more casual than LAX: no gleaming stainless steel juxtaposed against endless construction projects and angry, screaming commuters. People here move slower, laugh more, and the airport is decorated with images of orchids and ocean.

Frankie waits beside me in line for security, unrecognizable and nervous. The long brown wig I found for her this morning is cheap but the best I could do in a pinch. She's wearing a black beanie so you can't see the tragic fake roots. I'm in my blond Candace wig and baseball cap—equally tragic—and we're both wearing contouring makeup that changes our features a bit. It wouldn't hold up against facial recognition software, but we don't have to worry about that until we fly internationally out of LAX. I'm prepared, though; I have some special-effects makeup in my bag and learned how to do subtle nose and cheekbone extensions a few months ago.

I'm starting to feel back on my game again. What happened with Nathan is in the past. We're going to disappear into one of the biggest cities on Earth. We just need to get there.

A large family behind us in line distracts me from my worrying; the mom is trying desperately to control her kids while the dad fumbles through their bags, red-faced. When it's my turn to go through security, I show the TSA agent my Candace driver's license and boarding pass. He frowns at my license, and I hold my breath.

He brings it closer to his face. He's in his mid-fifties, a no-nonsense man with hair turning gray at the temples. "You're from San Diego?" he asks, reading Candace's address.

"Yep." I try to keep my voice normal.

"You go to college?"

"Yes, at UCSD."

"What's your birth date?" he asks, looking me up and down.

"March seventeenth," I reply, suddenly hoping Frankie memorized the birthday on her stolen ID.

He nods, scans the ID and boarding pass, and hands them back to me. "Have a safe flight."

I breathe out a huge sigh of relief and move through. Frankie is behind me, and she hands her ID to the agent. I'm putting my bag on the conveyor belt and removing my shoes, and I can't hear the conversation between them. It seems to be taking longer than it should.

I look Frankie over, scanning for any errors. She's got the small wheeling suitcase we bought and filled with a few days' worth of clothes this morning. She's tanned and looks like a college girl on vacation. I can't see any holes in my plan, unless she does something stupid and forgets her freaking birthday.

As the moment drags on, I try to think what I'll do if she gets caught right now. Move on without her? Pretend I don't know her and keep going to LA? No, she'll tell our parents, she'll rat me out. I'm panicking, breathing too fast, and someone bumps into me, impatient that I'm holding up the line.

And then the agent hands Frankie back her ID and boarding pass, and she smiles at him and wheels her suitcase toward the conveyor belt. She nods at me, and I can breathe again. We're on our way.

We're sitting in the airport restaurant, half-heartedly sharing some fries, when the local news comes on the nearby TV. A picture of our faces flashes on the screen, and we can't help exchanging a terrified look. The newscaster, a young woman with a morose expression, says, "Two Orange County teenagers lost in a boating accident near Kailua-Kona have been declared missing, presumed dead.

After two days of searching, they still have not been found, and local authorities say there is little chance of them being discovered alive at this point."

The camera pans out to include a second newscaster, an older man, who shakes his head in a display of grief. "You don't know us—don't act like you're sad," I grumble, and Frankie snickers.

"What can we take away from this?" the newscaster asks his colleague. "What can we learn from this tragic accident?"

"Well, there's an investigation going on around how they rented the kayaks," she replies. "They were under-age and rented from a local vendor, apparently with forged parental permission. There's talk right now of liability on the vendor's part, but because the girls did present parental permission, I'm guessing it's more an act of desperation on the part of the family rather than a serious legal claim."

"Darling family," I mutter, and Frankie nods.

I notice that a lot of people in the restaurant are watching the news. The loud family who'd waited in the TSA line behind us are eating burgers, the mom and dad talking animatedly, pointing to the TV every so often. Even the bartender is watching it.

"Um, Frankie? Do you think we should get out of here?"

"Yeah, I do," she agrees, looking around nervously.

We dump our fries in a nearby trash can and leave. We walk silently through the airport, and I pull her into a quieter corner, at a gate that doesn't have a flight coming, where we can sit with our backs to the flow of traffic. She settles in next to me, and I examine her wig, her makeup. She looks nothing like the Frankie on the news.

I still can't breathe.

Fifteen

ONE MONTH AGO

Frankie

IT WAS ELEVEN FIFTY-SEVEN, THREE MINUTES FROM lunch. Mr. Henderson was going on and on about the economics of World War II, and behind me, the baseball team guys were whispering, "Frank. Fraaaaaank. Frank." As a group, they snickered just quietly enough so Mr. Henderson didn't yell at them.

I glanced sideways at Gia, who was smirking. We'd been friends all through middle school and the first year of high school, but when the other kids had decided I wasn't cool, she'd gone along with it. Sometimes I felt like I was losing my mind, like I'd imagined our years of friendship.

I looked away from her stupid, traitorous face and made sure my backpack was zipped and ready to go. I was getting out of here at lunch. These assholes were in my fifth and sixth periods, too.

"Fraaaaank," one of the guys whispered, poking my back with something. The thing where they all called me Frank had started this year, when I'd decided I was done wearing the girls' uniform.

It was fine, I told myself. I didn't care about these people. I didn't need them to like me. I didn't need anyone to like me.

That felt like a lie. Of course I wanted people to like me. I'm not above human nature.

I glanced at the other queer kid in class, a boy named Armando. He was quiet and shy, and he shot me sympathetic looks from time to time when the jocks were really on a roll. Right now he was looking down at his desk. I'd tried to be friends with him, but I was pretty sure he worried that getting close to me would bring some of the teasing his way. I couldn't blame him for wanting to steer clear.

The bell rang. I stood up fast, grabbed my backpack, and was first out the door. I shot Gia a dirty look as I passed her desk. She didn't notice; she was turned in her seat to talk to her boyfriend, Matt, one of the baseball idiots. He caught my eye and went rigid. "What are you looking at, Frank?"

Instead of answering him, I turned to Gia, who was scrupulously focused on her phone. "Seriously, Gia? This guy?"

She snapped her head up to face me, eyebrows drawing together. She was so pretty these days, so polished and made up, I don't know if I'd have recognized her back in eighth grade, when we were best friends. Before she could get started, a few other baseball guys joined us, having at last figured out how the zippers on their backpacks worked.

"Frank," they cried in unison, then dissolved into giggles.

I kept my eyes on Gia. I held her gaze for a long moment, hoping she felt the weight of her betrayal, and then I turned and walked away. How could she date that guy? How could she stand to be around someone who treated people like that? If she didn't want to be friends anymore, that was her right, but I'd never understand her choice to align herself with the same people who made my school days a living hell.

The halls were packed full of uniformed students, and I slipped between them on my way out, determined not to cry until I was in my car. Juniors and seniors were allowed to leave during lunch; how else would people show off their cars and get sushi? I trotted down the steps of the expansive, Spanish-style front entryway and through a crowd of plaid skirts and green polos. "It's Frank!" cried a girl in the crowd, and a chorus of "Frank!" came from her friends.

I couldn't believe people were allowed to behave this way with no consequences. Then again, this was South Orange County—not LA, not New York. The gender binary was alive and well here, and these geniuses were living proof. But why should that be my problem?

If I were being honest, I wasn't totally sure I was a girl. I'd had plenty of time to think about it—endless hours alone in my room—and I was forced to confront my turbulent relationship to gender norms every day when the kids at school did this ridiculousness. I'd read a lot of blogs written by trans people about their experiences, and I truly wasn't sure.

Some days I felt fine with being a girl, albeit a super-queer, non-skirt-wearing variety, but other days, the idea of being female felt icky and awful. At the same time, I wasn't sure if they/them pronouns quite fit, but the idea of growing up, getting married, and being a wife made my skin crawl. The word *wife*—ugh. Or words like *miss, ma'am*—shudder.

I'd shelved all of this under *Things to Figure Out After I Leave High School and...*

And what?

I had no idea what was next. Unlike everyone around me, my future felt uncertain. I didn't have it in me to go to an Ivy League and study hard for some suit job in my grandma's real estate development corporation. But if not that, what? I didn't want to be like my dad, another family disappointment, but being a loser was attractive in a weird way. If you disappointed everyone in one fell swoop, you didn't have to worry about doing it incrementally your whole life.

In the student parking lot, I let myself into my rental Prius. I turned the car on and took a few deep breaths. I kept getting flashbacks to barreling down the hill, flipping, rolling...

I closed my eyes. I rested my head on the seat. I breathed away the vertigo.

I'd loved driving before, the feeling of escaping, the road an adventure waiting to happen. Now I kept hearing the *crash-crunch* of metal smashing, the muted explosion of the airbag. I decided to go home; no one would be there, and I could nap in peace.

I took the long way, avoiding the scene of my almost-death, going ten miles an hour under the speed limit and slamming on my brakes at the slightest provocation. By the time I pulled into the sloped driveway and parked in front of the garage doors, my whole body felt heavy. I trudged up the front steps, past the fountain and the rose garden and the stupid wind chimes, and I let myself in the front door.

Something was different. My skin prickled. I froze, hand on the doorknob.

I was hearing voices.

I followed the sound. It was coming from the study, an unnecessary room at the front corner of the house that was decorated like a fancy office. My dad almost never worked from home. I got the feeling he didn't work much at work, either.

"A complete disaster. Absolutely unbelievable. What were you thinking?" It was my grandma's voice; she was clearly laying into my dad about something.

I couldn't see him; the door was only half-open, and I couldn't get closer without their seeing me. I had a feeling she was yelling about my car; she'd been mad when he bought me the Mustang, a "reckless vanity purchase." I felt guilty about him getting ripped into for something I'd wanted. Besides, the Mustang was an example of the good side of my dad, the moments when he could be fun and make me feel like we were on a lifelong road trip, two kids alone for the weekend with no grown-ups in sight.

"So irresponsible," she was saying.

"I know," he replied. He sounded meek, totally unlike his usual self. A long pause. "What do you suggest?"

"What do *you* suggest?" she shot back. "You aren't my problem to solve anymore. You're a grown man. You have a *wife*." Her tone was sour, like the word *wife* made her sick. I couldn't help but crinkle my nose a little; there was that word again. *Wife*.

"Come on, Mom." His tone was pleading. "I could lose the house."

"Then get an apartment."

"Mom!" I heard him drawing in a deep breath. "What about Francesca? Think about her."

"Francesca will be fine. Her trust fund matures when she turns eighteen."

"Don't you think you should reallocate some of that to me? I need it to raise her."

"You need it to pay for your lifestyle. Those two things are not the same. You dug yourself a hole. Now you can dig yourself out of it. You're a grown man, Chris, a husband and a father. Act like it." Footsteps, heels on the wood floor. She was on the move. I panicked and ended up ducking into the powder room across the hall. I heard her *click-clack* out of the study, through the foyer, and to the front door. My dad was right on her heels, cajoling, arguing.

They were about to see my car in the driveway. I needed to make it clear I hadn't heard anything. I slipped out of the bathroom and around the back way to the stairs. I took them three at a time, fled along the open-air hallway to my room, and eased my door shut behind me. I caught my breath and plopped down onto my usual place on the carpet at the foot of my bed. I leaned back against the footboard and stared at my legs, stretched out in front of me. I was dizzy again and nauseatingly floaty, like a buoy on the ocean, bobbing on the surface of the endlessly deep water.

I felt my head drooping. I should crawl into my bed, but it was so far away.

A new dizzy spell hit me. I leaned my head back and breathed slowly. When I'd called my doctor to explain that I'd been feeling sick lately, he'd recommended an iron supplement and a multivitamin. Fat lot of good that was doing.

My door swung open, and my dad stood in the doorway.

"Dad!" I protested weakly. "Knock! What if I was changing?" The words sounded fuzzy. Was I slurring?

His arms crossed over his chest, he looked down at me. With the hall light behind him, he was in silhouette, and I could barely see his face. Or maybe that was the blurriness in my head. I felt unsafe suddenly, like a stranger was in the house. My head was swimming. What was happening to me?

"What are you doing home?" he asked.

"I wasn't feeling well."

"What's wrong?"

"My stomach. I told you, I've been having issues lately."

He didn't seem to hear me. "Did you listen to my conversation with your grandmother?"

I decided to play dumb. "Grandma's here?"

He shifted his weight, restless. "She's out of her mind." He stepped into the room and sat on the floor next to me, grunting as he did it. He leaned back against my bed frame and pulled his knees up, wrapping his arms around them like he was a teenager, too. I caught a faint whiff of his aftershave and realized I hadn't been this close to him in a long time.

"We could go to Europe," he mused. "Take a trip. We could leave tomorrow."

I felt too nauseous for this. "I have school," I reminded him, not sure if I actually cared.

"Right. I forgot." He leaned his head back and looked up at the ceiling. We sat in silence for a few minutes. "Remember when we bought the Mustang? That was fun, right?"

"It was." I closed my eyes. The room felt strange, the air thick.

"Those days might be over soon," he said, his voice soft. "We might be moving. Things might be changing."

"Moving where?"

"Your grandmother feels it's time to stop—" He interrupted himself to laugh, a bitter sound I didn't recognize. "To stop 'nurturing a generation that has been given more than enough.' What does that even mean? She doesn't want to waste her money on her own son? I can guarantee you she isn't cutting Todd off. I promise you he's getting a raise, not getting fired."

"Fired?"

He turned his head to meet my eyes. "She's giving you all my money, Frankie, because she doesn't trust me with it. She's given it all to you. And to the twins." He rolled his eyes. "If she thinks I'm useless, she should meet those kids in ten years."

I had no idea what to say.

Staring into the middle distance, he said, "I'm her son. That should mean something."

"Dad, I—"

"It doesn't matter. Forget it." He pushed himself up, grunting again as he stood.

"But, Dad, wait. Doesn't Leah have a job? You can look for a new one, right, and she can pay the bills in the meantime?"

He shook his head. "No, babe. Leah doesn't make real money." His blue eyes, dark in this light, held mine tight in their grasp.

"I…" I fumbled through my nausea for words. "I'm sorry. I wish I could help."

Shoulders slumped, he walked toward the door and left, pulling it shut behind him.

I wrapped my arms around my waist, and my eyes pricked with tears. Why did I feel so guilty, like whatever was happening was all my fault?

I fumbled for my phone and texted Leah. You should call Dad. He's in a bad place. Don't tell him I said anything.

After a moment, her reply came through: Oh no. What happened?

I think he had a fight with Grandma.

About me? 😬

Not this time.

Thank God.

Don't get excited yet. I think it was about money.

Okay, calling him. I won't tell him you said anything.

I set the phone aside, relieved she was here to help with this stuff. It had been nice, all the years of just Dad and me being irresponsible, skipping school and eating McDonald's, but it was nice to have another person to lean on, too.

I hated to think that just when my dad had his life together somewhat, my grandma was going to knock it all down. Why would she do that? She'd been supporting him all these years. Why today?

Another huge wave of nausea hit me, and I had to scramble to my feet and run for the bathroom to throw up. All the family drama evaporated for now.

Sixteen

THE LA BUS IS CROWDED AND HOT, AND I FEEL DIRTY, MY THIGHS sticking to the plastic seat beside Frankie, who sits slumped back with her suitcase tucked between her knees and her arms crossed tight over her chest. A pair of guys in their early twenties have been grinning at us, then at each other, then back at us, then at each other, for the last few miles, which is unnerving. It makes me wonder: What if we find ourselves the victims of a crime? We can't go to the police.

I keep my eyes trained on the city outside the window and track the stops closely. The motel I booked is in the southern part of East Hollywood, a seedy neighborhood I've gotten to know because it's a couple of miles from the place that made my fake IDs.

It's getting dark. Our flight landed at five o'clock, and it's seven now. It's incredible how long it takes to get across LA on public transit. I allow a few minutes of London fantasies. No more stinky asphalt-and-sweat bus rides. I'll be on the Tube, on double-decker red buses, visiting the London Gallery and the British Museum. The weather will be crisp, and I'll wear fashionable coats every day. And in the summer, when the days are long, I'll spend endless hours wandering through parks and taking day trips to Brighton and Oxford.

"What are you thinking about?" Frankie asks. "You look intense. Is your foot bothering you?"

I feel my cheeks heat up. "My foot's feeling a little better, actually."

"So what's on your mind?"

"Nothing."

"Oh, come on. I'm bored out of my mind. It's weird not having a phone."

"That reminds me. We need to get you a burner." She stares at me pointedly, and I say, "Okay, fine. I was thinking about London."

She nods, lips pursed. "What made you pick London as your destination?"

I glance around to see if anyone can hear us, but there's too much white noise and we're talking softly. "I don't know. I guess I grew up reading books set there, and it seemed like this amazing place. And then I got super into, like ..." I must be red-faced now. "This is stupid. Never mind."

"Oh my god. Just spit it out."

I lower my voice so she has to lean in to hear me. "I got really into Sherlock Holmes, Agatha Christie, all those

British crime novels, but especially Sherlock Holmes. I loved Moriarty and always imagined how I would catch him if I were there. I don't know. It just feels like the right place for someone like me."

"A criminal mastermind," she quips.

"See, this is why I wasn't going to tell you!" I turn so she can't see my face and look out the window, waiting for my cheeks to cool down.

She puts a hand on my shoulder. "I'm just teasing. You're a nerd, but it's okay. You're also a mastermind."

Damn right, I grumble silently, but then I realize we're approaching our stop. Relieved, I beckon to Frankie, and we roll our suitcases to the door, trying not to bump the knees and feet of the other passengers. I worry the guys might follow us, but they just make licking-kissing sounds as we exit.

Out on the street, cars inch by, stuck in traffic. The sidewalks are crowded, and the air is a mélange of exhaust, weed fumes, and the smell of Mexican food from a nearby taco truck. A long stretch of tents and piles of trash and furniture—a homeless encampment—occupies the area next to the sidewalk, leaving only a few feet for walking.

"Where's our motel?" Frankie asks.

I point north. "Make a right on Western, two blocks east."

"I can't wait to take a shower. I feel so gross."

"Same. And we need to find better wigs. I wasn't plan-ning on staying blond this long, but while we're in LA, so I need to match the Candace driver's license. And this thing won't fool anyone in Hollywood."

"Can I just forget the wig? I have the same hair color as this stolen license. And maybe it will be good if I look different from the security camera at LAX, just in case."

I consider this. "You know what? I think you're right."

"Let's get some clippers and buzz the sides. I want to go really, really short." Her mouth is set in a line.

"Okay, it's a plan," I agree.

The motel is similar to the one in Hilo: two stories, all rooms letting out onto outdoor hallways with exterior stairs connecting the second floor to the parking lot. Like in Hilo, I check in alone using my Candace ID, and I pay with a pre-paid Visa. It's sixty-nine dollars a night, the cheapest I was able to find, but still so much money. I'd considered a youth hostel, but it would mean too much exposure.

I shower first, and while Frankie's in the bathroom, I surf through news sites on my burner phone, foot elevated on a few pillows. The room smells like stale cigarette smoke, and I have the windows open to try to clear it out. From the street, the sounds of horns and sirens drift in.

I can't find anything about Nathan. I've tried a million search terms: "Nathan" "Hawaii" "Hilo" "missing" and all the other combinations of words I can think of. I find articles about Frankie and me, and I pause on a story with pictures of both our faces, soaking in the pleasure of knowing that, as far as the world is concerned, we are dead.

Dressed in clothes we'd bought in Hilo—jeans and plain T-shirts, nothing notable—and with my blond Candace wig back on for now, we take a bus down to MacArthur Park. With her shaggy hair, Frankie blends in with the Angelenos much better than I do.

I lead her through the busy shopping district, where vendors crowd the sidewalks, offering prepaid phones, money wires to Central and South America, DVDs, clothes, piñatas, party rentals, jewelry—you can probably get anything here. The park itself always struck me as shady, somewhere a young girl might hang out if she wanted to end up on an episode of *My Favorite Murder*.

We pass a loud shop offering car stereo equipment and then enter a shipping store. It's quiet in here, the walls full of cardboard boxes and envelopes, a row of PO boxes lining the back half of the store. The man behind the counter is young and has a diamond stud in his left ear.

"Hello," he greets us politely. His eyes are sharp.

I approach the counter. "Can I speak with Art, please?"

His eyebrows rise, just a little. "He's not here right now."

"Oh." I'm disappointed. "Can you get a message to him? I've worked with him before, and I was hoping to add one more thing to my order."

He starts texting. "What's your name?"

"Candace."

He points his phone at me. "Say cheese." He takes my picture.

Frankie watches this from a few feet away, eyes flitting back and forth between me and the guy.

He receives a text message and says, "Okay, Candace. Come on back." He beckons us to follow him behind the counter, and he opens a door to the back room. It's familiar to me now, but every time I've walked through this door, I've thought anything could happen to me back here.

Art is sitting behind his desk in the concrete-floored storage room. When we enter, he looks up and smiles. "Candace. I didn't expect to see you again so soon."

He gestures that we should sit in front of his desk, in two mismatched dining chairs. In the corner of the room, a man stands, arms crossed, watching. He's always here, or someone like him. Art is never alone. He's a balding, middle-aged man with the aesthetic of a dad who should be barbecuing in sandals and socks, not running a fake-papers ring. But then I suppose that's why he's successful.

"So how can I help you today?" he asks, eyes flicking over to Frankie.

"I thought you could help my friend with the same situation. She needs the same type of papers I got, ones that can stand up to scrutiny. An American passport for her, tied to a Social Security number, et cetera."

He purses his lips, then beckons the man in the corner over. "My friend is just going to make sure everything is okay. Can you please stand and put your hands on your head?"

"He's going to pat us down," I tell Frankie, standing and indicating that she should do the same. I hold still while the guy digs through the empty pockets of my jeans and feels my stomach and chest, something that makes me highly uncomfortable. I know he's looking to make sure I don't have a wire or something, but the feeling of his big hands on me makes me shudder. I hate to watch when he does it to Frankie, but I do, keeping a close eye on him, like that's going to do any good if he decides to cross a line. But it all feels professional, and he takes my purse and rifles through it before handing it back to me and nodding at Art.

Art indicates that we should return to our seats. He smiles again, like a crocodile. "You know the price. If you want real papers, not fake, that can pass inspection, you'll need to pay for them."

"I know. It's just one passport, though."

"Five thousand," he says.

"That's more than I paid," I protest. "Four thousand."

"Forty-five hundred."

"Fine." It's so much more than we can afford. "How long will it take? We need it as fast as possible."

"Two weeks? Three? You remember from last time."

My heart sinks. "We need it a lot sooner. Can you do it faster?"

He shakes his head. "I can try, but I can't promise."

I sigh, exchanging a look with Frankie. Two weeks in LA is too long. There's no question: We're going to have to find a way to earn some money while we're here. I mull it over while he takes Frankie's picture, thinking of different ways to get cash fast. I bussed tables in Santa Ana while saving up for this, but that had taken two years.

I slump in my seat. If I can't think of something, we're going to end up trapped in LA.

I glare at Frankie, resentment acidic in the back of my throat. She's the obstacle between my new beginning or a dead end.

Seventeen

"WHAT'S WRONG?" FRANKIE ASKS AS WE GET OFF THE BUS ON HOLLY-wood Boulevard. I've been quiet since we left Art's, my brain overheating while trying to solve this money problem. It's night now, the streetlights turning on, headlights bright as cars inch past in the traffic, store windows flaring with neon signs.

"Money," I reply, terse.

She looks confused. "Money, as in..."

"As in, we don't have enough and we need more." I check my phone, which has Google Maps open. The wig shop is a few blocks farther.

Hollywood is familiar; I've been here many times, but I can't say I'm used to it. Stepping on stars along the Walk of Fame, we pass restaurants, souvenir shops, smoke shops, and a trashy lingerie store. My spirits lift at the sight of the wig shop. It's huge, with a million selections.

Frankie contemplates a series of brightly colored pieces while I hunt down a realistic-looking blond one that falls to my chest. It costs a hundred and fifty dollars. Compared to the human-hair wigs, which cost thousands, it's a good price, but I wince as I hand the cash over to the bored-looking, pierced clerk. I put it on in a quiet corner before leaving the store, a little relieved to match my Candace ID again. Frankie fusses with the bangs, helping me get the wig on straight. "It looks really good," she says, checking the back. She grins. "You're a blond. Look at that."

Back on the street, as we walk toward Hollywood and Highland to get something to eat, Frankie asks, "What can I do to help earn money? Can we get jobs?"

I sigh heavily. "I mean, yeah, that's what I did when I was working toward this whole plan, but it took me two years to save a total of fifteen grand, and I stole some of that from my mom. We need to earn a lot faster. I have about nine thousand left, and almost five of that has to go toward your papers. It'll cost a thousand each for airfare to get out of the country, and I don't plan on landing in London with only a thousand dollars in my pocket." I had this all worked out. I was planning to arrive with twelve thousand dollars to get me through until I could find an apartment, a roommate, a steady job. Another wave of rage hits me out of nowhere. I can't believe I'm back in stinky, stupid Hollywood.

I was supposed to go from Hawaii to Bali on a cruise

ship—the cruise ticket another sunk cost—and lie low there for a month, until my disappearance was officially ruled an accidental death and my family was back home and settling into life without me. Then, having spent the month practicing my English accent and mentally becoming Elizabeth, I'd book a flight to London, where I'd arrive tanned and rooted in my identity, ready to begin my beautiful, shining new life.

As I mourn all this, we walk by a pair of men with neck tattoos who whistle at us and say, "Damn, that ass," to me in particular. It's like the universe is flipping me off. We ignore them and cross the street. It's packed over here, wall-to-wall flesh. Hollywood and Highland is always a madhouse, with street performers surrounded by tourists, people selling souvenirs and soliciting donations, groups of young women heading for clubs, couples out on dates, and everything in between.

We turn to the escalators and weave through the crowd. Near the entrance of the outdoor mall, a beautiful woman in a short black dress, fully done up as though for a night out, is handing out flyers.

"Hey, girls," she calls to us, smiling brightly. She has an accent, maybe Russian or Georgian. "What are you doing later? We have a great night planned." She offers us a pair of flyers.

I say, "No, thank you." We keep walking.

Frankie says, "What is she, like, a club promoter?"

I shrug. "I assume."

She pulls me to a stop. "We could do that. It probably pays more than bussing tables or cleaning houses."

I frown. "How? I don't think you can just walk up to the bouncer in a club and demand to be a promoter for them."

She stares at me for a minute and then spins around and walks back the way we came. She approaches the young woman and starts talking to her.

I curse her in my mind, thinking about the dangers of calling attention to ourselves, and hurry to catch up. Frankie's saying, "We were just wondering how you got into this. We're in town for a couple of weeks and really need to earn some money. We thought club promoting might be a good idea, but we're not sure who to talk to."

The woman looks back and forth between us. She has bright blue eyes and beautiful, long light brown hair, impeccably styled. "What are your names?" she asks.

I step forward. "I'm Candace," I say, hoping it reminds Frankie to use the name on her stolen driver's license.

"I'm Ivy," says Frankie, and I breathe a quiet sigh of relief.

"And you're both eighteen?"

"Yes, we're freshmen in college," I reply.

She smiles. "I'm Natalya. I promote for Blue, just up toward Cahuenga. Why don't we try you out tonight and see how you do? A test run. You have the look."

Frankie shoots me a delighted grin, clearly proud of herself. "That sounds great."

"Well, wait," I cut in, but Natalya is already responding.

"You can meet me there at ten o'clock. Be dressed." She indicates her own outfit.

I want to curse Frankie to the depths of hell. Now we have to buy clubbing outfits and tromp all over Hollywood basically naked.

"What's the pay like?" I ask Natalya, half hoping it won't be worth it.

"You'll get a cut of all the traffic you bring in the door. Tonight is a twenty-dollar cover, so you'll get five bucks a head." She smiles brightly.

If I get fifty people into the club, that's two hundred and fifty bucks. Between the two of us, we stand to make five hundred bucks a night. Damn. Worth it.

"We'll be there," I reply.

Hollywood and Highland is packed full of the exact kind of clothes we need, and we decide to hang out here until it's time to meet Natalya. We get Frankie a burner phone from one of the kiosks, find a hair clipper at Walgreens, and track down a couple of outfits like the one Natalya was wearing. We lock ourselves in one of the public restrooms, and I clean up the sides of Frankie's hair. She stares at herself in the mirror for a long moment after, running her hands up the short-cropped sides and through the longer, wavy hair on top. "I've been wanting to do this for so long," she says, and I sense that this means something more to her than just a change in hairstyle. I'm about to reply when she says, "Hey, you haven't mentioned your foot in a while. Is it feeling better?"

Surprised, I look down. "You know what? It's hurting a lot less." I slip my sneaker and sock off, and we take a closer look. The redness and swelling have gone way down.

She grins at me. "Maybe our luck is changing."

Superstition overwhelms me. "Don't say that. You'll jinx us."

"Says who?"

I look up at the ceiling, like I'm going to see the tsunami before it crushes us. "Just... don't get cocky."

"Not a problem."

We change into our new dresses, and when Frankie comes out of the stall in her black minidress and heels, I almost laugh. She's so hot with this haircut, it's truly unfair.

"What?" she asks, grumpily stuffing her jeans and T-shirt into the shopping bag. "I hate dresses."

"You look..."

"*You* look," she retorts, examining my dress and heels in a way that makes my face feel hot. She says, "Honestly, I wouldn't recognize you if I saw you in this. You're completely disguised."

I look in the mirror. She's right.

Do I like it? I like not looking like Maude, that's true, and being Candace is more liberating than being myself. I'm not looking forward to the gross catcalls the moment we leave this bathroom, but I do like the way Frankie seems to be averting her eyes from my body. I like that a lot.

Eighteen

ONE MONTH AGO

Frankie

"HEY, GRANDMA." I WAVED AS I APPROACHED HER.

She looked up from her laptop. "Francesca! To what do I owe the pleasure of a midweek visit?" She was sitting at the dining table on the patio of her Newport Coast estate. It was eight o'clock, and the sunset was turning into dusk, all the landscape lights twinkling against the dark purple sky.

I sat in a cushy chair across the table from her. She hadn't lived there very long, only since my grandfather died. She'd described it as "downsizing," which was pretty funny.

"I came over because I was hoping to talk to you for a second," I began.

"Of course. I'm delighted to see you. Do you want something to drink?"

"No, thank you."

She set the laptop aside and gave me her full attention. "How's school?"

Hell on earth. I want to set it on fire. "School's fine. Nothing new there."

"You're out of uniform again," she observed, looking me up and down. "They must tell you that every day."

"I'm not out of uniform. This is the boys' uniform."

"I support the feminist statement, but be careful. You don't want to give people the wrong idea."

"What wrong idea?"

She smiled with one side of her mouth. "There's nothing wrong with being a tomboy as a child, but you're almost a woman. People will start thinking..." She hesitated.

"Thinking what?" My heart was pounding a little harder. I was pretty sure I knew where this was going, and it wasn't good.

"Come on, Francesca. You know the world well enough by now."

"That I'm, like, gay?" I asked.

She nodded.

I sat there for a minute, trying to digest this. It wasn't news. She was a rich, seventy-year-old woman from South Orange County. She wasn't going to be joining PFLAG. Like everyone else, her love had limits, and I knew that the time was coming very soon when I would reach the end of the line.

One shitty family thing at a time. "Look, Grandma. Can I talk to you about my dad?"

She raised her eyebrows. "All right."

"Can you…not tell him we talked? Can this be confidential?"

She picked up her glass of sparkling water and sipped it. At last she nodded. "All right. Go ahead."

"I overheard your conversation the other day. About money."

She sighed and set her glass down. "Francesca, I'm not—"

"I think you should help him."

"Excuse me?"

I tried to say this exactly right. "Look. I understand if he's not doing a good job at work and you need to let him go. I know he's not a hard worker. But I don't want to be the reason anything bad happens to him. I want you to help him, even if it means taking some money out of my trust fund to do it. I don't want…" I hesitated, clarifying my thoughts to myself. "He's the only parent I have left. I don't want to mess up my relationship with him over something as stupid as money."

She sat there with her eyebrows raised. "Francesca, you should let me work this out with your father. You shouldn't be worrying about this."

I held my hand up to stop her. "I know he's a disappointment to you, that he's not a good businessman the way Todd is. But he's trying. And he and Leah are actually doing really well."

Her face darkened. "Do not bring her into this."

"Leah's not so bad. And my dad really loves her. Shouldn't you be sort of happy for him?"

She narrowed her eyes. Okay, maybe *happy* was a stretch.

I pressed on. "Well, I just wanted to see if you would consider helping him out for a while. I don't want him to resent me forever if you give me money but cut him off."

She leaned across the table and gripped my forearm. "Your father is a bad investment. He has a hole in his pocket. Why don't you come live with me for the rest of high school?"

"I can't do that," I replied. I couldn't stomach being a double disappointment to her, both gay and Ivy League–incompatible. I didn't know where I was going, who I was, but I knew I wasn't headed toward any path she had in mind for me.

She patted my hand. "We have our family trip coming up. After that you can think about coming home with me. It's not so bad here, is it?" She gestured at the house and grounds.

"No, Grandma, you know I love it here." I hesitated. "I feel bad, though. My dad's—"

"My son is not your responsibility," she said firmly.

As I walked back along the path through the darkened landscape, I felt like I'd swallowed a rock. My dad was going to hate me for the rest of his life if he lost his house. I considered signing the trust-fund money over to him when I turned eighteen, but I had a feeling that wasn't soon enough. By then the damage would have been done.

If he hated me, there'd be no one left. My mom was gone. Everyone at school hated me. My grandma would be done with me as soon as I came out. I was completely and totally alone.

Nineteen

THE CLUB BLUE IS ON CAHUENGA, JUST OFF HOLLYWOOD BOULEVARD.
Its sign is a single, blue neon *B*. A long line winds around
the corner from the entrance, managed by a few black-clad
bouncers and ending at a velvet rope that serves as a gate.
As we approach, I see Natalya standing near the front of
the line, in conversation with the bouncer in charge of lifting the rope and letting people in.

She spots us as we approach and breaks into a wide
smile. "Candace! Ivy! You look fantastic!" She air-kisses our
cheeks—she smells like perfume—and says, "Look at this
disaster." She waves an arm to indicate the line. "Can you
believe it? Horrible."

I'm confused. Frankie is, too. She says, "Is it...too many
people in line?"

"No! Look at them! They're all men!" She lowers her voice. "And older ladies."

I look back at the line, and she's right; it's almost all men in their twenties, with a few groups of women in their late thirties.

"So you're hoping to bring in more young women?" Frankie asks.

"Yes! Here, I'll show you." She beckons us toward Hollywood Boulevard, ignoring the stares of men in line as we pass. Her heels are two inches higher than Frankie's and mine, and she walks in them like a runway model. "As you know, Hollywood is full of clubs. Between here and Hollywood and Highland, this whole block, you'll see the kind of women you're looking to attract. There." She points down the crowded sidewalk at a group of young, dressed-up women waiting at the crosswalk for the light to change. "Stay with me so we're clearly a group," she instructs. She hurries toward the women, smiling her glossy smile. "Hi, hello," she greets them cheerfully. "Where are you going? Which club?"

They look at her in slightly unfriendly surprise. "The Starlight Room, why?"

"Wow. Okay," Natalya replies, with a look on her face like they've suggested they're going to the Dog Poop Room.

"Why?" asks one of the girls, a brunette with carefully manicured eyebrows.

"Oh, well, my friend works the door at Blue, and I can

get some more girls in free, so I thought I'd ask. Blue is a little more upscale than Starlight, so..." She trails off, clearly implying she may have misjudged them.

"Why is your friend letting people in for free?" asks a black-haired girl with a beautiful chin-length bob.

"There's an industry party in the VIP room tonight for one of the casting agencies, and they want to make sure they have the prettiest girls for their publicity photos."

The girls light up, and in four seconds we're walking back to Blue as a group, where Natalya escorts them with great honor straight to the front of the line. The bouncer lifts the velvet rope, and we all walk in together. As the girls go into the club, Natalya pulls Frankie and me into the alcove entryway. She raises her voice to be heard over the beat pounding through the wall. "For every girl that comes in, we can let in one guy. So you're not making five bucks a head off the ladies, you're making five bucks off the guys who get to come in after. Get it?"

There is something truly vile about this. From the curl of her upper lip, I can tell Frankie feels low-key sickened by it. But we agree, and Natalya takes us back outside and introduces us to the bouncer at the door. "This is Adam." The tall, broad-shouldered man looks us over, not even a little impressed. "They're working street tonight," she tells him. "Keep count for the books. I'm working interior." He nods, and she grins at us. "Adam isn't much of a talker. I'll be inside circulating if you need me. And remember my line about the casting-agency party. It works every time."

Frankie and I walk away from the door. "I can't believe you got me into this," I mutter.

She lifts a finger. "Just remember the money."

"Oh, I know."

We *click-clack* back to Hollywood Boulevard, our heels barely audible above the cacophony of street and crowd noise. A foursome of pretty young women is ahead of us on the sidewalk, dressed for a night out, and Frankie leaves me behind to catch up.

"Hey there," she says in a friendly, upbeat voice, tapping the shoulder of one of the girls.

They turn to look at her with suspicious eyes. "What?" the girl asks.

"I just wondered if you were heading to Blue." Frankie points back up the street.

"No," the girl answers, turning around to leave.

"Why do you ask?" asks one of the other girls.

I open my mouth to speak, but nothing comes out. Panic pounds in my ears. *I can't do this*, a voice screams in my head.

Frankie says, "They're having some VIP casting party tonight and are looking for pretty girls to be in the background for all the pictures, so there's no cover charge. I just assumed you were heading over and thought we could go in together. We'd make a bigger impact in a larger group." With her short hair and wide smile, her whole vibe is edgy and confident, and I'm ripped apart by jealousy and longing. Why can't I be like this?

The girls look at each other. "I've been to Blue—it's cool," says one of the four.

So we walk up the street, Frankie chatting animatedly with the prettiest of their group. I bring up the rear, feeling unattractive and uncharismatic next to Frankie. Also, my foot still hurts. It's not as bad as it was, but it's a constant, annoying soreness.

As we walk, I notice the girl in front of me has a tag hanging out of the back of her short red dress.

"You have a label sticking out," I tell her, showing her where it is. "I think maybe you forgot to cut it off when you bought the dress."

She fumbles to reach behind her. "Can you tuck it in for me?"

"Sure. Or do you want me to pull it off?"

"No, no, no!" She shoots me a bashful look. She's a well-dressed blond with waist-length hair and glossy lips. "I have a thing I do. I buy a dress, wear it out, and return it the next day."

I tuck in the tag, careful not to poke her with the pointy corners. The price of the dress is three hundred and ninety-eight dollars.

My wheels are turning. There's something to consider here.

Frankie leads the group straight to Adam, who opens the velvet rope. We follow the girls in, keeping with our story about going in together; I'm assuming Frankie plans to ditch them once we're inside. We run into Natalya in the darkened entry area. "Hey, nicely done!" she cries, eyes alight at the sight of the four attractive girls with us.

Frankie grins at her, and I try to follow suit. Natalya leans in to tell us, "If you can keep this up, I'd love to have you back for as long as you're in town." Frankie turns her smile on me, and I return it weakly. I hate this.

But the dress-return scam has given me a great idea.

Twenty

I'M QUIET AND MOODY AS WE TAKE THE BUS TO THE BEVERLY CENTER, A huge shopping mall about five miles west of our motel. I'm in my Candace wig, and Frankie and I are both wearing one of the three jeans-and-T-shirt outfits we bought in Hawaii. We'll need more clubbing dresses if we're going to keep doing Satan's work. I glance sideways at her. This super-short haircut is obscene; she looks like she was born to wear it.

"You sure nothing's wrong?" Frankie asks for the third time since we woke up.

"This is our stop." We get out onto the busy sidewalk and find the entrance to the three-story mall that takes up a whole triangular city block.

She says, "I thought you'd be happy today. We made two hundred bucks last night."

"I am happy," I snap, which makes her laugh. We get on

a massive escalator, and I turn to face her. "I hated it. I hated every minute of it."

"Of what?"

"Last night. I hate the club, the people, having to, like, chat up strangers and get them to..." I shudder.

"It wasn't that bad. I did most of the talking."

"I *know*. Don't you think I know?" The words come out louder than I meant them to.

"Did that upset you? I thought I was helping. You seemed uncomfortable."

"You were. It did. I..." I feel stupid, and pathetic, and small, but I'm not going to tell her that. "Whatever," I mutter.

We get off the elevator, and I head straight for Macy's. "Wait," Frankie says. She puts a hand on my wrist and guides me away from the people crowding the walkway. She peers into my eyes. "Tell me what's bothering you. I don't want to worry all day about what I did to upset you."

I look down at her hand, and I squirm against the discomfort, but I don't pull away. After all, her hand is warm, and I'm kind of starved for human contact. Pathetic.

"Say out loud the words that are in your head," Frankie insists. "I see you thinking a million things. Just open your mouth and say them."

I glare at her, anger flaring up, and I snatch away my wrist. "You don't get to tell me—"

"I know, I know, I cornered you, and now you're going to say something really mean. Like at the party in Hawaii. Right?"

I hate her for bringing that up. I thought we were pretending that never happened.

She says, "Just be honest. If it's something I did, I can take it."

I look down at my feet. "I'm not good at that kind of socializing."

"Like, on street corners? Or what?"

I feel my eyes going hot. I will *not* cry.

I may as well just spit it out. "I'm not good with groups of girls, or being popular or outgoing. I usually just strategically build relationships with one person or another or gradually work my way into a group, but I can't do spontaneous."

Frankie laughs. She actually laughs. It's so mean, I turn and start walking away from her, my face on fire.

"Stop. Maude. I'm not laughing like you think I am." She gets in my way and puts her hands on my shoulders, which again makes my insides squirm with discomfort.

"Whatever." I try to pull away.

"Maude. At school they call me Frank."

That makes me stop in my tracks. I look at her questioningly.

She laughs again, short and bitter, and I realize the tone of her laughter was sardonic, not mocking. "Yeah. I'm, like, an outcast. They make constant fun of me. When it comes to talking to groups of popular girls, I have zero experience."

I examine her face, trying to understand both her words and the emotion behind them. "What do you mean, they call you Frank and make fun of you? You're, like..." I feel myself flushing, my neck and cheeks hot with embarrassment. "You're cool," I finish, and god, it's so sad hearing the words come out.

She snorts. "I go to one of the ritziest private schools in Orange County. For girls, it's all about bleaching your hair and getting nose jobs, and for the guys it's, like, who can get laid and do sports and drive the best cars. And then there's me." She shrugs.

I glance around. We're tucked into a corner near Macy's, where no one can hear us, but I want to be sure. "What do you mean, and then there's you?"

"I don't know, honestly," she says. "I mean, sometimes I think I might be nonbinary, but sometimes I don't. And figuring it out hasn't really been a priority. It's not like I have anyone in my life who would respect it. I've sort of put that thinking on hold until college—at least that's what I've been telling myself. At school I wear the boys' uniform, and even that is a whole thing, but I'd rather be alone and be real than have to fake anything to be friends with those assholes." She says this last part with her chin held high and defiant.

I realize all at once that Frankie is so, so much better than me. She has principles. Her family is as messed up as mine, but rather than concoct some huge revenge scheme, she's stuck to her guns and stood by who she is until she can find a better situation.

And look where it's gotten her. This proves what I've always known: There's no point in being noble. The universe will not reward you for rising above. You have to look out for number one because no one else will.

"Why did you want to come with me?" I ask, the question flooding out. "Please tell me."

She sighs, and then she shakes her head. "In two weeks, we'll go our separate ways. This is something I have to carry by myself. You have enough baggage of your own."

Her eyes are deep brown, and I realize I'm looking directly into them. I glance down at my shoes again. I'm attracted to her. I suppose I already knew that. It makes me angry; it's just another point of vulnerability.

For the millionth time, I wish I had never gone into her hotel room. I wish I'd stayed with the twins. I'd be in Bali right now, and maybe there I'd have met someone I could actually hook up with, someone who didn't know Maude at all.

"Come on," I say, avoiding more eye contact. "Let's just get started." I lead the way to Macy's.

"So what's the plan?"

"I'm not totally sure. I have to feel it out."

Inside, I find the nearest clothing counter and ask the salesperson for a bag. He hands me a medium-size paper bag with handles, and I fold it and tuck it under my arm. Outside, in the crowded interior walkway, I unfold the bag and put my purse inside to give it some weight. Frankie watches this with curiosity but doesn't ask questions.

"I think the food court will be our best bet," I tell her.

We take the escalators to the packed food court, where a horde of people are having lunch. "So here's what I'm thinking, since you apparently have some latent talent at chatting with strangers," I say, and proceed to outline Frankie's assignment.

Our first target is a young woman with diamond rings, lip implants, and acrylic nails long enough that I marvel at her ability to use her phone and wonder about her ability to wipe her butt. She's sitting near Starbucks, surrounded by a pile of shopping bags, loudly talking to someone on Face-Time. I watch her for a minute, deciding which of her bags to target.

"FaceTime in public," Frankie muses, shaking her head as she puts on lipstick using my powder compact. I'd told her to try and look bougie.

"Anyone who does that deserves cosmic retribution," I reply.

Frankie chuckles. She snaps the mirror shut and fixes a piece of my wig. I squash the urge to flinch away from her hand.

I say, "Okay. I know which bag I'm going for."

She slides on a pair of fake designer sunglasses I'd picked up in Hollywood, completing her look. "Let's do it."

She walks confidently toward the young woman. I watch her go, heart pounding. There are two mall cops near the food court: one by the main entrance and one by the restaurants. I keep my eyes on them, but they're not looking our way.

Frankie stops by the woman and makes a show of recognizing her. She's clearly channeling the mannerisms of women like Leah. It almost makes me laugh.

While they're talking, I approach the woman from behind and sit at the table back-to-back with hers. I set my Macy's bag on the floor. I can hear Frankie now; she's talking

139

about some party she thinks she saw this girl at last week, and the girl is saying she didn't go to that party. "I know we know each other from somewhere," Frankie is saying. "Maybe you were at the Hotel Beverly brunch last weekend?"

Whoever the girl is FaceTiming chimes in. "Let me see her—maybe I'll recognize her," says the tinny, bratty voice, and Frankie waves to the image when the camera is turned her way.

"Hey," she says, hilariously bubbly. "I'm Elle. Where did you guys go to school? I went to Beverly." I feel like she's trying to make me laugh.

While this is going on, I lean down like I'm going through my own shopping bag and extract things from our target's. I get a dress, a handful of cosmetics, and a pair of designer sunglasses, all with corresponding receipts. I do this slowly and carefully while Frankie makes up a long story about hanging out with D-list celebrities at some club and almost getting busted by TMZ.

Finished, I get up from the table and head away from the food court, pretending to be absorbed in my phone. No one nearby even glances my way. I walk past the mall cop, heart pounding, but he says nothing. I feel high, like I'm spinning.

I wait for Frankie near the exit, and she comes around the corner a few minutes later, grinning widely. "I got us an invite to a party if you want to make some friends," she says.

"I would rather peel my face off."

She cracks up. "So how'd you do?"

I let her look inside the bag. "I think I got about five

hundred bucks' worth. I figure I'll come back tomorrow and return them. I'll say they were gifts and get the return money in cash."

"Five hundred! That's amazing!" She holds a hand up for a high five, which I return weakly. "Seven hundred bucks so far. If we can make that every day, we'll have, like..." She does mental math. "Almost ten grand at the end of two weeks. Split both ways, that's enough to get us where we need to go and finance a decent landing."

I nod. It's nowhere near as much as I'd hoped, but it's better than nothing. And this return scam is a good skill to have in my back pocket. It's something I can lean on if I'm ever in a bind again.

"Do you want to go return this stuff now?" Frankie asks.

I consider. "I think it might be weird, right? From the store's perspective?"

"True. So we'll come back in a few days?"

"That sounds good. We can hit a different mall tomorrow, mix it up so we aren't in the same place too often."

We leave the mall and head for a nearby fast-food place to eat lunch. The air is warm and the city is bustling, loud with cars and buses. I feel like I've disappeared into a busy ant hive. The city is safety; it's invisibility.

I feel good for now, like maybe things will work out after all. This detour is merely an inconvenience.

Twenty-One

ONE MONTH AGO

Frankie

IT WAS DARK AND SILENT, THE MIDDLE OF THE NIGHT. I needed to throw up, but I couldn't move. How long had I been awake? What was I doing on the floor? I didn't remember lying down here. Why wasn't I in my bed? Nothing made sense.

My cheek was smashed into the rough fuzz of the carpet. The texture dug into my face. I felt weary of it, like I'd been here for a long time. I tried to recall memories of the evening. It was a black hole. I remembered being at school, then nothing.

My phone was down here with me, by my face. I reached a slow, numb hand out and fumbled with it. I couldn't grab it. I felt like I was wearing baseball mitts.

In a thick, faraway voice, I said, "Hey, Siri. Call my dad."

My phone said, "I'm sorry. I don't see anyone named My Dad in your contacts."

The room spun wildly, a roller coaster, a carousel. I pushed myself onto my hands and knees and then collapsed.

The darkness had stars in it. I floated around, weightless.

"Help," I tried to yell. It came out as a whisper-croak. "Help!" I cried louder. I didn't, though. The word never left my mouth. My mouth didn't make words anymore.

This is how I die.

The thought was wild, a snake coiling its way through my brain.

The stars faded, and then there was only darkness.

———

I opened my eyes. The spinning had stopped. So had the nausea. I felt sore and worn out. I was alone in a room, in a bed. I lifted my head, trying to stitch memories together.

This was a hospital. The dark sky outside the window told me it was nighttime.

I looked down at myself. I was in a hospital gown, my arms resting on my stomach. My left hand had an IV hooked up to it, and monitors beeped nearby.

"Hello?" I said, testing my voice. It was hoarse.

I noticed a white remote-control thing lying on the bed beside me. I picked it up and pushed the call button.

A woman in scrubs hurried through the door, followed closely by my grandmother. When my grandma saw me, she rushed to my bed and started ordering the nurse around. "Page the doctor. Check her vitals. How is her urine output?"

"Ma'am, please have a seat," the nurse said firmly, and I instantly liked her commanding tone.

"What happened?" I asked Grandma.

She sat on the foot of my bed. "You overdosed on Valium," she said, blunt as usual.

The nurse shot her a look. "Ma'am, she just woke up."

Grandma waved that off. I said, "Overdosed on Valium? Like, the medication?"

"Don't play dumb with me," she snapped.

I was so confused, I felt myself starting to tear up. "What's going on? Where's Dad?"

"He's talking to the police."

"The *police*? Why?"

My grandma and the nurse looked at each other.

I said, "Can I call him? Can you give me my phone? Do I have my stuff?"

"The police have your phone. They found your texts."

"What texts?" I felt like Alice in Wonderland, down a deep, dark hole.

"I didn't know you were doing drugs. Pills. I didn't know you had gotten that from your mother. We'll get you help."

I sat straight up. "What? Drugs? No."

"Francesca. They *found* your *texts*."

"Texts I sent? Or someone sent me?" I was trying desperately to understand.

She leveled me with a glare. "They found all of them, Francesca."

I stared at her, more confused than I'd ever felt in my life.

"But I don't take Valium," I managed.

"According to your drug tests, you do."

Something terrible was happening. Texts didn't just appear; an overdose didn't just happen. I had never willingly taken any Valium, and I couldn't see how it was possible to have accidentally ingested enough to overdose.

Someone had dosed me with it. On purpose. It was the only explanation.

But who? And *why*?

My skin was full of goose bumps. I pulled the blanket over my chest and arms, like it could shield me from danger.

Twenty-Two

I CAN'T DO IT.

I feel this panic every single time we approach a group of girls.

"Hey," Frankie calls out, friendly as ever, each time like it's the first. "Are you guys on your way to Blue?"

The girls turn around. There are three of them, and they're young, maybe nineteen years old. Blue is eighteen and over, so this is fine. One of the girls, a pretty brunette with streaky, highlighted hair, gives Frankie a head-to-toe once-over.

"No, we're on our way to Monarch," she replies, which I've learned is a club on the next block. God, this is tiresome. I'm adding nightclubs to the list of things I am permanently not interested in.

"Oh, okay." Frankie shoots me a disappointed look that I know she's faking. "It's just that we get into Blue free if we bring more than two people, and they're having this massive VIP party tonight with these industry people who are casting extras for a new movie. We were hoping to find some friends." She's wearing red lipstick, and she twists her smile into a pout.

The girl detaches her eyes from Frankie's lips and turns to her friends. "We could try a new place," she suggests while one of her friends says, "I'm in for a casting party. I haven't auditioned in two weeks. I need to get in front of some people."

The third friend, a fair-skinned blond with short, shaggy hair, shrugs. "Fine with me. I don't care where we go."

I force a smile and say, "Great." They all look at me like they didn't realize I was here. Awesome.

We walk together up the sidewalk, Frankie falling into step beside the brunette. The blond stays by my side and murmurs, "Honestly, I hate clubbing."

I'm surprised. "You do? Why do you do it?"

She casts me a rueful look. "Because I don't want to be alone on a Friday night. Do you like it?" She seems like she already intuits the answer.

I admit, "Not really."

"But your girlfriend does," she guesses.

"Oh, we're not together." I feel my cheeks warming. It's the first time a stranger has guessed I was queer. I'm weirdly pleased.

"Oh." She sounds surprised. She gestures to her friend and Frankie, who are chatting animatedly ahead of us. "I guess I should have known your girlfriend wouldn't be flirting it up with my friend right in front of you."

It stings, and I have to force a laugh. "Yeah," I say, which is all I can think with my head swimming. Is Frankie flirting? No, she's just doing her job. Right as I dismiss it, she puts a hand on the brunette's back and makes a "right this way" gesture at the entrance of Blue.

Adam lets us in, and I follow Frankie and the other girls, feeling bitter and angry. I hate her for being so self-possessed. And I can't stand to see them flirting. Maude, Candace, or Elizabeth: I'm obviously a bad person. I can't be happy for Frankie. No way.

Natalya spots us as we walk in, and she crows with happiness and comes to say hello, stunning in an ice-blue minidress and white heels, her hair wavy and long down her back, golden-tan legs endless. "Look how pretty these girls are," she tells me in my ear. Frankie remains in conversation with the brunette, leaning in so they can hear each other above the music.

Natalya is still talking to me. I force my attention off Frankie and onto her. "You're doing so great," she goes on. "Why don't you come to my after-party later on? I'm going to head over there at one. You can leave early and come with me. I want you to meet some of my friends. Maybe a new boyfriend?"

I'm nodding along, and Frankie still has a hand on the brunette, this time on her forearm. They're talking intensely while the other two girls head off to the dance floor. Why doesn't Frankie cut her loose so we can get back to work?

Natalya says, "Candace? Candace?" She has to say it a couple of times before I remember it's my name.

"Sorry. I thought I saw someone I knew," I fib, pointing vaguely at the crowd.

"What do you think? You want to come to my after-party later? There will be lots of cute guys."

"I don't think so, but thank you," I reply, wincing at the disappointed look on her face. "We have to be somewhere in the morning," I explain.

"Okay, well, let me know if you reconsider. And don't forget to hydrate! Get ice water from the bar." She gives me a dimpled smile before disappearing into the crowd.

Frankie is *still* talking to the girl. I march over so she can see me wave, indicating that we should get going. She doesn't notice me. I sigh heavily and join them, hating the idea of busting into their cozy little bubble.

Frankie shoots me a smile. "Hey there! Sorry, we got talking." The brunette smiles at me, too. Why is everyone so goddamn smiley?

"Sorry to interrupt," I say, the words a little sharp despite my best efforts. "Can I borrow you for a minute?"

"Of course." Frankie shoots an apologetic look at the girl. "I'll catch up with you soon, okay?"

"'Kay." The brunette hugs her and says, "I didn't get your number yet. Make sure you find me. I'm Allison, by the way."

"Frankie." She holds her hand out to shake, and while I watch, dumbfounded, they shake hands and hug one more time. Frankie turns to me, a little flushed, and says, "Okay, let's get back to it."

"Frankie?" I repeat, shocked.

"Yes...?" She crooks an eyebrow. Suddenly it dawns on her. "Oh no. My name is supposed to be Ivy."

"What the hell is wrong with you? You see a pretty girl and suddenly have amnesia? Are you trying to get us caught?"

"Of course not. It was just a mistake. Habit. I was off guard."

"Yeah, I could tell."

My passive aggression stings, and her face darkens with anger. "I just forgot for a minute. It could happen to anyone."

"Anyone who was too busy flirting to do what they're supposed to do," I retort.

"I wasn't flirting—"

"Give it a rest. Even her friend thought you guys were flirting."

"You're talking about me with random people now?"

We stop, glaring at each other. I can't believe I ever trusted her. I can't sit here all night and watch her hook up with Allison. The betrayal physically hurts.

"I think it's clear you don't need me," I say, my voice simmering with anger. "Why don't I leave you to it? Go ahead and have fun with *Allison* tonight. Don't worry about paying off your passport. I'll handle that, like I handle everything else. You can just do whatever the hell you want."

Before she can reply, I disappear. Alone. The way I was always meant to.

Twenty-Three

PURSE SLUNG OVER MY SHOULDER, I *CLICK-CLACK* ANGRILY DOWN Hollywood Boulevard, cursing the stupid heels I wore for this stupid job. I'm furious, my brain racing from one angry thought to the next. She's probably dancing with Allison right now. I say the name in a spiteful, childish voice in my head. *Allison.*

A pair of shady-looking guys whistle at me as I walk by them, and I realize I've gone past the touristy part of Hollywood into the sketchy eastern section. Ahead is a long homeless encampment, and a group of young men watching me with glittering eyes while they smoke weed.

I turn and hurry back the way I'd come, heart pounding, suddenly very aware of my short skirt, blond wig, and heels—and the fact that I'm alone and have no one to call if something goes wrong except Frankie. No parents. No friends. No cops.

As I think this, a male voice says, "What's the hurry?"

I jump out of my skin. It's one of the guys from the group. He's caught up to me and is walking right at my side, like we're on a date. I ignore him, mind racing. I can't scream or make a scene; what if someone calls the police?

"Hey, slow down, honey. What's the rush?"

I do a frantic one-second search for options. The business next to us is closed, its picture window covered with a retractable iron grate. Across the street is a restaurant, its patio half-full of diners. Traffic is medium busy, a car coasting by every few seconds.

I jump off the curb into the street and run. A car honks at me and screeches its brakes. Slowed by my heels, I hurry across the street, up the sidewalk, and into the restaurant. Only when I'm inside do I look behind me. The man is standing on the opposite side of the street, glaring at me with narrowed, dangerous eyes.

I turn away from him, toward the interior of the restaurant. It smells like pizza and garlic bread.

"Are you meeting someone?" the hostess asks. She's a little older than me, maybe nineteen or twenty, and has short-cropped hair and lots of tattoos.

"It's just me," I reply. She looks surprised; I'm clearly dressed for a night out. "I'm eating before I go clubbing with my friends," I explain, and she nods.

"Right this way." She begins to lead me to a small table at the front of the restaurant by the window.

"Is it okay if I sit farther back?" I hesitate, then imagine she's not the type of person to call the cops over something like this. "There's a creepy guy sort of bothering me out there, and I don't want him to be able to watch me through the window."

"Of course." She walks me the opposite way, toward the back. "Assholes," she commiserates quietly.

She waves me into a seat at a small, tucked-away two-top and hands me a menu. I sit there for a minute, just breathing. I need pepper spray. Or a Taser. And a knife. I can't be wandering around so unprotected. I'm supposed to be a spider, building a web, but spiders are venomous. I'm unarmed and helpless. For the first time, I really under-stand: I'm prey.

When the waiter, an older man who doesn't give me a second glance, arrives, I order fettuccine Alfredo as a spiritual affront to my mother. To cheer myself up, I look through news stories about my own death on my phone, pausing on one of my mom's interviews.

I zoom in on her face. She looks tired, worn out, wan.

I sit with the image for a minute.

Is this what I'd hoped for?

I feel sorry for her. That's not right. I should enjoy her suffering.

My pasta comes, and I toss my phone into my purse and

start eating. But my appetite is off; I keep seeing my mom's traumatized face.

I push the plate away and get my phone out again. I surf through other stories, trying to restore the feeling of righteous vengeance.

But then I picture Nathan's dead body, the image I've been hiding from. I remember rolling him into a ditch. I remember the look on his dead face as he'd gazed up at the night sky. It wasn't fair, what happened to him. He hadn't been a nice guy, not in my short experience with him, but he didn't deserve to die like that.

I'm filled with pity and remorse. It could have just as easily been me getting hit by that car. The universe is so cruel, so random.

Now I'm definitely not hungry.

I look around the restaurant at the other diners. It's past midnight, and they're mostly couples on dates and friend groups in their twenties. At the table next to me, a pair of men saw away with steak knives at what looks like veal parmesan.

After my encounter with the guy, I see how important it is for Frankie and me to stick together, even if we're in a fight. I should go meet her at the club so we can get a cab home. It's the sensible thing to do. I pull out my phone and call Frankie's burner, having programmed the number in when we'd bought it. It rings out and beeps, an anonymous voicemail we don't even know how to check. I hang up and try again, but no luck. She must be inside Blue, unable to hear over the music.

As I stand and grab my purse, I notice the empty table next to me; the men left a few minutes ago, but their dirty dishes haven't been cleared yet. Thinking about the guy outside, I grab one of the steak knives, wipe it clean on a napkin, and slide it into my purse. It's stupid, but it makes me feel a little better.

The hostess waves goodbye, and I breathe a sigh of relief when I emerge onto the sidewalk. He's not out here.

I walk fast; the sidewalk is emptier than it was, but it's still as busy as any daytime street in Orange County. I keep my eyes straight ahead and try not to itch my scalp, which is hot and sweaty under the wig. The air is cool, but the fumes from cars and vape pens create a mustiness that makes me feel claustrophobic. Twenty minutes later, I arrive at Cahuenga and turn right to head up to the front door of Blue. I approach Adam, who acknowledges me with a faint lift of his chin.

"Is Ivy inside?" I ask him.

He shrugs.

"I'm going to go check."

He opens the velvet rope for me, and I pass the line of guys and move into the packed, bass drum–booming club. I wind through the dance floor until I find Allison and her group, but Frankie isn't with them.

I tap Allison on the shoulder. She turns to look at me, glowing with sweat and bright with alcohol, a guy basically superglued to her butt. "Heyyyy," she says. "Where've you been?"

"I'm looking for my friend. Have you seen her?"

"She went to some after-party! She invited us, but we were having fun here."

"When did she go?" I ask, trying to process that Frankie would leave without me, without even calling or texting to tell me where she was going.

She shrugs.

I turn and push through the crowd. My heart is starting to speed up again. I find the girl who collects the cover charge behind her little booth in the dark entry hall, and I say, "Hey, you know my friend Ivy? Did she go to an after-party or—" I suddenly remember Natalya's invitation. "I think it's Natalya's party," I tell the girl.

"I dunno." She shrugs, looking annoyed like this is a stupid question.

"Well, do you know where Natalya's house is?"

She shakes her head. "Ask Adam. They hang out sometimes."

I turn and hurry out the door to Adam. "Did Natalya go back to her place for an after-party?" '

He's busy carding a group of girls. "Yeah."

"Well, Ivy went there, apparently, so I have to go pick her up. Can you please give me the address?"

He looks up from the ID he's analyzing like he's on *CSI*. "Yeah. Okay."

I pull out my phone and type the address into Google Maps. It's a house up in the hills. I call a cab, my stomach in knots. I don't like this. Not at all.

Twenty-Four

THREE WEEKS AGO
Frankie

THE MORNING WAS BRIGHT AND SUNNY. I LAY IN BED for a while, snoozing my alarm, and watched the stripes of light from my blinds dance on the high ceiling. I felt clear-headed and clean, and I realized I'd been living in a nauseous fog for weeks. It had crept up on me slowly, and I tried to think back to when I started feeling weird. Christmas?

Someone had been dosing me for months.

Since I returned home from the hospital, a stifled silence had fallen over the house. My dad and Leah didn't seem to know what to say to me. Leah had spent a horrible hour talking to me about her own teenage struggles, and my dad was doing that guy thing where he didn't know how to help, so he kept very busy elsewhere. No one had let me see the texts I'd supposedly been sending, but apparently I'd been trying to acquire and sell drugs. The police had kept my phone, and my grandma, in her trademark way, was trying to use lawyers and money make the whole thing disappear.

The alarm on my new phone went off again, and I silenced it. This phone was restricted; I could only call or text my dad and grandma, and I wasn't allowed to download any new apps.

I'd been registered for mandatory, twice-weekly addiction counseling. I'd told the therapist the truth, that I'd never taken any drugs, that I thought someone was dosing me. She'd looked at me scornfully and acted like I was trying to get away with a preposterous lie.

I couldn't stall anymore. I had to get ready.

———

I stood in front of school for a minute, backpack slung onto one shoulder, considering everything I could do to avoid going inside.

"You okay?" Gia's voice startled me. She was walking toward the school and had paused near me.

I looked her in the eyes, not in the mood for games. "Suddenly you care?" I replied.

She looked hurt. "What are you talking about?"

"We used to be best friends, and the second everyone decides to make fun of me, you act like you barely know me. But now you want to know how I am?"

She frowned and flicked her long, straight hair behind her shoulder. She was neat, every strand in place, every eyebrow hair combed. "I heard you OD'd."

"I didn't OD." I sounded defensive.

"Right." She turned away.

I grabbed her arm, pulling her back around. "What is your problem? Seriously, Gia, what the fuck?"

She yanked her arm away from me. "God. You're so ridiculous. Everything for attention. Everything about you, all the time."

"Attention?" I echoed, confused.

She did an imitation of my voice. "'I'm so edgy and depressed. No one understands me, even though I'm, like, some European heiress, and I live in Coto de Caza and have a billion-dollar inheritance.' Maybe if you didn't spend every day wanting everyone to feel sorry for you, you'd still have some friends." With that, she turned and flounced toward the front of school.

I noticed we were being watched by groups of people milling about. They whispered to each other now, little jittery snickers and mean eyes pointing at me like guns.

Face blazing hot, I moved past my audience. A group of football players called out, "Frank!"

I stopped, suddenly out of fucks to give. What did I have to lose?

I turned to them. "Do you have something you want to say?"

They giggled like children.

I felt like I was in a fishbowl, like I was on a stage, stripped apart by a hostile crowd. I felt surrounded by enemies. Was someone who dosed me here at school now? Was it one of these guys who always made fun of me? Who would want to do that, and why?

Gia's words came back, haunting me. I didn't know why she thought those things about me. I missed her so much; I desperately wished I could rewind back two years and tell her everything like I used to.

———

I thought about Gia all day long while I pretended to take notes in class and while I ate lunch alone in my usual corner of the quad. I watched her from afar, jealous of the easy way she moved from group to group, always polished and sharp, always with Matt's arm around her. I couldn't squelch the urge to reach out again, to grab her arm and make her talk it out with me.

We had last-period US history together, and I hung around after the bell rather than fleeing for the door as usual. I put my laptop and book into my backpack with painful slowness, observing her from the corner of my eye as she chatted with Matt and his friends. I followed her out into the hall, watching from a distance as she headed for cheerleading practice in the gym. An idea was brewing. If I could just get her alone, maybe after practice, I could confront her. We could hash it out.

Having confirmed she'd be practicing for a couple of hours, I headed out to the town car that was waiting for me. All the way home, I tapped my fingers impatiently on my knee.

The house was empty. I changed out of my uniform into my usual T-shirt and baggy jeans, chugged some chocolate milk, and trotted downstairs to my dad's study. In the top drawer of the big executive desk that he almost never used, I found my car keys exactly where I'd expected, behind the little drawer divider with all the other sets of keys to the gardening shed, my grandma's house, and whatever other assets he had access to. I also found the set of keys to his second car, a truck he had for weekend trips when he wanted to tow the boat. It was an F-350 and way bigger than anything I'd ever driven, but my Mustang was too recognizable. I'd have to wing it.

"Yoink," I whispered, pocketing the keys.

I hurried out of the house to the garage and opened it with the key code: my father's birthday. I'd always thought that was kind of narcissistic, using your own birthday as a password.

The truck's radio was tuned to some cheesy dad rock, and guitars came blaring out of the speakers when I turned it on. It made me remember the last time I'd ridden with my dad in this truck; he'd been doing one-handed air guitar while driving.

I drove carefully back to school, afraid of getting pulled over and shipped off to military academy or rehab for real. It went smoothly, and I pulled onto the side street adjacent to the school parking lot to wait. I checked the time. It was quarter to five. Cheerleading practice would end in fifteen minutes.

Sure enough, girls started trickling out of the gym alongside boys in basketball and volleyball uniforms. Around the other side of school, swim team and track were letting out, and the parking lot started filling up with people as they got into their expensive gas-guzzlers. No Gia, though. I wondered if I should just go to her house and wait for her. It was only a few miles from mine, and I'd been there a million times, but it had been a few years, and I wasn't sure I'd be able to find it.

At last, once almost everyone had cleared out, she came walking toward the lot alone. She had sweats on under her cheer skirt, and her posture told me she was tired.

I was about to get out and wave her down, but I thought it might be better to talk to her at her house. It was neutral territory. Fine, I'd follow her home.

She got into her car, which was an eight-year-old Lexus hand-me-down from her big sister (I was sure she was on a relentless mission to get her mom to let her upgrade), and when she pulled out of the lot onto the street, I eased the truck away from the curb and followed.

She didn't seem to notice me. She was texting and driving, stopping at the stop sign too long, making the person in line behind her impatient enough to honk. I was surprised when she turned right instead of left, toward the hills. She continued straight and then got on the freeway heading north.

That was weird. Maybe she wasn't going home.

I almost turned around, afraid of the wrath I'd face when my dad realized I'd taken the truck, but I kept going. I was determined to have this out with her today.

She was on the freeway for five miles, and when she pulled off, we were in a landscape of newer, middle-class developments, mostly townhome and condo complexes interspersed with Targets and Walmarts. She drove another few miles and turned right into a subdivision of beige, cheap-looking townhomes.

She must be visiting someone, I decided, and was looking for a place to turn around when she pulled into a driveway behind a car I recognized as her mother's. It was unusual that I'd recognize her mom's car; most mothers I knew changed vehicles every year or two, and I hadn't seen her mom since freshman year. I pulled up to the curb a few houses away and watched Gia get out of her car, collect her bags, walk up the walkway to the front door, and let herself in.

I was shocked. It wasn't a bad neighborhood, not by any stretch, but this was a far, far reach from the mansion she'd lived in when we were friends.

I took a deep, shaky breath, nervous. At last I gathered my courage, got out of the truck, and rang the doorbell. I caught the aroma of marinara sauce, dinner cooking. Her parents never used to cook. They were a restaurant family. Her dad worked in Newport Beach as a lawyer, and her mom stayed home and did Pilates.

The door swung open, and her mom looked out at me. She was tall and blond, with large breasts and a skinny, wiry frame. She looked the same as I remembered her, in bootcut jeans with sparkly bling on the pockets and a V-neck turquoise top.

"Frankie," she cried, looking me up and down. "Oh my god, I haven't seen you in years! Look how tall you are!"

She pulled me in for a hug—fake boobs always felt so rock-hard—and then pushed me back out so she could get a better look at me. "You look— Your hair…" She trailed off.

"I know, I chopped it," I replied, smiling ruefully. "I'd go even shorter, but my grandma won't let me. Is Gia here?"

"Yes, of course. Come in." She looked hesitant. "Did she…invite you over?"

"Um…"

Gia trotted down the stairs then, having changed into shorts, and was just starting to say something to her mom when she saw me. Her eyes bugged out. "Frankie? What the hell?" She rushed toward me, and I thought she was going to hit me, but then she turned to her mom with scared eyes. "I didn't tell her where we lived."

I realized her mom looked angry. Clearly, Gia wasn't supposed to share her address with people. Why? "I followed you after cheer practice," I explained. "I wanted to talk to you. I didn't realize you'd moved. When—"

Gia and her mom were staring at me with such intensity, I trailed off into silence.

"This is temporary," her mom said, gesturing to the room around us. It was neatly but plainly furnished, like they'd gone to a generic furniture store and picked out the showroom basics.

"Okay," I replied, not understanding.

"Gia's father and I split up."

"Oh, I'm so sorry," I murmured uselessly.

Gia said, "Outside. Now." I thought she was kicking me out, but she beckoned me deeper into the townhouse and led me through a small kitchen, out onto an even smaller patio that had no furniture on it. She slid the glass door shut behind us and turned on me. "Now what? You're going to blackmail me? Get revenge?"

"Revenge?"

She was looking at me with arms crossed, nostrils flared, hair in a just-messy-enough bun. She was put together and feminine and everything Orange County wanted a girl to be, but in that moment, I realized she felt small.

"What happened?" I asked gently. "Your parents divorced? Why didn't you guys stay in the house?"

She lifted her chin. "Because Dad's a lawyer, and he took almost everything. So my mom is having to, like, redo our lives, but she's working as an administrative assistant."

"Shit," I breathed. "That sucks. I'm so sorry."

"Yeah, it does."

"Are you going to have to transfer to public school?"

She shook her head. "Dad says he'll pay through graduation."

"Good."

We stood there awkwardly, and then we started speaking at once. I said, "I came here to ask if you're the one who's been—" and she said, "I don't know how everything got so—"

We stopped. We looked at each other and laughed.

I said, "Remember our *Hunger Games* phase? When we used to put on costumes and go out into the greenbelt?"

She snorted. "We were such dorks."

"Totally." I paused. "What happened, Gia? Why are you such a dick to me now?"

She leaned on the patio railing. On the other side, a walkway wound between townhomes. It was all very claustrophobic, all these houses shoved into such a small space.

"Frankie...," she began.

"Yeah?"

"I know your mom left and your dad is kind of out to lunch. But, like, you have no idea how good you have it. You walk around under this dark cloud, like everyone is supposed to feel sorry for you. If I had what you have, I'd be queen of the school."

"Someone's been dosing me with Valium," I said, the words bursting from me. "I don't know what to do. Can you think of anyone at school who would want to do that to me?"

The look on her face was priceless. "Excuse me, what?"

"Someone's been slipping me Valium. I almost died, Gia."

"Why would someone do that?" she asked, skeptical.

"That's what I want to know. I thought it might be you."

She gave me an are-you-serious look I recognized from our years together. "First you crash your car and almost kill yourself, and then you OD. Maybe you should take some responsibility. Stop blaming your problems on other people. Stop making yourself the center of attention and then getting mad when it doesn't go how you wanted."

"You're not listening to me," I protested.

She lifted her chin, haughty. "Really?"

"I don't want attention, Gia. That's the last thing I want. I'm not trying to be weird or different or whatever else you said. I'm just gay." There it was. Out loud for the first time.

She lifted her eyebrows. "Like…you've…" She seemed to consider this for a few seconds. "I mean, I'm not surprised. But…"

"I'm not even sure I'm a girl. I don't know anything. I'm—" My voice chokes, and I can't say any more.

She stepped forward and reached for my shoulder. "Frankie, I don't know what to say. I didn't know. I mean, I suspected. Because you look…I mean, it's kind of…"

"Kind of what? Because I cut my hair and wear pants to school? Is that really so awful?" My words are sharp. "Because I don't look like you and your friends? Because your loser boyfriend doesn't think I'm femme enough?"

"You could be beautiful if you wanted to. Some of us can't afford to act out and do whatever we want. There's so much more pressure on me—" She held her hands up. "You know what? Never mind. You wouldn't understand."

My temper flared. "*You* wouldn't understand. How can you be with someone who treats me like that? What happened to you?"

"Survival happened to me." Her voice was low and strained.

I felt like I was going to start crying and never stop. I turned and slid the patio door open, stepped into the kitchen, and hurried away. Gia called after me, but I couldn't look back. I felt like I'd already said too much.

In the truck, I rested my forehead on the steering wheel.

Suddenly I remembered something she'd said, about the chain of disastrous events. She was right. I'd just had two near-death experiences back-to-back. First, my car had malfunctioned. Then the overdose.

There was no way the overdose had been an accident. Someone had been drugging me for months. It was very much on purpose.

Maybe the car was, too.

Twenty-Five

OUTSIDE THE WINDOWS OF THE TAXI, HOLLYWOOD LOOKS SPARKLY and festive. It's weird how the seediness doesn't translate into two-dimensional imagery; you have to be on the sidewalk in order to feel the grit.

I'm calling Frankie's burner phone for the thousandth time. It rings out and goes to voicemail. Frustrated, I push the end button and dial again. I can't believe she went to some party without even texting me. A little voice of humility reminds me that I stormed out and left *her*, so there wasn't much reason for Frankie to think I cared where she went. *Shut up*, I tell the voice. I hate it when my conscience suddenly decides to get involved. *Where have you been this whole time? I've been leaving dead bodies in the Hawaiian wilderness and conducting wanton thievery, but* now *I need an intervention?* Honestly.

We leave the strip and drive up into the hills, into residential neighborhoods with gates that branch off the street behind which I glimpse long driveways leading up to mansions. I check the address on my phone and confirm—we're headed in the right direction. If Natalya lives up here, why does she work at Blue? This must not be her house. I must have misunderstood. It has to be a friend's place or something.

The taxi pulls over at one of the gates, which stands open. "You want me to drop you off here or go up?" the driver asks.

I peer up the driveway and see lights, cars. "I'll walk up."

I pay him cash and get out, straightening my dress. Before walking up, I freshen my lip gloss and comb my fingers through the wig.

At the top of a hill, in front of the two-story modern mansion is a huge circular driveway full of vehicles stacked almost on top of each other, a nightmare if anyone has to leave. A valet is running around between them, and I see that he's moving a few cars so one can get out.

I take a nervous breath, straighten my shoulders, and walk up the path, between square-cut hedges, and through the front door.

The foyer has a two-story ceiling and leads straight into an open-concept great room with a white marble fireplace that travels all the way up to the ceiling high above. The room is furnished entirely in black and white, and people function like decorations chosen to offset the colorful abstract paintings hung judiciously on the walls.

In this front room, a handful of men in their late twenties are grouped onto a pair of leather couches, earnestly talking about something while throwing back shots from a bottle of what looks like scotch. Young women in a variety of short dresses surround them, not much older than me but beautiful and sophisticated in designer clothing and full faces of makeup. Scattered around the room, men in suits talk among themselves while their high-heeled, miniskirted dates hover nervously around them. Horrified, I remember Natalya telling me there would be lots of cute guys here tonight. Yuck.

I shake my head minutely and square my shoulders. I have to look like I belong here. I actually do fit right in; there are a lot of blonds, and my club dress and heels are apparently the uniform. I make my way through the room, waving cigarette smoke out of my face, and turn into a hall.

That takes me to another living room, this one with a massive TV playing music videos and couches full of people lounging around and drinking. I feel the appraising eyes of older men on me as I walk through, trying not to call attention to myself. *Frankie, you're really dead now.*

A figure steps forward out of a corner: Natalya, smiling but looking confused. "Candace?" she asks, approaching me.

Relieved, I reply, "Oh, hi! There you are. I heard Ivy came here after work, so I thought I'd meet up with her."

She smiles brightly, but something is weird; I've clearly surprised her. She says, "Of course! She's around here somewhere. Let me get you a drink." She leads me to a bar set up at the side of the room. It's professional, the kind you'd see in a nice restaurant, not a house. Behind it, a man with huge biceps is shaking a martini for a gray-haired man in a suit.

"Something sweet for my friend," Natalya tells him and gives me a wink.

I smile in return, but it's more of a grimace. The bartender makes something pink and hands it to me with a flourish. "Thanks," I say. The gray-haired man is still standing here despite having gotten his martini, his blue eyes studying me. Creeped out, I tell Natalya, "I'm going to find Fr—Ivy, okay?"

She's already busy with someone else, a tall, dark-haired man in jeans and a button-down. I slip away with my drink, back into the smoky crowds.

Determined to find Frankie and get the hell out of here, I start searching the house. I find the kitchen, which is full of people pouring themselves drinks from a self-serve station at the center island. I discover bathrooms, an office, and head upstairs, where I find a bunch of bedrooms, some of them occupied with the doors locked. Gross.

Back down in the great room, I'm struck by the difference between the men and women at this party. The men are noticeably older, mostly in their late twenties and up; these are not college-aged guys. The women are much younger; I'd be surprised if any of them is over twenty-two. They're all very, very pretty, and the way they focus on the men, laughing at their jokes and hanging on their every word...

On my second lap through the room where I'd gotten

the pink drink I'm still holding, I notice the men who hang back at the periphery. They were in the great room too, but I hadn't noticed them because they blend in with the other men—they're wearing blazers with jeans or full suits, and they have a certain edge to them. In each room, I spot three or four of these types. They're watchful, eyes sharply passing from one person to the next. Their hands are either clasped in front of them or behind them.

They're bouncers, I realize. Security.

This seems like a lot of security for a private party. I estimate there must be a hundred people here, and there are at least eight of these guys.

As I watch, a man sitting at one of the couches pulls a girl onto his lap, laughing loudly with his friends. She screams, but it's a fake scream of protest. She looks like she's kind of into it, if a little embarrassed. But her scream startles one of the bouncer guys, and he moves the lapel of his blazer aside. His hand makes it partway to a gun in a holster, but then he sees it's just a game between this man and the girl, and he relaxes.

What the hell kind of party is this? Again, I remember Natalya mentioning I could find a boyfriend here.

Okay, Frankie, we need to get out of here. Where are you?

A back door opens, and I realize I've been so absorbed in studying the people, I haven't noticed the pool and patio through the back windows. At least fifty more people are out there, some in the pool, some hanging out around it. I hurry for the glass door.

A man in his forties opens it for me. "Hey, hey," he says, blocking the exit with his body. "Why are you in such a hurry?"

"I'm just going to meet my friend. Thanks." I squeeze past him, grossed out by the smell of his cologne and feeling less safe by the minute.

There's a mile of patio between the house and the pool, and I pass a few clusters of men arguing and young women laughing in high-pitched voices. No Frankie.

A handful of beautiful girls in bikinis are swimming while fully dressed men watch from the deck. I search the people clustered around, and still no Frankie.

My eyes travel away from the pool, up the dark lawn that wraps around to the driveway in front. As my eyes adjust to the darkness, I see a small shape, that of a woman walking on the grass.

I take a couple of steps away from the pool. Could that be her?

As I watch, the figure passes in front of a bank of low landscape lighting at the base of a palm tree, and I see her silhouette. Short hair, heels in hand.

Frankie.

Twenty-Six

I START AWAY FROM THE POOL, INTO THE DARKNESS BEYOND THE party lights, walking fast onto the close-cropped lawn, trying not to let my heels sink into the grass. "Frankie," I call softly. I'm out of breath by the time I finally get to her. "Frankie!"

She turns, loses her balance, takes a wide step, and recovers. Her shoes dangle loosely from her right hand, a plastic cup in her left. "Whoa," she says, starting to laugh. "Wait. Are you here? No way."

"You're drunk." I sound like a furious parent. "Give me that." I snatch the cup out of her hand and smell it. It's strong enough to set my nostrils on fire. I throw the cup aside. "Come on, we have to get out of here."

"Screw you. I'm having a nice time. I'm making friends."

She scowls. Her hair is messy, her skirt riding up her thighs. She's a disaster, but I kind of enjoy the unchecked anger on her face.

"I like the energy, I really do, but there are guys with guns here, Frankie, and it's time to go." I take her by the elbow.

She yanks her arm away from me. "Stop bossing me around. Why are you even here? I thought you left. Remember? You were *so mad*?"

"Yes. I remember. We can talk about this on the cab ride home." I try pulling her again.

"You do *not* get to tell me when—"

"Hey, girls," a man's voice interrupts Frankie's rant as he emerges from the darkness. "How you doing? You having a little argument?" I recognize him from inside. He's wearing a blazer and jeans, has a shaved head, and looks strong and wiry. He's one of the rich-looking men in their late twenties I saw when I first arrived. I wonder what happened to the rest of his entourage and why he's all the way out here on the lawn in the dark.

"We're good," I say, blood rushing in my ears. "We're just getting ready to head out. My friend wanted to take a little walk."

"I'm not leaving," Frankie slurs, lifting her chin stubbornly.

The man cocks his head and looks back and forth between us. "Seems like your friend wants to stay."

"We'll figure it out. Thanks for checking on us." I give

him a forced smile and put a hand on Frankie's back. "Come on, let's get your shoes on."

"Stop telling me what to do," Frankie retorts, taking a step back from me and stumbling. The man jumps to help her and wraps an arm around her waist. In the darkness, his eyes glint white.

"I'll take you inside to lie down for a while," he tells Frankie. "Sound good?"

White-hot fear rears up inside me remembering the locked bedrooms upstairs. "Nope. We're good. Thank you, though." I try to pull Frankie away from him. I look around for anyone to help us. We're a hundred yards from the pool, out of earshot of the crowd and shrouded in shadows. Besides, none of these people would help us. Instinctively, my hand closes around the handle of the steak knife inside my purse.

"You can go home if you want," the man says, shouldering me out of the way.

I get in front of him again. "Get your hands off her."

A dangerous expression takes over his face. "You're going to want to get out of the way."

Frankie's eyebrows furrow. "I don't feel so good."

In a fluid motion, he ducks down and lifts her over his shoulder, holding her there with a hand on the backs of her knees. She squirms a little, but he has her in a vice grip. "Move," he says to me. "Go home. Or go get a drink and join the party."

I can't let him take her in there, but what am I going

to do with a steak knife against this hulk of a man? I pull at Frankie's ankles, trying to wrestle her away from him. He punches me in the chest, shoving me back. He turns and starts walking toward the house, and again I run to get in his way. "I'll call the cops," I bluff. "She's underage. You'll get in trouble for having her here."

Something in him seems to snap, and he whips his free hand up to my neck. He grabs my throat, thumb under my jaw, fingers clasped to the other side. My head swims. I try to draw in breath. I can't. Everything is getting blurry. I know what this is; I've read about it. It's a trick used in martial arts. He's going to make me pass out. Then what will happen while I'm unconscious? His hand is so strong; I tear at it but can't make it budge.

The knife.

As my vision fades to black, I fumble it out of my purse, get as good a grip on it as I can, and stab him in the stomach with all my strength.

It catches him just under the ribs, angling up. He releases me, crying out in pain. I haven't let go of the knife; an irrational fear tells me he's going to pull it out and use it on me. He struggles, dropping Frankie like a sack of potatoes onto the grass. The movement makes the knife shift position, and it pushes through some barrier and sinks all the way into his chest.

He makes a horrible groaning noise. Blood pours out of the wound. I snap my hand open and trip backward away from him, landing on my butt on the cool grass.

He grips the knife handle. His face is blank, shocked, blue eyes wide.

I gulp in huge breaths of air. Frankie rolls onto her hands and knees and throws up on the grass.

The man stands above us, clutching the knife. Blood soaks his white T-shirt. I feel myself shaking to the core.

He takes a step toward the pool, trips, and falls to his knees. After a moment, he slumps to the grass, where he lies quietly on his side, curled in the fetal position.

Twenty-Seven

IT'S QUIET BUT FOR THE DISTANT SOUNDS OF THE PARTY. FRANKIE IS done throwing up; she's silent and still, passed out on her stomach. I crawl to the man to see if he's breathing. His eyes are closed. With a shaking hand, I feel his neck, his wrist. I can't tell if there's a pulse, but I'm not exactly a doctor.

I'm hyperventilating, the edges of my vision blurry with panic. I need to get a grip. I need to figure out what to do.

I glance toward the pool. They can't see us here in the dark, but if someone decided to take a little walk like Frankie did...

All those men inside with guns.

I crawl to Frankie. "Hey. Hey!" I shake her. "We have to go. Frankie? Wake up."

She mumbles something incoherent but doesn't open her eyes.

"Shit," I moan. "Come on, Frankie. Come on!" I take my shoes off and try to lift her, try to pull her to her feet. She's limp. "Wake up!" I slap her across the face. Her eyes flicker open, but then she falls back into unconsciousness.

Desperate, I look around. Behind us the lawn leads around the side of the house to where the valet is playing Tetris with the cars. We could feasibly get out that way and sneak down the driveway, if I could only get Frankie to walk.

"Come on, Frankie," I mutter. I get my hands under her armpits and drag her, then drop her back onto the grass, panting. Frankie and I had lugged Nathan's body, but this is twice as hard alone. How do murderers do this? I try pulling her by the ankles, but that's no good, either.

And then it hits me—an idea.

Abandoning my shoes but holding onto our purses, I sprint across the lawn, up the slight hill through the darkness.

This lawn leads up to the circular driveway, which is packed full of cars. I scope out the area, examining the row of vehicles parked at the end by the grass. There's a fancy Expedition, a Mercedes coupe, an Audi...They're all stacked in, which sucks. But the driveway is bordered by a ten-foot stretch of grass. You could drive on that shoulder if you needed to, down to the street.

I decide on the Expedition. It seems most likely to be able to off-road a bit.

Crouching behind cars, heart pounding, I creep toward the valet stand. He's busy, off on the other side of the house getting someone's keys. Quickly I go through the keys he has hanging on the little pegs. I find a few sets that have Ford fobs. I grab all of them and duck back down, sharp little handfuls of keys stabbing my palms.

Still hidden, I start pressing Unlock on all the different keys. At last one lights up the Expedition, and I wheeze out a half laugh, half sob. I'm sweating so hard under my wig, I'm almost ready to tear it off.

I return the other keys to the pegs and crouch-run to the Expedition. I climb in and look out the window. The valet is nowhere in sight.

I turn the car on and look for the gearshift and emergency brake. I release the brake, put it in gear, and press down on the gas. It revs forward, gets hung up on the curb, and then lifts and hops onto the grass. My heart is pounding out of my chest. Any second now, someone could sound the alarm.

I keep the headlights off and inch over the grass, past the garage, aiming downhill toward where I left Frankie, careful not to overshoot and accidentally run her over.

There. I see the faint silhouettes of two bodies slumped onto the lawn, almost invisible in the darkness. I pull the Expedition toward them and throw it in Park.

I get out and cross the ten feet of grass toward Frankie. "Come on. Time to go." I grab her arm and pull her to a sitting position. "Just have to get into the car," I tell her, and she helps me a little as I heave her to her feet. I drag her around to the passenger's side; she's flopping against me, feet stumbling uselessly on the grass. I rest her on the side of the car, pull the door open, and heave-push her up into the seat, where she slumps over sideways. I slam the door behind her, run to grab our shoes off the grass, and race around to the driver's seat. I throw our purses and shoes on the floor by her feet and pull my seat belt on. Frankie groans miserably, and I hit the gas.

The grass is bumpy beneath us. I go way faster this time, less committed to stealth than to getting the hell out of here. I stay on the grass shoulder down the driveway until I clear the cars, at which point I steer left and bump onto the concrete. In the rearview mirror, I see a group of people leaving the party, faces turned to stare at the Expedition.

I flip on the headlights and go, screeching out onto the street, down the hill toward Hollywood. I'm not paying close attention to the roads, and I take a wrong turn, end up in a cul-de-sac, and have to flip a quick U-turn to get out, which sends me into a full-on anxiety attack. Finally, the narrow lane opens up onto a larger street, and I'm speeding down Highland with a million other cars.

What do I do? Where do I go?

Frankie moans again, and I spare a glance to check on her. She's trying to sit up, which seems good, and both hands are clutching her head.

"You're okay," I tell her in a voice that does not sound okay.

"Maude?" she whispers, voice rough.

"I've got you. We're going somewhere safe."

She falls asleep again, head bobbing limp. At the next red light, I reach around her and pull on her seat belt.

The music is on in the car. I had no idea. How did I not notice? It's hip-hop, something dark and loud. I fumble for the controls and turn it off.

I need a plan, and I need it now. This car has got to have GPS. We need to ditch it as fast as possible.

That's only one of the many problems. The knife in that man's gut is going to have my fingerprints on it.

That's fine, I argue to myself. My fingerprints aren't on file anywhere. When the police run them, they won't get a match. And I'll be out of the country soon enough. The cops work slow, right? I remember hearing that on one of my crime shows.

First things first. I need to ditch the car. Where's a good place to do it, somewhere the police would waste a lot of time searching for us, giving us more of a chance to escape?

The airport? That's smart, but too far. I need somewhere close.

A hospital.

I pull onto the shoulder of the road and get my phone out of my purse. My hands are shaking so bad I almost can't unlock it. I find the nearest hospital, which is down Vermont, only ten minutes away.

"This is good," I mutter, reassuring myself. This is so much worse than what happened in Hawaii. "Shut up," I whisper to myself. I keep feeling the knife pushing through his skin, the muscle, that last horrible release where it slipped deep into his chest. "Shut *up*," I command my brain.

Frankie mumbles, "I'm not talking."

"You're awake!" I'm so relieved, I want to cry. "Oh my god. Okay, that's good."

She stretches, groans, her skirt riding up to reveal her underwear. I look away, back at the road, and reach across to pull it down for her. "Try to wake up. You're going to have to walk a little."

The plan materializes while I drive: We'll ditch the car at the hospital and catch a taxi to . . . to where? I have to imagine the cops will trace the taxi, so I should have it drop us somewhere far from our motel, somewhere that will make them waste even more time searching for us . . .

My brain is busy, but my stomach is sick. Is something wrong with me that I can stab a man and still come up with these whole, intricate plans? Am I a sociopath?

Maude is used to plotting and planning. She's ruthless and secretive. Elizabeth won't be like that. She's a nice person, someone who works honest jobs and lives a quiet life. Once I become her, this will all be someone else's nightmare.

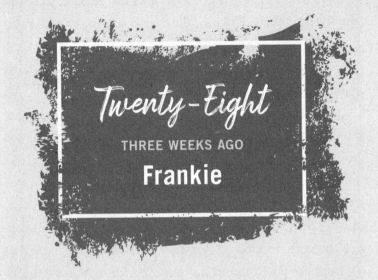

Twenty-Eight

THREE WEEKS AGO

Frankie

IT WAS SIX THIRTY WHEN I PULLED INTO THE DRIVE-way, having rushed home from Gia's place to return the truck, hoping to beat my dad and Leah to the house. I groaned to myself; Leah's Mercedes was parked in the spot of honor, the covered space between the garage and the house. I pulled the truck carefully into the garage and hopped out.

When I let myself inside, music was blaring from the back of the house. I tiptoed through the kitchen and laundry room—the music blared louder, some horrible squeaky pop—and poked my head into the gym. Leah was in there with her trainer, strapped into the Pilates gear.

Leah noticed me and smiled, sweaty and red-faced. "Help me," she mouthed, and her trainer laughed.

I returned through the kitchen, in a hurry now, not sure when my dad would show up. I let myself into his study, flicked the lights on, and returned the truck keys to their place in the drawer.

I sat at his desk, contemplating.

He tended to use paper files rather than digitizing and scanning things in. My best chance to find what I was looking for was probably in the desk file cabinet drawers. I tried the one on the right. Locked.

Hmm.

I checked the box of keys and tried three likely candidates before landing on the correct one. I slid the drawer out, eyes flitting nervously to the windows in anticipation of a flash of headlights. I squatted down and riffled through the files, reading the tabs. Triumphant, I extracted a file marked "Mustang."

It was almost seven o'clock. My dad would be home any minute. I hemmed and hawed, then put the key back into the drawer and hurried out of the study, turning the light off. My feet pounded on the stairs as I rushed to my room and shut the door behind me. I retreated to my bathroom, locked the door, and sat on the floor.

The folder looked disappointing at first; there was the paperwork from the sale of the car, the title in my dad's name, insurance paperwork listing me as a driver. I set each document aside, starting to think what I wanted wasn't going to be in here.

And then I found it: records from the accident. My heart pounded faster as I leafed through a solid twenty pages. There was the police report with photos of the car all banged up, along with the insurance claim.

Then there was a report from the mechanic. My heart sped up even faster as I unfolded a blueprint of a car with hand-scrawled notes beside it that read: *Brake line wear and tear/accidental damage.*

I considered that. Yes, clearly something had gone wrong with my brakes.

I flipped to the next page, where the insurance company had attached a Summary of Findings.

Cause of Malfunction: Brake line dislocation. And then a highly technical description that confused me.

I got my phone out of my pocket and Googled "brake line malfunction causes."

I poked through the results page and found that brake lines can erode over time, or they can be damaged if the brake mechanism is under your car and you drive fast over a massive bump. But if the brakes just suddenly die, that usually means there was interference. As in, someone damaged them on purpose.

I stared at that for a while.

Who would want to do that? And why? I considered the fact that the brakes had given out on the one steep hill I drove daily, and the fact that I'd almost died in the accident.

What good did killing me do anyone? I thought about all the people at school. They didn't like me, but they didn't care about me enough to plot a whole actual murder. I didn't have any exes, no spurned love interests.

Something was starting to eat at me.

I pulled up Google again and typed in "Can you get life insurance on someone under 18?"

I scanned through the results. No. Life insurance on kids wasn't a thing.

Well, but wait. Was life insurance really necessary? Somewhere, a bank account with millions of dollars was waiting for me to turn eighteen. What if...

I pulled up Google again and typed in "What happens to a kid's trust fund if they die?"

This answer wasn't as easy to find as the last one. It seemed like a lot of different things could happen. But the most common was that the money went to the next of kin.

My skin went cold. My chest went cold. The blood inside my veins went cold.

My dad.

No. That was stupid. Impossible. He was my *dad*. He loved me. He wasn't perfect, but he wouldn't do *this*.

Knock-knock-knock. "Frankie?" His voice boomed through my bedroom door.

My heart fell out of my chest. I opened my mouth but couldn't speak. I cleared my throat. "I'm in the bathroom!"

"Do you want pizza for dinner? Leah's doing Pilates. This is our chance to go rogue."

"Sure," I called back.

A pause. "Hey, have you packed for Hawaii yet? Your grandma wanted me to check."

"We're still going?" In the midst of everything, I'd completely forgotten about the upcoming trip.

"Her Highness insists. Gonna order from Marino's. I'll let you know when it comes." His footsteps faded away.

I felt numb. I had to be wrong. My dad would never.

But who else could it be?

Twenty-Nine

THE WOMAN SITTING IN THE SEAT ACROSS THE AISLE SHOOTS US another worried look, then stares at the floor like she's afraid to make eye contact. She's grandmotherly, dressed in a worn Dickies shirt with the icon of a cleaning company embroidered on the breast.

It's five thirty in the morning. From the hospital, we'd taken a cab to Santa Monica, which I chose because it's on the complete opposite side of town from our motel. I figured the cops would find the cab driver who'd picked us up and get our destination from him, so I'd had him drop us off at a large hotel by the beach. I thought they'd have a big job searching that place, and by then we'd be clear across town.

So here we are, on the smelly LA bus at the crack of dawn, heading east. Frankie's eyes are contemplating a homeless man slumped into a seat by the rear doors. Our nearest seatmate is a guy working his way through a bucket of Kentucky Fried Chicken a few rows away. He's eating the chicken slowly, then spreading the bones on the empty seats around him, constructing a series of runes with the slender, greasy remains.

I shudder and look out the window. As the sun comes up, the city is awakening, and it's a little bit beautiful. It's clean and peaceful in a way I've never known LA to be.

The bus stops with a screech, and a new pair of older women get on, buckets full of cleaning supplies in hand. A young man with a hoop earring follows them. He's wearing a Ralph's shirt and has a black apron slung across his shoulder.

This is a different LA, a softer version of the city, full of normal working people, all the party people at home sleeping off their hangovers. These women shoot us wide-eyed looks, then sit as far away from us as possible.

What must we look like? I haven't given it a single thought. I must be in shock. It's only in this moment that I realize I'm freezing in this stupid dress. I shiver, rubbing my hands together.

"Cold?" Frankie asks. Her voice sounds low and hoarse.

"You're awake." I look her over carefully. She seems much more alert than she was, but her eyes still have a heavy-lidded look.

"Kind of. Are we on the bus?" She stretches, back arching.

"You don't remember getting on?"

She frowns. "A little. I feel more normal now. Wait. Maude?" She sits straight up and grabs my hand, staring at it intensely. "Uh, Maude?"

Confused, I look down at my hands and gasp. "Oh my god, I didn't even..."

My hands and forearms are streaked with dried blood. Even the fronts of my pale thighs, exposed in this stupid clubbing dress, have tracks of blood on them. "Oh shit," I whisper. My eyes shoot over to the woman who was staring at me with worried eyes. She's now looking out the window.

I can't help but laugh, a short burst of incredulous sound. No one said anything, not the taxi driver, not the bus driver, not a single person on the street. I wonder if they thought we were filming a movie.

I scramble to get my small container of hand sanitizer out of my purse. I squirt some on my palms and do my best to wash off the blood. The sanitizer dilutes it, and I wipe the excess on my dress. Frankie holds out her hand, and I pass her the bottle. When she's done, I take the bottle back. I put more sanitizer on, rub it in, wipe my hands on my dress, and do it again. I feel hysteria taking over; I rub my palms against the cloth until they feel hot, then rough.

"You okay?" Frankie asks.

I can't answer. I can't breathe. I'm remembering the way the knife felt sinking into that man's flesh. I shudder, feel like I'm going to throw up. I have to stand up and run—

She grabs my hand and clasps it tightly between hers. "You're okay," she whispers into my ear. "Everything's fine."

I close my eyes, humiliated as tears escape, hot and wet. "I didn't want to do that," I squeak, like a child.

"I know." She pulls me into a hug, pressing a hand to the back of my head. "Shh. It's okay."

"I didn't want to," I whisper, grateful to be able to hide my face in her shoulder.

"Of course you didn't. You had no choice."

I pull away, sniffling, and wipe my eyes, casting embarrassed looks at the other passengers. No one is looking directly at us, but I feel like they're watching out of the corners of their eyes.

"We'll need to check out of the motel," I say in a low voice. "We can check into a place in a different part of town using your Ivy ID, just in case they trace us to this motel and discover my Candace identity."

"Natalya knows the name Ivy," she murmurs.

"But she doesn't know your last name."

"True, yeah."

"We should really get out of LA. Maybe Art can speed up your papers."

She squeezes my hand. "Maude. Hey. Look at me."

I obey, looking into her brown eyes.

"Thank you. And . . . I'm sorry. This is really all my fault. Natalya said there was another opportunity to earn money. I was stupid. I was remembering what you said, about how you have to do everything, and I felt . . ." She shrugs. "I'm an idiot. I shouldn't have gone."

"It's okay," I lie. Everything is the exact opposite of okay.

I feel like we're in quicksand. Every time we struggle, we sink deeper into the pit.

Thirty

IN THE MOTEL ROOM, I HEAD STRAIGHT FOR THE SHOWER TO GET THE blood off, and it feels amazing to be clean and purge the horrible Candace wig. I slip on my pajamas, not sure if we'll have time to get some sleep.

When I get out, Frankie smiles at me and says, "I'm happy to see your brown hair." It makes me flush.

While she showers, I Google around, looking for a story about the stabbing at the Hollywood Hills mansion. Nothing yet, but it's still early.

I lie on the bed, debating. Should we get a few hours of rest? Or should we get moving now? I retrace our steps and all the precautions I took to keep the police from being able to find us here, and they seem solid, but someone on the bus could have reported us. To be safe, we should get moving.

But I'm so tired. Every inch of me is limp with exhaustion.

It doesn't matter. I force myself to get up and dig Ivy's ID out of Frankie's purse and a prepaid Visa out of mine. I flop back on the bed, get online, and start looking for a motel. I decide on Glendale, which is a totally different part of town but accessible to MacArthur Park on the bus. There's also the Glendale Galleria mall, which will be a good place to do my return scam.

I'm just finishing up the booking when Frankie comes out of the bathroom. She's wearing loose jeans, a T-shirt with no bra—not that I'm looking—and she's towel-drying her short hair.

"I booked a motel for us in Glendale under Ivy's name," I tell her, setting my phone aside.

"Good. Thank you." She tosses the towel aside and sprawls out on the bed beside me.

"We can't check in till three, and I'm trying to decide if we should stay here or go hang out somewhere until then. I'm so tired."

"Same. But someone could remember us from the bus."

"That's what I was thinking."

"So we should leave soon." She rolls onto her side and looks at me. Her voice lowers, like she's trying to keep from being overheard. "I keep thinking about last night."

I fling an arm over my eyes. "I know. Me too."

"About you stabbing that guy."

"Frankie, stop. I'm not some murderer."

"That's not what I mean." She pries my arm away from my eyes. "I keep thinking—what would have happened if you hadn't come back for me?"

I don't say anything. We both know the answer.

She goes on. "You didn't have to go to that party. You could have just come back here and gone to sleep. It's not like I told you where I was. You must have had to, like, hunt me down, ask people at Blue, right?"

I don't know what to say.

"Maude, I . . ." She looks away from me, at the wall, then returns her eyes to mine. "You got mad at me because I was flirting with that girl. Allison."

"I got mad because you told her your real name. You can't do that. You could ruin our entire—"

"You were pissed about the name thing. But that's not where all the heat was coming from. I think you were jealous."

I sit up, heart pounding with anxiety. "What is wrong with you? I saved you. Why—"

She sits up, too. "I'm trying to say something. Can we just be honest for a minute?"

I snap my mouth shut and glare at her, fuming.

"You get mad. I like that about you. Where I just pretend everything's fine, pretend nothing bothers me, you get angry. You get *pissed*." She laughs a little, like she's remembering something. "It's good. You don't pretend. You make a plan, you get revenge. You *do* something. I admire you so much for it."

I shrug, uncomfortable.

"But here's the thing: Sometimes you lie."

"Okay, are you my therapist or—"

She scoots closer. "You're a liar. I like it. You're great at it. But you lie to yourself sometimes, too, Maude."

I crook an eyebrow, annoyed that she thinks she knows me this well.

"What I'm trying to tell you is this: You were jealous. It's okay. I want you to know that I feel the same way. I feel that for you, too." Her eyes are dark, earnest, searching my face. "I know you're going to London and you never want to see me again after that. I know we're not going to be together. It's cool. I just..." She looks down at her hands. "You stabbed someone to save me. I thought it was only fair I gave you this, so you don't feel like you're the only one." Her half smile is kind of sad. "And in the spirit of honesty, I was kind of flirting with Allison to make you jealous. I wanted to see." She winces. "It's awful. But it's true."

After an empty, awkward silence, I say, "In the spirit of honesty, I did stab that man to save myself. He was choking me. In that moment, it was self-preservation."

She laughs. She looks at my face and then laughs harder. "Maude, you're such a—such—"

"I know." I can't look at her. "I'm the worst."

"You *are*." She giggles again. "You really are."

The reality of what she's just said is creeping over me, and I feel hot inside my chest. She feels the same way? I hadn't even realized I felt that way, not really. I mean, of course she's hot, and I've wondered if we could just sleep together for convenience, but...

I feel stupid, remembering how I yelled at her in the club. She's right. I'm so embarrassed. Why did she have to catch me? Why did she ever have to be a part of this? I could have been in Bali right now, lying on a tropical beach. Alone.

She sees me. It's such a weird feeling. No matter what face or wig I put on, she sees right through it. I've never had anyone look, let alone *see*.

She touches my arm. "You okay? Did I make it weird? I just thought if I laid everything out on the table, we could move forward."

I need, I want—something, her, some heart-pounding thing—and I'm bitterly angry at that need, at her for being here in the first place. The wanting is a weakness and I hate her for it.

"Hello?" She nudges me.

I can't breathe. I look at her helplessly, and then I lose whatever battle I'm fighting and reach for her, a hand on her shoulder, another on the back of her head. The short hair is like I remember it from dancing together in Hawaii, soft and prickly, and I run my nails across it gently, heart raging.

She freezes for a moment, and then she leans forward and kisses me.

Time stops.

Her lips are warm, full, tasting faintly of toothpaste. She kisses me once, softly, and then pulls back an inch. Her face is so close I can smell the lotion on her cheeks. My heart is pounding, everything blurry. I'm dizzy from not breathing. Her arms wind around my waist, and we fall into kissing, slowly at first, tongues finding each other, chests pressed together, breath uneven, and then faster.

She pushes me back onto the pillows, her body between my legs. She kisses me again, soft and hard, and I feel myself winding around her, pulling her closer. Thoughts pop wildly into my brain: *Why did we not do this sooner? I'm definitely gay. There's no question.*

I get my hands up under her T-shirt and start to pull it off slowly, giving her time in case she doesn't want to go there, but she reaches down and yanks it off, throws it aside, and resumes kissing me, lips moving down my neck, making me gasp out little breathing noises that I'd normally find embarrassing but that now seem normal and fine. I run my hands down her bare, smooth back, and for this moment all my millions of worries are held at bay.

Thirty-One

TEN DAYS AGO

Frankie

IT WAS BEYOND SURREAL, WATCHING EVERYONE ACT normally like this was our usual family vacation and I hadn't just overdosed. I sat at dinner, eyes on the table-cloth, while my dad and his brother engaged in constant one-upmanship. Maude, across the table from me, wrestled with her little brothers, trying to get them to stop throwing tortilla chips. Her mom kept shooting her angry looks, as if her daughter was personally responsible for the rowdiness of the twins.

It was a glorious, postcard-worthy setting. We were in this open-air restaurant attached to the hotel that my grandma loved, and the Pacific stretched out before us, a glimmering carpet to the horizon. Below, gondolas filled with tourists wove through the resort's chlorine-scented river.

When my eyes drifted back to Maude, she was staring at her mother with a look I couldn't quite define settled onto her pretty face. It wasn't sadness or anger, really. I got the distinct impression that her face was a mask concealing a seething ocean.

Her eyes snapped onto mine. "What?" she asked.

"There's something different about you. Are you going through something right now?" I was weirdly hopeful she might be struggling, too. Maybe we could talk. She'd always been standoffish, but maybe that would change on this trip.

"No. Why?" Her expression was angry and challenging.

"You're still with that boyfriend? Everything's okay at school?"

She looked down at herself like I had pointed out a spill on her dress. "Everything is great. We have big plans for junior prom. We're, you know, in love and stuff." The words did not match the irritated tone of her delivery, and her cheeks were turning red. I'd always gotten queer vibes off her, but I could have been wrong. It made me wonder if the boyfriend might actually be a girlfriend or a theyfriend.

I tried to backpedal. "I mean, you look good. Put together. Everything *looks* fine. But something's off." *Talk to me.* I realized in one horrible moment how profoundly lonely I was. Why was it always like this?

I knew why: I was constantly in these places that were filled with jerks. It was them, not me. They sucked.

But Maude had never seemed like someone to write off. Her aloofness felt different, like shyness or fear rather than meanness. And besides, she wasn't raised with money like all the assholes at school. She was from Santa Ana, something she'd mentioned at a few dinners clearly because it made her mom so uncomfortable. She loved to reminisce, like, "Remember that little apartment we lived in when Dad was working at the gas station?" Her mom always tried to shut it down. "Oh now, honey, that was ten years ago," and "No one needs to hear about my college days." It totally worked; my grandma would inevitably narrow her eyes at Maude's mom, reminded that she was a social climber after one of Grandma's precious golden boys.

"Francesca," Grandma called from her throne at the head of the table. "Come here."

Oh god. This was going to be something embarrassing. I set my napkin by my plate and got up, allowing her to pull me to her side and wind an arm around my waist. She only made gestures like this in public, where everyone could see what a loving matriarch she was. "Tell us about school," she said, gesturing to the table full of attentive eyes.

I squirmed. "It's fine."

"Are you doing any extracurriculars?"

"Not really." Was she trying to humiliate me? She had to know my grades weren't high enough anyway.

"You should be doing as many extracurriculars as possible! It's very important for college applications that you show yourself to be well rounded. Chris, why isn't she in any sports, any clubs? This is your responsibility."

Now I understood. This was about digging the knife deeper into my dad. I shot him an apologetic look.

He seemed to flip through different scripts before landing on, "I'm on my own, Mom—it isn't easy. I'm a single working parent." Down the table, Maude rolled her eyes, and I almost smiled.

Released, I hurled myself back into my chair. Maude was studying me with interest. "What?" I asked, defensive.

She smiled, and it was like a different person was animating her face, someone calculating and simmering with a long, cold fury. She shook her head and went back to tending to her brothers. I was left with the feeling that everyone and everything around me was a mirage, a facade, and that the real underworkings were more dangerous than I could understand.

My phone buzzed, and I pulled it out of my pocket. A reminder: Sunset Jet Skiing with my dad and Leah. I remembered my dad booking this a few months ago, another one of his adventures.

I studied his profile. He was brooding, staring into his water glass. I met Leah's eyes, and she shook her head at me sympathetically. I could tell she felt bad for both me and my dad. We didn't ask for my grandma to be this way. We were all just along for the ride.

———

"Try to have fun," Leah told my dad quietly, clearly under the impression that I wasn't paying attention. We were gathered with two other families on the dock of a sheltered cove near the hotel. The sun was starting to sink, and on the horizon, I caught a glimpse of dolphin fins as they followed a school of fish.

A line of Jet Skis waited for us, and the instructor, a man with tribal tattoos, gathered us together for a safety talk. "Has anyone here Jet Skied before?" he asked, and everyone raised their hands. The other two groups were a young couple on their honeymoon and a family with two jock-looking teenage sons.

"Good." The instructor beamed. He hopped onto a Jet Ski and began going through a brief tutorial on these particular vehicles, and my dad stared moodily at the dolphins on the horizon.

"You okay?" I ventured.

He glanced down at me and forced a smile. "You know it."

Leah's brow furrowed in concern. She was magnificently pretty in a bikini and life vest, every inch of her trim and tan.

The instructor led us along the dock where a row of Jet Skis was secured in numbered slots. There were ten of us counting the instructor. "Morales family, I have you right here," he called, and the teenage boys pushed each other, excited to go first. The newlyweds were next, and then the instructor called my dad's name and showed us to the last three Jet Skis. He met us at the edge of the dock and offered to help us climb on, but my dad was already getting on, playing with the handles. Leah was right behind him, saddling up on a hot-pink Jet Ski like she'd done it a thousand times.

I stared down at the pink Jet Ski that was left for me and sighed. Here we were again.

"Is anything wrong?" Tribal tattoo guy was at my elbow, annoyingly helpful. "I can give you a hand getting on if you want?"

"No, it's just…" I shook my head. "Pink is not my favorite."

"Oh." He looked down at his clipboard. "I'm sorry, but that's the one we have reserved for you."

The older of the two jock guys had gotten off his own Jet Ski and was suddenly there with us. My heart sped up, ready to be mocked.

"Is my life vest buckled right?" he asked, turning around so the instructor could inspect it. "I feel like it's too tight."

Tribal tattoo guy made a few adjustments. I stood there with my face on fire, waiting for the jock to say something rude. Once his life vest was fixed, he seemed about to head back to his family, but then he did a double take and asked, "Is everything okay?"

"She doesn't like the color," tribal guy said in a tone that made me want to smack him.

"It's fine," I protested.

"I'll switch with you," the guy offered cheerfully. "I look hot in pink." He struck a pose in front of the pink Jet Ski. Indeed, his bronze skin and thick, dark hair looked pretty amazing against the bright pink.

"Okay, then. Right this way." Tribal tattoo guy led me to the black Jet Ski that had been assigned to the jock, who in turn hopped cheerfully onto the cotton-candy one I'd abandoned. I tossed him a grateful smile, and he winked at me. Where were all the guys like this at my school?

Now that everyone was happy, we got started pretty quick. My dad and Leah whipped around the smooth cove, gliding over the tiny waves and laughing to each other in the breeze. I took it slower, cruising around and admiring the sunset. The Morales family split up, and I cast thankful glances at the guy who'd rescued me.

I was watching him slice through the water on the other side of the cove, the sun a glowing orange disc at the horizon, when the pink Jet Ski skidded, slowed, and started smoking.

His mother screamed. I choked on a gasp. The jock guy leaped from the seat, diving into the water as the engine burst into flame, releasing a plume of coal-black smoke.

I stuttered to a stop. Hand clapped to my mouth, I watched as tribal tattoo guy raced to rescue the teenage boy, who was swimming away from the burning Jet Ski with clean, steady strokes.

I looked for my dad. He was stopped beside Leah, watching the burning Jet Ski as it tipped over and sank into the ocean. He turned and met my eyes, and in that moment, I knew there was no escape for me. I was going to die.

Thirty-Two

I PAUSE AT THE DOOR, GRIPPING THE ROLLING SUITCASE. I LOOK BACK.

Frankie is sleeping peacefully, one arm flung out, palm up. It's painful to look at her. Her cheeks are so soft, her lips full, parted slightly in sleep. Her long, dark lashes brush her cheeks, eyes flitting left to right behind closed lids. I wonder what she's dreaming about.

Tears are stinging my eyes. I blink hard and fast.

Here's the thing: My fingerprints are the ones on the knife. The police will be looking for me, not Frankie.

I need to get out of the country. I can't stay another two weeks.

My former rationalizations about police investigations taking a long time and my fingerprints not being on file spring to mind. I recall Frankie saying I'm not always honest with myself.

Fine. That isn't my only reason for leaving.

I left Frankie money to pay Art, and the motel room in Glendale is under Ivy's name, so she can check in on her own. I'm going to leave her all set up for the next week, the room prepaid, money for her ID, and even an extra thousand dollars for her next step. I've done everything I can. She doesn't need me to sit here with her like two fish in a barrel, waiting for that passport to be ready.

Again I feel a nudge. Maybe it's because I'm staring at her so intensely, flooded with memories of her lips, her skin on mine. The nudge pushes me closer to the truth.

Truth: I'm worried if I don't leave now, I never will.

And if we stay together, it doesn't matter what my passport says. I'll always be Maude. No fresh start. No escaping myself.

I stay Maude for just another moment, running my hand through my chin-length hair, remembering Frankie doing just that a few hours ago, whispering, "I love your brown hair."

That's enough.

I let myself out onto the walkway and close the door behind me. It automatically locks. I don't have a room key with me. I did that on purpose. No going back.

A bus downtown, a transfer to the Metro, and then a cab to LAX. Los Angeles is better than Orange County for public transportation, but this whole endeavor takes me four hours, and I'm starving and exhausted as the taxi lets me out at the curb of the international terminal. As the driver gets my suitcase out of the back, I check the time. My red-eye to

London leaves in five hours. That's all right. For starters, I can get something to eat.

My heart palpitates. I'm finally doing it.

I enter the terminal through the sliding door. It's chaotic, just like the day I went to Hawaii, which feels like a thousand years ago. My stomach is growling painfully, so I find a café on this side of security.

I select a limp-looking chicken sandwich and a bottled iced coffee and consider when I should start workshopping my British accent. Here in LA, since my passport is British? Can I pull it off? I was supposed to practice during my month in Bali.

I pay cash for my food, roll my suitcase to a small corner table, and sit down with my burner phone to check the news one last time while I eat. My plan is to ditch it and buy a new one at the London airport. I check my texts first. Nothing. Frankie has to be awake by now. I'd expected her to text or call, upset, angry, something. Instead...silence.

That's for the best.

I unwrap the sandwich, feeling nauseous with sadness. I shove the feelings down and take a huge bite. As I chew the flavorless mouthful, I check Google with my usual search parameters: "Francesca" "Maude" "Hawaii." The search results that populate shock me into sitting straight up.

I click on one of the links at random. It takes me to an article in the *LA Times*.

The headline: "Missing OC Teenagers Apparently Not Dead."

Oh no.

My horror is so huge I have to close my eyes and breathe for a few seconds. Then I read the article. It begins:

Two famously missing Orange County teenagers were presumed dead after an apparent boating accident in Kailua Kona, Hawaii, ten days ago. Footage of their devastated parents pleading with the Coast Guard to locate their bodies played across Hawaiian news, sparking conversations about tourist safety and more stringent regulations for water sports.

Now, new evidence has come to light. Hawaiian authorities confirm the two girls were at a party in Hilo days after the boating accident. Even stranger, they seem to have been in disguise and using false names, which indicates the boating accident may have been staged.

The story gets more bizarre. The girls were identified on the heels of an investigation into the death of Nathan Rangel, age 20, from Santa Barbara. Rangel was living in Hawaii, and he attended the same party at which the two Orange County teenagers were seen. His car was abandoned on the other side of town, and his body was found yesterday when it washed out of an apparent hiding place on private ranch land during a storm.

The investigation into Rangel's death revealed that, after attending the party in Hilo, he went back to a friend's home with a handful of close friends and two new additions, whom the authorities believe are Maude Hendricks and Francesca Maxwell from Orange County. One of the tenants of the apartment, Ivy Balbuena, has since reported her driver's license missing.

"Oh no," I whisper. I can't feel my hands or feet. Not at all. I almost can't keep reading, because I know what comes next and I don't want to shift into a world where this is real. I can just get up, I tell myself. I can gather my belongings and get on my plane. I can leave this behind.

Except I can't. I read on.

The investigation into this increasingly convoluted situation led authorities to discover that Balbuena's ID was used to board a flight from Honolulu to Los Angeles five days ago.

There's a photo of Frankie passing through security, and there I am—Candace, with my stupid blond wig and baseball hat.

Maude was traveling under the name Candace White. It's not known at this time whether this is also a stolen ID. The two are currently assumed to be in the vicinity of Los Angeles, and the FBI has taken over jurisdiction.

Wide speculation about the girls' motives for these crimes instantly abounded across the internet. Are they involved in drug smuggling, working for the Southern California cartels, or is there a more personal motive behind this crime spree?

The FBI is asking for tips. The two are assumed to be traveling under the names Candace White and Ivy Balbuena. Tips can be sent to info@fbi.gov.

I search my name on Twitter, and sure enough, a dozen articles about us have gone viral, and people are speculating wildly. This is my nightmare. This is the opposite of escaping quietly into oblivion.

My mom. Oh god. What must she be thinking right now?

Grief washes through me, a tsunami. It's all ruined. It's over.

They think we killed Nathan? Can't they tell it was a car accident? Maybe he was too badly decomposed for them to determine how he died.

I realize suddenly that I am at LAX, precisely where they will be searching for me.

Another brick falls out of the sky to hit me on the head: last night. Natalya's party. The dead man. The knife with my fingerprints on it. The people at Blue know us as Candace and Ivy.

I need to warn Frankie.

I don't know what we're going to do.

Thirty-Three

TEN DAYS AGO

Frankie

I GASPED, PANTED, HYPERVENTILATING, WALKING AS fast as I could along the corridors of the hotel.

I passed a family with small children. The parents cast me a concerned look. I forced a smile. That seemed to make it even worse.

Finally, my room. I pulled the key out of my back pocket, beeped my way in with shaking hands, and shut the door behind me. I snapped the deadbolt and the manual upper lock.

It was time to face the truth.

My dad was trying to kill me.

There was no running. There was no escape. I was trapped in this hotel, just a few rooms away from him. When we got back to Orange County, I had very few choices. I could move in with my grandma.

But he had a key to her house. He was there all the time.

I could run away.

Where? How? With what money?

I sat with my back against the door and drew my knees into my chest.

If I told anyone about this, they'd think I was lying, unhinged, unstable.

Outside, I heard a slam and then a few seconds of yelling.

I got up to look through the peephole. Maude was sitting on the carpet in the hallway, messing with something on her phone.

Oh, please. Please keep me company, I thought, getting up and scrambling for the door handle. I couldn't be alone for another minute.

———

After we finished the movie, it got dark and quiet. Maude was passed out, breath coming in even intervals, but I couldn't sleep. I kept jumping at every little sound. The words *What am I going to do?* kept circulating around my brain. Could I get Maude to stay with me for the rest of the trip, keep me safe, be a witness? What about when I got home?

A creak and rustle told me she was getting up to go to the bathroom. I didn't want to seem weird, so I kept pretending to be asleep. But then I heard the soft zip of her suitcase and the sound of her fumbling around inside.

Apparently she found what she wanted, because she pulled it out and took it to the bathroom. The door clicked quietly shut behind her.

I opened my eyes, considering this.

Drugs. That had to be it.

Did I have any right to an opinion?

I was worried, though. I'd learned from personal experience how dangerous this could be.

And then I remembered her at LAX, sweating bullets as she waited for her bag to go through TSA.

I grabbed my phone and got stealthily out of bed, lowering myself onto the floor by her bag. It was unzipped, so I easily pulled it open and shone my flashlight into the contents. It was just clothes and shoes, but if *I* were going to hide something major, I'd stash it in the lining. I felt around and, sure enough, my hand identified something square and hard hiding beneath the silky fabric. I felt a slit in the cloth, reached in, and grabbed the hard little square. It was a passport.

Why would she hide her passport like this? I flipped through it, and sure enough, it was Maude. But she had a different haircut, a cute brunette bob, and the name was different. A California driver's license fell out, and I turned it over. Another Maude, this time with blond hair. When I closed the passport, I noticed it wasn't American. It was British. In the dim light, I hadn't noticed the difference.

I stared at these things for a long moment. Candace White and Elizabeth Lewis? Fake identities?

She'd been acting weird this whole trip.

I flashed back to every time I'd hung out with her. She was always so tightly laced, always so careful. I'd assumed it was because she was a little fake, like most of the people I knew.

But her behavior tonight—totally different, like she was mourning something.

And then it clicked. Her plan was to escape. She was going to use this trip to run.

Oh my god.

She was brilliant. How had she gotten these? I was painfully jealous. She had to have a whole plan in place for getting off Hawaii and to…England? I looked at the name again: Elizabeth.

If she could set this up for herself, she could set it up for me.

Thirty-Four

I JIGGLE MY KNEES IN THE BACK OF THE TAXI, MY EYES FOCUSED OUT the window. I keep telling myself I don't have to worry about the driver recognizing me; my hair is short and brown, not long and blond like they showed on the news. The ride from LAX to Glendale is going to cost a hundred dollars, an expense I can't afford, but I don't have four hours to spend on the bus.

At last we pull up next to the motel on a crowded, run-down street in eastern Glendale, where a pair of homeless women have set up an elaborate campground situation on the sidewalk. I thank the driver, grab my bags, and hurry out. "Wait here," I tell him.

"Meter's running," he grumbles, settling in with his coffee.

The sun is low in the sky. Palm trees toss in a delicate

wind, and the aroma of tacos drifts across the street from a food truck parked in the lot of a 99 Cent Store. I turn to the motel, rolling my suitcase away from the tents. The women are huddled around a bag of food and cast me suspicious looks as I pass by.

I hurry up the exterior stairs, my suitcase bumping on each concrete step, and stop outside room 215. I knock, hard and fast. I'm holding my breath, anxious to get in off the street.

A rustle behind the door, and then a shadow passes in front of the peephole. "It's me. Let me in," I say as loud as I dare.

The chain clinks, and the door opens. A hand on the knob, Frankie stands before me, lips set in an angry line. "Did you forget something?"

I push past her. "You can be mad later. We're in too deep." I pull my phone out, find the *LA Times* article, and hand it to her. While she reads, I survey the room. She's already unpacked a little; I see her toiletries in the bathroom and a few shirts on the bed.

"Oh, shit," she whispers.

"The cops could be here any minute. Get your stuff."

"But...where will we go?" I can see she's still in shock. It took me a few minutes to absorb the article, too.

"We'll get a room under my Elizabeth ID or something. Let's go!" I make rushing hand motions at her.

While I look out the window to make sure the taxi hasn't left, she stuffs everything back into her suitcase. We hurry to the door and let ourselves out onto the exterior walkway. "Let's leave through the back," I tell her. "There are two women out front, and I don't want them to see us."

We cross the parking lot and emerge onto the street from the other side of the building. As we walk, she says, "It didn't sound like they'd put the Hawaii stuff together with what happened last night."

"Or they just didn't tell the news yet," I reply, having already thought this through. If they're really looking for us, they'd keep some things to themselves, things that would make Frankie and me feel confident and more likely to make mistakes. Am I paranoid?

We hurry across the sidewalk, throw our suitcases into the trunk of the taxi, and get in.

"MacArthur Park," I tell the driver. As he pulls away from the curb, I keep my eyes on the back windshield, still nervous about those women.

As we stop to turn right at the corner, a pair of police cars pass us. I grip Frankie's arm. Her eyes go wide. "It's a coincidence," I whisper.

We look through the rear window as the cab hits the gas. The cop cars stop in front of the motel.

We face forward. Frankie is pale, eyes huge. I'm sure I look the same.

We are so, so screwed.

Thirty-Five

MY BRAIN IS GOING A THOUSAND MILES AN HOUR, RICOCHETING from one option to the next. I make a mental list of our situation: We can't go through LAX. We'll have to leave the country from another city, somewhere they'd never expect us to go.

I wonder...

I get out my burner phone and Google "What cities' airports use facial recognition?" I'm reading through the results, Frankie peering over my shoulder, when the driver says, "Where do you want me to drop you off?"

"Another few blocks up, there's a restaurant," I tell the driver, not wanting him to know our real destination.

He leaves us at a little sandwich shop, and we head down the crowded street. Frankie asks me, "So we're going to see if we can get my papers early?"

I explain what I'm thinking, that we need to get out of LA as soon as possible, and she nods. "We should look at bus and train lines and see what cities are a straight shot that have international airports," she suggests.

"Good," I agree. "And we should research whether the buses and trains have security cameras on board."

"We don't want to go through Union Station or one that'll have security cameras inside."

I smile wryly at her. "Now you're thinking like I think."

"I guess you're rubbing off on me. Maybe next I'll hook up with someone and abandon them in a motel room while they're sleeping."

I pull her to a stop by her elbow. "You said you knew we weren't going to be together. You said—"

"Don't even try me, Maude." Her eyes flash black in the reflected light from a store window.

"I'm just saying—"

"Seriously. Knock it off. I appreciate you coming back to warn me. We're cool. I just can't stand being bullshitted by you right now."

***

The inside of the mailbox and shipping store is exactly the same as it was last week. We approach the counter, where a young man greets us, eyes lingering on our suitcases. Another man lurks by the door to the backroom, leaning on the counter with his arms crossed.

"I'm looking for Art," I tell the guy at the counter.

He lifts his chin and says, "I'm not sure we have an Art here. Let me check. What's your name?"

"Candace."

He turns and disappears through the back door. We're left with the second guy. He says nothing, and his silence unnerves me. I shift my weight uncomfortably.

The man pokes his head out and beckons us. "Come on back." The other guy opens the waist-high door in the counter.

He's the one who pats us down and searches through our purses, and I have to hold my tongue when he lingers too long on Frankie's chest, which is absurd; there's no room to smuggle anything in her A cups. He asks the other guy, "Do I look through their suitcases?"

The guy mulls it over, then tells us, "Leave the suitcases out here. You taking a trip?"

"Going on vacation," I reply, rolling it to a spot by the door. I don't like leaving it behind, but my passport and money are in my purse. If they decide to steal our bags, they'll end up with a bunch of cheap clothes and some toiletries.

Art is at his desk, and he looks up from his computer when we enter. "You changed your hair," he tells me.

I force a friendly smile. I need to butter him up. "It was time for a change. Do you like it?"

"The long hair was sexier. But now you match your passport." He grins. "So I guess we know where you're going next. England."

Frankie glances at me to see my reaction to that. I'm not worried about Art. He can't want the cops around any more than I do. I ignore the England comment and say, "I'm sorry to bother you. I know the new papers aren't supposed to be ready for another week. I'm wondering if there's any way to get them sooner. Like, as soon as possible. I remember with my passport, it came in earlier than you expected."

"We got lucky with that one."

"I just thought maybe you could make a phone call and ask, if it's not too much trouble." I smile my sweetest Maude smile.

He gets up and comes around the desk. I cast a glance at Frankie. She's doing good, looking casual. The young guy who let us in watches from his post by the door. I might be imagining it, but I think he tenses up a little. Something is off.

"I hear you have suitcases with you. In a hurry to get out of town, Maude?" To Frankie, he says, "And you're Francesca? How was Hawaii? Seems like you two had a hell of a time."

We say nothing.

He laughs, a little giggle like he's delighted. "You should see your faces. When I saw the news, I was like, that's my rich girl! And her friend who suddenly needs good papers. You ladies have been busy."

I'm frozen. I don't know what to say or do.

He half-sits on the edge of his desk. "Well, good news for you is I do have the papers early. You're in luck. Which doesn't seem like something you've had much of."

My heart races. This is good.

"But here's the thing. I like to get lucky, too. And I'm thinking, wow, I'm doing these ladies a big favor, keeping this secret for them. I could tip off the FBI right now, introduce the cops to Elizabeth." He grins. "Imagine that."

After a breathless silence, I say, "But then I'd tell them where I got the fake passport."

He holds his hands up. "This is a mailbox and shipping store. I don't know anything about fake papers. These girls are probably just trying to get back at me for turning them in. I saw the passport when she came in here, trying to ship something to England." His smile is dark and dangerous now. "And you're naive to think I don't have friends on the inside. How do you suppose good fake identities are made?"

I glance at Frankie. Her eyes are wide, her mouth pinched shut.

"But that's okay, everything's cool," Art says. "We can come to an agreement. You can have your passport early, and I can forget the names on the passports I got you."

"Okay . . . ," I reply, not sure what's the problem, then.

"For an extra five thousand."

My jaw drops. That's almost all the cash we have. That would just leave us whatever is on the prepaid debit cards, which is maybe five or eight hundred bucks. We'd have enough to get out of town and get a room in a motel for a few nights. That's it.

"I can't," I protest.

"Come on, rich girl, I think you can."

"It's literally all the money I have."

"You'll figure something out. You have things you can sell." He winks lecherously.

I stare at him for thirty long seconds, going over things in my head, jumping from choice to choice. I've never felt so desperate.

But then I remember the mall scheme. That was a potential five hundred dollars, although we never had time to go cash in the merchandise I stole. And we earned a thousand bucks in just a few days of club promoting. We can earn money. What we need more than anything is a fresh start with no connections in a city big enough that we won't be noticed, and not so far that it's expensive to travel to.

The right answer comes to me, just like that. I know exactly where we should go.

Grim, I start digging around in my purse. "Let me see the passport before I pay you," I tell Art.

"Yes, ma'am," he replies, a self-satisfied smile on his stupid face. He hops up and heads for the safe, and Frankie mouths the words *I'm sorry* at me. I shake my head. We're past that now.

Thirty-Six

THE ROAD RUMBLES BENEATH THE BUS. OUTSIDE THE WINDOWS, THE desert is an endless stretch of darkness, turning gray at the horizon. I've always liked the desert. My mom has a thing for Palm Springs, and so do the Todds; I think Morticia has a house out there, and with all that golfing, they're bound to love the place. That's not why I like it, though. I like the emptiness, the brutality of the land, the way you feel disconnected from the city and its highway cage bars. And the sky at night—it's incredible, full of stars.

Frankie's looking out the window, too. When I refocus, her face clarifies, luminescent, a ghost overlaid against the greasy windowpane.

The bus is half full, and we have our row and the one in front of it to ourselves. The people on the dawn bus to Vegas are not the nosy, curious type. They're either workers wearing cheap business clothes or they're older retirees, maybe going to play the slots. Only one person has given us more than a glance: a middle-aged, truck driver-looking man who probably has teenage kids and thinks we're running away from home. That worries me, but I put it out of my mind. He's not going to call the cops because he saw teenagers taking a bus.

I realize that since we've been on the run, we've been surrounded by working-class people. No bougie, douchey OC suburbanites ride the city bus or hang out around discount motels. I feel grounded, centered, like I've escaped something stifling. This is the rest of my life.

"What are you thinking about?" Frankie asks quietly.

"I'm thinking about how I'm happy not to be in Orange County anymore."

She nods.

"But you want to ask me something else," I guess.

Her eyes flick down to the burner phone in her hand. She was looking at it a lot earlier, toggling through news articles. She says, "You know the guy at the party? The one you..." She stops, like she's going to offend me by saying the word *stabbed*.

"What about him?"

She clears her throat. "There are a bunch of articles about him right now. He, um..."

I frown at her, trying to read her facial expression. "He what?"

"He died."

My eyebrows shoot up, and I try to decide how I feel about that. On one hand, I killed a man. This isn't like Nathan; he didn't die by accident. I stabbed him in the gut. I remember the feeling of the knife penetrating his stomach muscle, of the soft flesh beneath.

I shudder.

"Are you okay?" she asks.

I nod, maybe a little too fast. "I'm fine. I guess I expected that."

"It was self-defense."

"Tell that to the FBI." I return to staring out at the brightening dawn sky.

My dreams of being dead are dead themselves. The best I can hope for is to salvage some half-assed new start, tainted by the fact that my family knows I'm alive.

She touches my arm, and then her hand moves down and wraps tightly around my wrist. "You left," she murmurs, barely audible.

It feels like this is her holding me here, keeping me from leaving her again. "We were always going to part ways in LA."

"Not like that. Not with you sneaking out and leaving me naked in bed like some awful movie."

I wince. I wish she wouldn't confront me. I was hoping to leave it unspoken and unexamined.

Her hand moves off my wrist and onto my hand. She presses her palm against mine and laces our fingers together. All this touching is making me feel things I don't want to feel. I look down at our intertwined fingers, my head full of conflicting emotions.

"Maude," she says, squeezing. "Say something."

I raise my face to look at her. My stomach is in knots. I hate the cliché of it all—I can't stop looking into her eyes; they're deep and dark, and I can't help feeling warm and mushy, remembering that she feels things for me. This isn't *me*. I don't have time for this now.

I pull my hand away from hers and go back to looking out the window. I can feel her anger and hurt like they're a third person sitting in our row, but I can't engage. Feelings won't save us. I need to keep moving forward.

Thirty-Seven

TIVOLI VILLAGE IS A MASSIVE OUTDOOR SHOPPING MALL IN THE eastern Las Vegas suburbs, which I selected on the six-hour bus ride by searching "upscale Las Vegas shopping" and "where to buy designer clothes in Las Vegas." It takes us two more buses to get there, and when we're ejected onto the sweltering street corner, I have to laugh because I feel like I'm right back in Orange County. It has that upscale, faux–Mediterranean Orange County vibe that attracts wine moms and sugar babies alike—prime demographic targets for thievery.

Already sweating, we pay ten bucks at an adjacent hotel to stash our suitcases at their front desk and find a bathroom to put on makeup and spruce ourselves up enough to look like we belong here. It feels amazing not to be wearing the horrible Candace wig anymore. I consider whether I should dispose of that driver's license and passport, which are in the suitcase. Both Frankie's and Elizabeth's passports are in there, too, and I hate being separated from them, but I worried if we had those with us and we got caught stealing, the police would tie us to those identities, and we'd never be able to use them.

Frankie puts some water in her short hair, smoothing it into place. My brain keeps trying to distract me, popping up images from our night together when I'm not ready. I feel my face go hot, and I focus on my lipstick.

We look tired, but we'll fit in. We're just wearing jeans and T-shirts, but with our hair and makeup done, we look a bit upscale, maybe even like college students.

"Ready?" I ask her.

She nods. She won't make eye contact with me.

We walk down the street to the entrance, which is magnificent in its commitment to the Mediterranean aesthetic. Two-story pillars covered in ivy, warm shades of orange and cream, arched doorways...the place is huge. On the grass by a series of fountains, a group of women are doing yoga. They're so Orange County I almost feel homesick.

The air is interesting: so dry the sweat evaporates off my skin with a not unpleasant prickling sensation. It smells different, too, earthier and like something I can't quite place. Gasoline? No, but close.

We follow an outdoor walkway between a gym and an art gallery to a maze of sidewalks, shops, restaurants, and fountains. It's crowded, groups of women with shopping bags sitting on outdoor patios and standing around talking.

"Well, this is perfect," I murmur. Frankie doesn't respond. Apparently, she's giving me the silent treatment.

I duck into the nearest retail store and ask for an empty bag. I thank the clerk, collect the bag, and head over to one of the groups of chatting women in their thirties. They've set their purchases down and are deep in conversation. There are seven of them, four blond and three brunette, and they're all tanned and toned and wearing Lululemon. I use Frankie as a shield while I pretend to drop my phone, bend down to pick it up, and snatch a few things from some of the bags. Mission accomplished, we walk casually away, and I make notes in my phone of what we've stolen and what store it's from.

Our day continues like this, getting hotter as the sun heats up the desert. I end up with a few bags full of clothes and accessories, and at four o'clock, I turn to Frankie. "I'm starving, and we can't return this stuff until at least tomorrow. Are you hungry, too?"

She nods stonily.

"Do you want to, like, point to where you want to eat, or should I just pick the place?" My voice is dripping with sarcasm.

She shrugs and looks away.

"If it's up to me, we'll eat cheap. I saw a fast-food place

outside the mall, down the street on the corner. We'll walk over there."

She says nothing but follows me. If that's how she wants it, fine.

We eat burgers inside by the window while I browse stuff on my phone. "I should check the return policy on the stores this loot is from," I muse. "I wonder if it will be a problem, asking for cash." I Google around, and I gasp when I see the search results.

"Frankie, this is not good. Listen." I read her a line from the article. "Over the last five years, most major retailers have been getting increasingly restrictive with their return policies. For recipients of gifts, it's most common to be refunded in the form of store credit unless the original credit card is present, in which case the balance will be refunded to the card. Cash returns are almost nonexistent."

I look up at her, wide-eyed. She's staring at her fries, eyebrows drawn together. "Frankie, this ruins our whole plan. What are we going to do now? Pawn this random crap? Just straight up steal money from people?" No sooner have I said it than I realize that's exactly what we'll have to do. My morals are getting looser every day we're on the road.

I sit back in my chair, winded like I got punched in the stomach. Frankie's still avoiding my eyes. "We can't spend any money," I tell her. "Maybe we should just keep moving our suitcases around, stashing them in hotel lobbies like we did today, and be homeless for a bit, just until we get enough money to leave the country. I was thinking—have you been to Vegas before? Have you been to the Strip?" She doesn't answer. "Okay, well, there are a lot of places inside the casinos where you could sort of tuck yourself off to the side and take a nap. And plenty of bathrooms where we could change, and it's so crowded we'd be like a needle in a haystack. Plus, there are a lot of nightclubs on and off the Strip. I'm thinking we could do this during the day and maybe find a club-promoting gig at night. A week of that and we'd be good to go. What do you think?"

She sips her soda silently.

"I need you to say something, Frankie. This is life and death here. It's not fair for me to make all these decisions alone."

She looks up at me, eyes flashing. "Isn't that how you like to do things, though? Alone?"

It hurts for some reason I don't understand. She isn't wrong. "All right, then, if it's up to me, we'll try this and see how it works."

"Super," she mutters, back to eating her fries.

I let my eyes drift out to the street. I don't know how everything got so messed up. At the same time, my whole body is crying out to reach over the small table and touch her. I'm about to do it, just for one moment, to feel her skin. It doesn't have to mean anything. My hand is reaching without my permission. I can't even look at her. My eyes are on the people waiting under the shade of the bus shelter. My hand connects with Frankie's inner forearm and rests on the soft, tender skin. I feel her freeze.

I let my fingertips stay for just a moment while a battle wages inside me. *Stop*, I command myself. But this reminds me of all her other skin, how it felt pressed against me, and I want to scream. I can't stand this. *Stop*.

At last, my body obeys. I pull my hand back and look down at my lap, humiliated by my own weakness.

"Maude," Frankie says. "Look at me."

I feel tears in my eyes. God, I hate myself. I look out the window, blinking hard to clear my blurry vision. One of the men waiting for the bus turns and looks back at us, almost like he could feel my eyes on him. He reminds me of the truck driver man who sat near us on our ride to Vegas.

"Look at me," Frankie repeats, her voice soft like she's going to be nice to me.

That makes it so much worse. I shake my head. I take a few deep breaths, and then I get my phone out again for something to do. Out of habit, I Google our names to see if there's any news.

The article at the top of my feed reads: "Orange County Teenagers Linked to Murder in Hollywood: Killing Spree Continues."

"Oh no," I hear myself whisper.

I don't click on it. I can't handle any more bad news. Is this burger joint cursed? It's a wild, irrational thought, but suddenly I'm convinced that we should never have come in here.

"Maude? What is it?" Frankie's voice feels far away.

I pass her the phone. "I can't read the article," I say.

She's scanning it. "They know it was you who stabbed that man. He was apparently some kind of rich finance guy. They're looking for Candace and Ivy all over LA. We got out just in time."

It takes me a few minutes to answer. "We're not Candace and Ivy anymore. We're in a whole other city. They're not looking for us here. We're okay."

"You're right. Let's just stick to the plan. Make money fast, leave the country."

I stand up. I have to get out of here. I feel like I'm being buried alive.

Thirty-Eight

CASINOS ARE WEIRD; IT'S IMPOSSIBLE TO TELL IF IT'S DAY OR NIGHT once you're inside. They have the feeling of a vacuum, of being suspended outside space and time. It's ten o'clock at night, but it could just as easily be six in the morning; everything runs twenty-four hours a day, seven days a week in here, a perpetual motion machine.

In the lactation room where Frankie and I had stolen a few hours' sleep curled uncomfortably on a small divan, I confront the wreck of my reflection. I can't remember ever being or looking this tired. I splash water on my face, dry it with a paper towel, and open my makeup bag.

The bathroom stall door opens and Frankie comes out, wearing her black club dress. "I forgot how much I hate heels," she grumbles.

"The worst." I apply concealer to the dark circles under

my eyes. Frankie gets her own cosmetics bag out of her purse and starts putting on eyeliner. After a few minutes of working in silence, I say, "I did some research on clubs. I think we'll want to take a cab a little bit further down the Strip to a promising one called Moonshine. I don't want to walk five miles in heels."

"Same."

"Hopefully we'll find work." My stomach churns with anxiety. I go through the numbers even though I've gone through them a thousand times. "I have about eight hundred left on prepaid Visa cards. We need a thousand each for plane fare. And we probably need another thousand each to get started once we get to our new locations. So we need at least four thousand dollars. I don't want to steal money from people, but at this point, I'm not sure what else to do. Maybe we could take some credit cards and use them to buy Visa gift cards or something. Ugh. I just don't know. It feels over the line. But maybe my conscience is just reacting to the manslaughter and, like..." I gesture helplessly. "All the other crimes."

She meets my eyes in the mirror. "What if we went to Mexico for a little while? We could get down there for a few hundred bucks, lie low, and have more time to earn money. We could work actual jobs using our fake passports, take a few months, and then you could go to London and I could go wherever I want."

I apply mascara for a minute, then blink my eyes to dry it, considering the idea. I can't deny the practicality of her suggestion. Finally, I reply, "I don't think so, Frankie."

She turns toward me. "Why not?"

"I can't." I don't want to go into it any further. I don't want to tempt myself with the idea of three months with her. I have my plan. I need to stick to my plan.

She steps closer. "Look at me."

I clench my jaw and look down at the sink. "Let's just get ready."

"We have to talk about what happened between us."

"No. We don't." I start shoving makeup back into the pouch.

She huffs a frustrated sigh. "Can you please—"

I walk away and sit on the bench to organize my purse. She kneels on the carpet in front of me, pushes my purse aside, and takes my hands in hers. "You don't sleep with someone and then run away to the airport afterward. It's mean. Do you understand that? How do you think it feels knowing how bad you can't wait to get away from me?"

I feel my cheeks flush red with the memories her words stir up. Words are flying around inside my head. Finally, some of them escape. "I don't want to get away from you, I want to get away from *me*. Can't you see that? This whole thing is about becoming a new person, and I can't be this bright, shiny new person when you're right here in front of me always seeing *Maude*." I say my name with disgust.

She frowns. "You can't just decide to be a different person."

I laugh, incredulous. "What do you think we're doing here?"

She looks like she feels sorry for me. She pushes herself up and sits right beside me, so close our thighs are touching. She puts an arm around my shoulders and squeezes. "I like Maude," she murmurs.

The words are like poison. They get inside me. I shrug away from her. "I don't want you to like Maude. I don't want you to *know* Maude." I'm going to cry. I blink the tears back hard; I just put makeup on.

Her voice soft, she says, "I'm so sorry you've been in pain for so long. I don't know who made you feel like this, but Maude is amazing. Maude is perfect."

I turn to face her and say something snappy, something to make her stop saying nice things to me, but then our faces are close, and the next second we're kissing. Really kissing, all our pent-up anger and fear and uncertainty in this kiss. Her lips are soft on mine, hands just like the other night— on my neck, my waist, my back. I swear at myself, cursing my inability to do anything right. I should tell her to stop, should run out and leave her, should . . .

I lose the thread. The kissing feels too good. I'm pushing her back onto the divan and winding our limbs together, and it's happening again, everything gone except this moment.

Hands entwined in my hair, she whispers in my ear, "Stay with me."

It puts a picture in my head of us together in a new place, figuring out a new life.

I rest my forehead on her breastbone. I breathe in the

smell of her skin. Everything about her is delicious. I could stay here all night and forget everything else.

"Why are you even here?" I ask. I sound broken, destroyed, which I am. She has destroyed the new me that was supposed to be in Bali, then London, ten grand in her pocket.

A hand tightens on the roots of my hair. "My dad is trying to kill me," she whispers.

I prop myself up and look down at her. "What?"

She smiles sadly. "He's broke. If I'm dead, he gets my trust fund."

I search her face for signs of deception. "You're kidding."

She shakes her head, the back of her short hair rubbing against the cloth. "My car's brakes were sabotaged, and I almost died in a car accident. Then I was progressively dosed with Valium and OD'd. I think he was putting it in my chocolate milk."

I'm shocked. I don't have a single thing to say.

"And then in Hawaii, the Jet Ski I was supposed to be riding caught fire. I had traded with this guy, and he made it out in time, but..."

Her voice breaks. I'm filled with fear picturing her on that Jet Ski, filled suddenly with gory, horrifying images.

She goes on. "I didn't know what to do after that. Go back home with him and then, what? Wait for him to kill me for real? Then I found out what you were planning, and I knew that was my only way to escape." One corner of her mouth tweaks into a wry half-smile. "I thought if I was dead, he'd get my trust fund and I'd be safe. But now that everyone knows we're alive, I don't know what that means for him. Will my grandma just give him the money? Or will he try to find me and kill me? I want to disappear as bad as you do, Maude. Maybe even worse. I need to get out of the country as soon as possible."

I sit up, detangling myself from her. "I can't believe you're only just telling me this now."

"Did it matter? You wanted to get rid of me. What do you care?" Her voice is bitter, and she sits up and straightens her dress.

"I care," I say, and I realize it's true. How am I going to do this—let her go, never know what happens to her?

She puts a hand on my chin and turns my head so I'm facing her. She kisses my lips softly, gently. "We don't have to split up. We can stay together."

I pull back. My head is going to explode. I feel panicked, my chest tight.

I stand up. I put a hand on the wall to steady myself. "I can't," I tell her, barely breathing.

She looks devastated. She stands up, grabs her purse, unlocks the door, and yanks it open. Helplessly, I watch as she walks out. The door swings shut behind her.

Ten seconds click by. Twenty.

I feel her getting farther away, disappearing into the casino crowds.

Thirty.

I can't stand it. The idea of her off in the world, uncharted and alone, is worse than losing my dream of being Elizabeth. I realize I'd rather stay Maude if it means keeping Frankie.

I grab my purse and follow her.

The lactation room is off a long, quiet hallway that connects the casino to a wing of the hotel. I follow it out into the larger hall, which is wide enough to drive a car through and full of people in every different kind of outfit imaginable. They seem to be on their way back up to their rooms or out for the evening. I push through them, searching for Frankie's familiar silhouette.

The hallway lets me out onto the casino floor. It's organized chaos, with slot machines dinging, the roar of conversation, and waitresses carrying drink trays around. The size of these casinos is unimaginable; it's like being inside a series of connected malls. I hurry to the exterior doors. She either left the building, or she's going to the concierge to get her suitcase. I pass the concierge desk, don't see her, and burst out into the warm desert night.

The street is full of foot traffic, cabs, limos full of partyers. I stand there for a minute, searching the sidewalk.

And then I see her, over by the valet. She's with a man. He looks like the truck driver guy I'd noticed on the bus, and I realize it was the same guy outside the fast-food restaurant. He's got a hand on her arm and is shoving her into the back of a car. He slams the door behind her, gets into the front passenger seat, and drives away.

Thirty-Nine

"FRANKIE," I SCREAM, HORROR AND FEAR RUBBING MY VOICE RAW. People turn and stare at me. I'm frozen for a second, and then I break through it and run, trying to catch the car. It's pulling away from the curb. I can't see well enough to get a license plate number, or even a make and model. It's a plain white sedan. Here, then gone.

Frankie. The scream reverberates in my brain even though my jaw is clamped shut. People walk past me. I'm in their way.

The FBI. It had to be them, or someone like them, following us since LA. But why hadn't he just arrested us on the bus? Or at the fast-food place?

My chest is heaving. I feel helpless. A valet is approaching me. He says some words. I don't have a reply; I can't hear anything above the pounding of my heart.

I back away from the valet and through the sliding doors, into the casino. The sounds of slot machines and roar of conversation envelope me again.

I don't know what to do.

That sentence gallops around inside my panicked brain for a while, and then it's replaced by another thought: Why would they only take Frankie?

I glance around, paranoid. No one's looking at me. No SWAT team converges upon me. They could have gotten me, too, just as easily. They could get me right now. It really seems like it was just that one guy shoving Frankie into a car.

So was he, like...connected to Natalya in LA? Or is it a random kidnapping? I dismiss that immediately. It can't be random; what are the odds? Besides, this guy has clearly been following us since we left LA.

"Miss, can I help you?" A security guard stands in front of me, a worried expression on his face. I'm acting strangely.

"No, thank you," I murmur. I turn away and hurry through the casino, searching for a bathroom. I need to hide. I need to regroup.

By the time I find a ladies' room off the main hallway, I feel dizzy with fear. I rush through the marble foyer and lock myself in a stall. I sit on the toilet seat, breathing raggedly. This can't be happening. This can't be real.

It's stupid, but I get my phone out and dial Frankie's burner. It goes straight to voicemail.

I end the call and stare at the phone, thinking hard. If it wasn't law enforcement who took Frankie, that leaves someone connected to Natalya, but again, they'd also want me. Who would want just Frankie?

And then hits me. Her dad.

The whole reason she wanted to fake her own death was so he would get the trust-fund money and stop harming her for real. The second they discovered we were really alive, he'd...

He'd want to kill her.

I could call the cops, but I didn't get a make or a model on the car. I'd just be giving my own location away. I could... I could...

What can I do?

An idea flashes like an explosion. I fumble for my phone, open up the browser, and start searching around for Frankie's dad's phone number. I'm going to go straight to the source. I'll call him and tell him I know what he's up to, and I'll make sure everyone else knows, too, unless he calls off his guy and lets Frankie go. I'm Googling his name, hoping his cell will be listed online somewhere. When I enter his name, a bunch of news articles about Frankie's and my disappearance come up. I'm about to make my search more specific when the top one catches my eye.

"Live Now: Press Conference with Family of Missing Orange County Teenagers."

I click on the image, which takes me to a live feed from a news station. It's our family, standing in front of what looks like a police station or some other government building. There's my mom and Todd, tired and drawn, and Frankie's dad, his face completely blank. Morticia is about to speak; she's having a cop lower the microphone to her level. I don't see Leah, which is weird. She's usually hanging on Chris's arm, giving him concerned looks like Morticia will love her if only she's nice enough.

I consider Frankie's dad as Morticia takes her place behind the mic and starts speaking. I guess this is what a psychopath looks like. I'd expect him to be better at feigning emotion. I thought psychopaths were supposed to be good at that.

Morticia begins by summarizing the situation, describing her family's journey from grief to confusion to disappointment. She talks about being shocked and horrified when she heard we were potentially involved in the death of Nathan in Hawaii, but her speech was clearly drafted by lawyers, because everything she says hints at the allegations against us being ridiculous. "The idea of our girls committing any crimes after a lifetime of spotless records is bewildering. We're sure the FBI will uncover the truth as their investigation proceeds." She's kind of backing us up, which is interesting. Then again, she's really just protecting the Maxwell brand.

"We know they're somewhere in Los Angeles County," she continues. "The investigation into the death of Mr. Avery in Hollywood is still ongoing, but the police have reason to believe they haven't left the city." Morticia goes on to tell people to be on the lookout for us, to give us the benefit of the doubt, and a bunch of other stuff. I stop listening closely and focus in on Frankie's dad.

Something is nagging at me.

I go back through Frankie's descriptions in her mind. He had messed with her brakes, trying to kill her in a car accident. He'd dosed her for months, eventually OD-ing her and framing her for a drug addiction. He'd sabotaged a Jet Ski, causing it to catch fire.

With two fingers, I pinch the screen and expand, zooming in on his face. He looks blank, stupid, like he's shocked and overwhelmed by this whole thing.

I realize what's bothering me. This whole plan Frankie described—it's complex, requiring mechanical knowledge and intensive research and planning. Chris has never seemed that smart; he's a grown-up frat boy, a rich kid partying away his family money. Can I picture him coordinating with some hired guy to snatch Frankie out of the casino while keeping it together enough to do this press conference? Can I picture him learning about Jet Ski mechanics and getting into the rental facility's garage to tamper with the exact one Frankie would be using? Can I picture him with enough attention to detail to get the Valium dosage right over a period of months, to cut the brakes on her car in such a way that it wasn't immediately flagged as intentional?

No. I can't.

She must have been taken by the FBI, then. Either that, or there's some solution I'm not considering.

I'm watching Chris so closely it takes me a minute to

realize the press conference has stopped. A man in a suit has come in to whisper something in Morticia's ear. She's covering the mic and listening to him with a frown. He seems like he wants to take the mic from her, but she waves him away imperiously. He doesn't take this well; he literally grabs the mic and turns to face the cameras and reporters. He's a serious-looking man in his thirties or forties, carrying the distinct air of a public official.

"We have some breaking news," he says.

A moment of silence.

"It seems the girls have been spotted at a bus station, heading to Las Vegas. They were captured on security cameras at the terminal."

The screen fills with a grainy black-and-white video in which Frankie and I are hurrying through the rows of buses. At one point I look up, and the camera freezes on my face. As it zooms in, making it clear that this is me, I remember this moment. I'd been worried about security cameras there.

"Oh, shit," I whisper.

There must be security cameras all over the casinos.

I can't help Frankie if I'm in jail. I need to get out of here.

Forty

FIFTEEN MINUTES AGO
Frankie

ABANDONING MAUDE IN THE LACTATION ROOM, I RUSHED through the casino, weaving between people, purse bumping my hip. I cursed the heels and my own stupidity in equal measure. Why did I keep trying with Maude? Why did I keep asking her to be with me? I was so stupid. Who threw themselves in front of a train over and over again? She didn't want me.

I needed to get some air and think about what was next. I turned toward the main entrance and walked faster. Through the sliding doors, out into the warm, busy Las Vegas night. I took a few deep breaths, wandering away from the door.

What now? Get my suitcase, then what?

My eyes were turned inward, and at first, I didn't notice the white sedan. It pulled up to the curb right in front of me and a man got out, approaching me with a hand in his back pocket. He had a mustache and a working-class look, like the man I'd seen on the bus to Vegas. I assumed he'd walk into the casino, but he pulled out a wallet and showed it to me. It was a badge that read *FBI*.

"Francesca Maxwell?" he said. "You need to come with me."

My heart plummeted into my stomach.

It was over. We were caught.

Well, I was. Maude was still in the lactation room, presumably.

"Francesca?" the man repeated. He put a hand on my elbow. "Come on. Get in the car."

I debated wrestling away from him. I could run—but no. I was in heels. He was six feet tall and probably twice my weight. Besides, couldn't I get in trouble for running from the FBI?

It happened so fast: The back door popped open, his grip on me tightened, and he yanked me toward the car. I tripped, unbalanced in my shoes, and he used the momentum to sweep me into the back seat. The door swung shut behind me, and I grabbed for the handle, jiggling it, a whimper of fear rising from my throat.

"Hey. Calm down. It's okay." The voice came from the other side of the back seat. I whipped around to face the person talking, and when I recognized her, all my emotions were replaced by one: confusion.

"Leah?" I asked. "What are you doing here?"

She was wearing jeans and a white T-shirt, a much more low-key outfit than usual. Her long hair was pulled up into a tight bun, and she had no makeup on.

The FBI agent slid into the front seat and closed the door behind him. He pulled the car away from the curb and sped forward into traffic.

Leah said, "Frankie, god, I'm so glad you're okay."

"What's going on? Why are you here with the FBI?"

"He's not actually FBI. I just needed someone to help me find you." Her voice was shaky. "It's been so awful. I'm just glad you're all right."

"Leah, what's happening? Are you taking me to the cops?"

She took a deep breath. "I thought we could talk about that, figure it out together."

"About what?"

"I know what your dad did to you. I know what he *tried* to do to you. Frankie, I…" She shook her head, eyes bright with tears. Behind her, outside the window, Vegas sparkled like a Christmas tree.

"I think he's trying to do the same thing to me."

"What do you mean exactly?" I asked.

"He's trying to kill me."

"What?" I gaped at her. "Why? How?"

"Um…" She wiped tears away from her cheeks. "A few different ways. I didn't realize what was happening at first, until I put it together with what you've been going through, all the close calls. I'm sorry I didn't believe you about the overdose. There were all those texts. Do you forgive me?"

I had no idea what to say, so I just nodded and let her go on.

"There were accidents. Well, almost accidents. Things that felt coincidental but weren't. You know?"

"Like what, specifically? What accidents?"

She looked at the man in the front seat. "Let's talk about it in private. We need to figure this out. They might not believe either of us on our own, but they might believe us together."

"But what about all the trouble I'm in? The FBI are looking for me, for real. And I can't just leave Maude back there." *I should text her,* I thought, but then I realized I didn't have my purse. The man had taken it from me when he'd shoved me into the car.

Forty-One
Frankie

THE MOTEL IS A HUMBLE PLACE ACROSS FROM A COUPLE of the big casinos on the south end of the Strip, and Leah's room has that Vegas seediness that makes me picture sad old men gambling away their kids' college savings. It doesn't seem like anywhere she'd ever stay.

As soon as the door shuts behind us, I tell her, "I really need to call Maude. Can that guy give me back my purse?"

"Just hear me out first," Leah says. "We can think about what to tell her and everybody else. Can we sit down and talk?"

There's a small table with two orange chairs by the window. I take a seat, still confused. She sits across from me and rubs her eyes with her fingertips. She looks exhausted and scared.

I glance toward the door. The man who'd caught me at the casino is stationed outside the room. "Who is he, anyway? He's creeping me out."

"He's a private investigator. I hired him to help me find you."

"He did a better job than the police."

She makes a wry face. "They've been one step behind you, that's for sure."

"So tell me—how did you know my dad was trying to kill you? Are you okay?" I stop myself from asking more questions. I could go on all night.

She takes a shaky breath. She looks so much more fragile than I've ever seen her. Usually, she's a bombshell of energy, the prettiest, best-dressed woman in any room.

"I wasn't feeling well," she says. "At first I started feeling almost high. I thought I was drinking too much coffee or eating too many carbs. I felt sort of light and floaty. And then I started feeling nauseous and...well, just terrible. Dizzy, weak, like I could faint any minute."

"That's how I was. I felt that way for a couple of months."

"For me, the feeling started in Hawaii."

I process that. "He was dosing you on vacation?"

She holds her hands out in a helpless gesture. "I guess so."

"But why?" I lean my elbows on the sticky table. "With me, I figure he wants my trust fund. With you, what does he have to gain?"

"Have you heard of family annihilators?" In response to my blank expression, she says, "People who kill their partners and children. Sometimes the motivation is financial, and sometimes it's that they feel their family is a burden, a heavy weight they're trying to get out from underneath. Usually, it's one incident, like Andrea Yates drowning all five of her children, but with this one man named John List, he actually killed two of his kids, went to the third kid's soccer game, then took him home and shot him, too."

"That's horrible." I feel my gut clench up, imagining my dad doing this.

She gets up. "I could use a real drink, but since we have to keep our heads clear, let's have a soda." She squats by a mini fridge and digs around inside. "Diet Coke okay?"

"Sure."

Her back to me, she pulls two plastic cups out of their sanitary wrappers and cracks open the soda can. "I'm sorry you've been through all this. I know it must be hard with your mom being gone and everything. Were you planning to go to Italy and find her? Is that where you were headed?"

My mom has a big extended family in Italy, it's true, but I hadn't planned on visiting them. For one, they'd be sure to tell my dad where I was. For another, they're not very nice people. There's a reason my mom is so messed up. But because I don't want to betray Maude's plan, I say, "Yeah. That's where I was going. But I don't have a passport, so I was trying to maybe steal one."

She turns, a cup in each hand, and steps around the bed to return to the table. She sets the cups down and slides into her seat. "What happened with that dead guy in Hawaii?"

"He got hit by a car. Maude and I didn't do anything to him. We got scared and hid his body, that's all."

"I know. You're a nice girl. You would never." Her eyes are earnest, warm. She's always been kind to me, never rude or competitive. How could my dad do this to us?

"What are you thinking about?" she asks.

I find myself blinking back tears. "I don't know. It's just...the Jet Ski. That's a horrible way to die. He wanted me to die like a circus act?"

She nods, sympathetic. "I know. But you have to remember you didn't do anything to deserve this. You're a good kid. It's him."

"So what do you want to do?" I ask.

She sits back in her chair and sighs. "I think we should figure out who we want to tell our story to. Maybe we should hire a lawyer? Or call the media?"

I grimace. "I don't think the media is a very good idea."

"Drink your soda," she says. "You look tired. We both need a pick-me-up."

I lift the cup to my lips. She does the same and takes a little sip. Usually, she leaves a ton of lipstick on the rim of all her glasses, but she's wearing no makeup today.

Something is nagging at me.

I don't know why, but I pretend to sip instead of actually sipping and set my cup down.

Why did I do that?

But I know, don't I?

My dad isn't the only one with access to my food, to my phone, to my car. My dad isn't the only one who would benefit from the millions in my trust fund.

This thought pumps ice-cold fear through my veins. She's looking at me, head cocked, like she's trying to read the thoughts going through my head.

"I thought I heard something," I tell her. "At the door."

"Oh, well, our guy is out there."

"No, like, I thought I heard a struggle. Could someone have gotten him? Could the cops be out there?"

She frowns. "That's not likely, they've only just...Well, hm..." She gets up and crosses the small room to look through the peephole.

The second her back is turned, I switch our cups.

Forty-Two

I HAVE TO GET OUT OF HERE. THE CASINO IS FULL OF EYES WATCH-ing. My head is swimming. Who took Frankie? What's happening to her right now?

If it was the FBI, they're looking for me next. If it wasn't the FBI, it could be someone connected to that man I killed at Natalya's house. That crowd wouldn't want to do something as benign as arrest us. They'd have other, much worse plans.

For the first time I can remember, I have no idea what to do. *Think, Maude. What's next?*

First things first—I have to get out of the casino.

I exit the ladies' room into a busy, crowded hallway. Nearby, a restaurant lets ambiguous food smells out into the sea of people, making my stomach groan; I haven't eaten since the fast-food meal with Frankie.

I hurry along the hallway and into the casino floor near the slot machines. Old and young gamblers have gathered to try their luck while cocktail waitresses shuffle around, pretty in their bustiers, shorts, and black stockings. I snake through the massive gambling arena toward the front entrance, eyes on the security guards peppered throughout the crowds.

I'm about to reach the end of the gambling floor and move out into the hotel lobby when a pair of uniformed cops enters through the sliding exterior doors. I halt, almost tripping over my feet. A second pair of cops follows them. Behind them, two men in suits rush to the concierge.

It was the FBI who took Frankie. They're here for me.

Heart pounding, I turn around and hurry back the way I came. There must be a rear exit through which staff members come and go. There's probably a break room, somewhere to store their personal belongings, somewhere that lets out into an employee parking lot. I flag down the nearest waitress, a beautiful woman in her late twenties with a short haircut and bright red lipstick. "Excuse me," I tell her, and she turns to me, maintaining her grip on her drink-laden tray with calm professionalism. "I'm a waitress—I'm new," I explain, making it up as I go along. "I'm starting today, and I'm supposed to drop my purse off and change, but I don't know where to go."

She brightens. "You'll need to check in with John. He's the big guy with the walkie-talkie and the black shirt." She searches the crowd. "I'm not sure where he is right now..."

"Do you mind telling me where the employee area is before I check in with him? I'm kind of having a period emergency, and I want to handle it before I, you know, talk to the new boss." I wince, hoping my desperation rings true.

She says, "Ahhhh," and I know I've struck the right note. "Sure, of course. Go back there, behind the blackjack tables, and make a left. Take the hallway toward the kitchen, and it's the third unmarked door on the left. That's the entrance to the locker room. Just knock; someone will let you in. You'll get your key card later. Good luck!"

"Thank you so much." I speed-walk, letting out a string of whispered "Please, please, please," because I don't know what I'll do if this doesn't work. I guess I'll try going through the kitchen. There have to be fire exits, right? But those might be alarmed. My heart is pounding so loud, blood rushing in my ears, I can't think straight.

I find the door just like she'd said and knock on it loudly. A young woman swings it open. She's pretty like all the other waitresses, a petite blond with deeply tanned skin.

"Sorry, I'm new and I need to get in. They said someone could open the door for me," I explain. I drop my voice and say, "Period emergency."

"Oh, sure, of course." She beckons me into a musty corridor that leads to a locker room where three women are changing into their uniforms. "Bathroom's back through that hallway," the blond says, pointing. "Showers, too, if it's a full-on situation." She grins, round cheeks dimpling. I like her. She seems funny.

"And just for next time, is there a back door we're supposed to use instead of going through the whole casino?"

"Yeah, totally. It's all the way back, past the bathrooms. You'll need your key card to get in that way, but John should give you that today."

"Thanks." I hurry away, leaving her behind. *Thank God,* I chant to myself. *Thank God, Thank God...* It's weird how humans are reduced to prayer in desperate circumstances. If there is a God, he sure as hell doesn't care if I make it out of here or not. I'm sure I'm not on his good list. Wait, that's Santa. I'm fully losing it.

The door has a big EXIT sign, and I feel like I've found a mirage in a desert. I push it open and find myself looking out at a small parking lot full of humble cars—an employee lot just as I'd hoped. The evening sun is hot, beating orange-red light down onto the asphalt, and the air has a desert-dry aroma that feels wonderful in my lungs after all the air-conditioning. I inhale gratefully, deciding which way I should go, and then a pair of squad cars pulls into the parking lot. The asphalt grinds under their tires, and they pull to a stop.

I pull the door shut. EXIT, the sign on it reads, taunting me. Now what?

"I thought you needed to use the restroom." The voice comes from behind me. I swing around. It's the blond, looking at me with furrowed, suspicious brows.

I don't have a story. I'm trapped.

"Are you okay?" She steps closer, looking concerned.

I'm scrambling for an answer. I have no ideas. I'm drawing a total blank.

She pushes past me and peeks out the door, obviously wondering what I'm so freaked out about. "Don't," I protest, but she pulls the door shut as soon as she sees the cops. They're out of their cars now in deep conversation, gesturing to the casino.

She turns to me with raised eyebrows. After a long moment, she says, "You're one of the girls they're looking for."

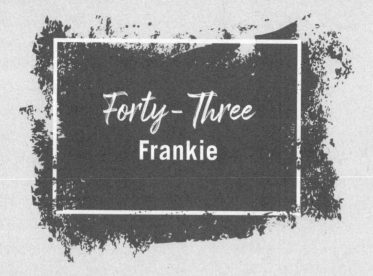

Forty-Three
Frankie

HAVING CHECKED ON THE GUY STANDING GUARD OUT-side the door, Leah returns to the table. "Everything's fine. He's on the lookout. Don't worry."

"Sorry. False alarm, I guess."

She settles into her seat and lifts her cup. "Cheers. To us. To justice."

I touch my cup to hers and take a sip. She does the same, eyes on me as she drinks a little more deeply this time. She says, "We need to be sharp if we're going to protect ourselves."

I make a show of taking another sip, and she does the same. My stomach is in knots. "So you think my dad is after your money? Isn't there paperwork that protects you from that? A prenup or something?"

She twists her mouth into a sardonic expression. "That's why your grandmother has always been a bitch about our marriage. We eloped; we didn't sign one. She thinks I'm after his money, but it's the other way around at this point."

Interesting. Without a prenup, she'd have access to any money my dad inherited.

I say, "You could have just gotten a lawyer and told your story to the cops yourself, and you could have told them what happened to me."

"Who's going to believe me? I'll be a hysterical woman. And now they think you're off the rails, a murderer. I wanted to protect both of us." She lifts her cup and indicates that I should do the same. I drink the cold soda, eyes on her. She sets her almost-empty cup down and casts her gaze out the window at the Venetian across the street. "I always thought Las Vegas was a romantic city," she murmurs.

"Really?" I ask.

"I used to come here a lot. My friends and I would get dressed up, looking so hot, we'd go to clubs and men would buy us drinks all night…days by the pool…" Her words trail off.

Am I imagining it, or does she sound a little strange?

"Tell me more about that. How old were you when you used to come here?"

"Oh, since high school, but in my twenties, at least once a month. Your father loves Las Vegas. He loves to show me off." She beams, cheeks pinking. "You know I'm thirty-two? Did you know that?"

I shake my head. "You never told me your age. But I figured it was about that."

"Really? You didn't think I was younger?"

I stammer a little, and then I realize she's not listening. She's glazing over, staring out the window. "Leah? Are you all right?"

She looks at me, and then her eyes widen. She shakes herself, looks down at her the remnants of her Diet Coke, then back up at me. "How are you feeling?"

"Fine. Why?"

She frowns down at her cup. It's like her brain is slow; I can see every thought passing through her head. She's wondering why she's feeling this way, remembering pouring the drinks, wondering if she'd accidentally switched them.

"Are you feeling okay?" I ask. "Do you need to lie down?"

"No." She pushes herself to an unsteady standing position and crosses the room to the bed where she'd tossed her purse. Her steps are uneven, and she has to lean on the bed to dig around in her bag.

Why did she want to drug me here in this crappy motel? What would be the point of that?

Purse in hand, she stumbles back to the table. I can see how woozy she is; she's weaving, like she's on a ship bucking in the waves.

From her purse, she withdraws a gun. She uses both hands to point it at me. "Did you switch the cups?"

My heart stops.

The gun's point, a hollow, empty circle, is unsteady, but it's only a few feet away from my chest. She could be the worst shot in the world, and she'd still hit me.

"What are you doing?" I hear myself ask from far away.

She steps closer. The muzzle presses against my breastbone. My heart, formerly silent, pounds like a drum. "I'm not doing anything. You're doing this to yourself."

Forty-Four

THE WAITRESS IS STARING AT ME, WIDE-EYED. "YOU'RE ONE OF THE girls they're looking for."

I turn and run away from her. I don't know how I'm going to get out of the casino. If there are cops stationed in the back parking lot, that's a bad sign. A very bad sign. Maybe I could hide up in a room. But then what?

"Hey. Hey!" The waitress catches up with me and grabs my arm. "Wait. You have to help me."

That surprises me enough to stop my mad rush down the hallway. We're at the entrance to the locker room, and no one else is changing right now; we have the room to ourselves.

"Help you with what?" I ask.

She hesitates. "Don't tell anyone. Promise."

"Sure, yes. Look, I have to get going."

"How did you do all of it? The news said you were using this other identity. Did you steal someone's ID? But if you did, how have you not gotten caught?"

I narrow my eyes at her. "Why?"

"Because I need to do it." Her bright blue eyes are haunting. Her funny, quick-tongued demeanor had been a mask. This is her, and she's terrified.

"You want to fake your own death?"

"No. I'm..." She lowers her voice. "I have this ex. I've tried everything, but no one will help me. I keep moving around, but he always finds me. I've been here for a month. I have to move on soon. But I feel like I'm losing my mind; I can't keep running forever."

"He's stalking you?"

She smiles wryly, sadly, and it makes her look a hundred years old. "Honey, he'll kill me if he gets the chance."

"You can't go to the cops?"

She snorts. "Why didn't I think of that?"

"Sorry. I just mean—"

"They won't do anything. I've tried in three different states. So tell me how you got your ID. Did you buy a fake, steal one, what? Do you have a contact, someone who can get me good fake papers?"

I want to help her, but I have to get out of here. "I know a guy in LA who does really good, legit, fake identities, yeah. I can give you his info. It costs about five grand."

She brightens. "I have that! I save almost everything, and I make good money here. Can you give me his number?"

And now I know what to do. The idea hits me like a tidal wave.

"I'll give you his number. I'll put you in touch with him. But you have to help me, too."

"How?"

"Let me wear your waitress outfit. I'll have a chance of getting past the cops in it."

She smiles. "I can do better than that. I have a spare in my locker. I'll help get you out of the casino. We can go through the side door in the bar. We'll just look like two cocktail waitresses taking a smoke break."

"Okay, let's do it. And I'll need that five grand up front if you want me to handle the papers for you. And let me take your picture with my phone. I assume you want a United States passport, right?"

She hurries to one of the lockers and starts turning the dial, then stops. She slumps. "Wait. I just realized. I'm so stupid. I've always been gullible. My friends used to call me *such a blond.*"

"What are you talking about?" I'm feeling frantic. The minutes are ticking past. I picture cops infiltrating the casino like cockroaches.

"If I help you get out of here, you aren't going to put me in touch with your guy. You're going to disappear with my five grand."

This whole thing is a moot point. The second I walk onto that casino floor, the cops could catch me and take me off to . . . jail? Juvie?

I remember that I have our passports, the Elizabeth one for me and the new one for Frankie. If I get caught by the cops, they'll get these.

She's looking at me with big, sad blue eyes. She can't be more than twenty-two.

"I know what we have to do," I say, grim. I take the passports out of my purse and hand them to her. "Hold on to these for me. When I get yours, we'll trade."

She accepts the passports and briefly glances through them. "What are these?"

"My ticket to freedom. Without a passport, I can't leave the country. That's your insurance."

She looks them over, looks at me, and nods. "Okay. Let's do it."

"What's your name?" I ask.

"Katie. What's yours? I forget what they said on the news."

"Maude."

And there it is. Frankie was right. I'm still Maude. I think I always will be.

Forty-Five
Frankie

I TAKE A DEEP BREATH, READY TO SCREAM, AND LEAH
says, "I'll have to kill you now if you're going to start yelling." She digs the gun into my breastbone hard.

I snap my mouth shut. A thousand thoughts are bouncing around my brain: Should I try to take her by surprise, jump away from the gun, fight? Can she shoot that fast?

It's a split second of indecision, and the right answer doesn't come to me, so I'm still frozen when she says, "Walk slowly backward to the bathroom."

I cast a glance over my shoulder at the open bathroom door. "To the—but why?"

She presses the gun in harder. "Do it."

"What's wrong—you don't want to get blood on the carpet?" It's a ridiculous thing to joke about, but here I am, doing stand-up at death's door.

Her eyes are steel. She looks out of it, foggy and unsteady, but her hand on the gun seems pretty freaking stable.

I take a step backward. "Good," she says. "Nice and slow."

I realize I'm waiting for something to happen, for someone to come help me. I remember the party in Hollywood, how Maude showed up when I needed her. Maude isn't coming now. I'm on my own.

"What's the plan?" I ask. "Why the bathroom?"

The pressure of the gun doesn't let up. "It's a sad story, actually. You've been struggling for so long, right? The drugs, all the trouble at school. The boy clothes." She presses her lips together and shakes her head. "Keep walking backward."

I take a few tiny steps, trying to buy time. "So, okay, I'm all fucked up. Why the bathroom?"

"You'll see." She smiles like she has a secret.

And then, all of a sudden, I know. She's setting a scene. That's why she's having me walk myself to the bathroom, why she isn't touching me and leaving her DNA on me. I realize—the bun—she never wears her hair up. She's making sure not to drop any telltale long hairs here in the hotel room.

I wonder whose name is on the reservation.

She's going to make it look like I died by suicide. Will she shoot me as soon as she can get me to lie down in the bathtub?

"Maude will never let your story fly," I tell her. "She'll make sure everyone knows I didn't do this to myself."

She raises her eyebrows, and her grip on the gun seems to weaken for just a moment; it swerves to the left, then recenters on my chest. "Babe, Maude doesn't have a lot of social capital right now. She won't be able to argue with forensics."

"You don't know Maude."

Her jaw tightens. I feel like I'm watching her desperately trying to stay with it; whatever meds she took would have no doubt put me to sleep, or at least made me loopy enough to be docile and easy to manage. She's off script, trying to patch up her plan.

Maude would seize that advantage and come up with some counterplan on the spot. How does she do that? I'm almost at the bathroom door now; this isn't a large room.

Leah can't shoot me from afar. She has to make it look like I did it to myself. The angle of the bullet, everything, has to be right. Not just that—my body has to be spotless, no evidence of her on me. She hasn't touched me once since I got in the back of the car.

These things all click into place as I reach the bathroom door. I'm out of time to stall. I have to do something.

Running on instinct, I drop to the floor suddenly, like a rock. She doesn't shoot. She's smarter than that. I attack her legs, counting on her being off her game. Sure enough, she stumbles back and trips, landing on the carpet with a muffled *thunk*. She tries to aim at me, but I'm feral now. I come up under the gun, grab the wrist that holds it, and climb on top of her, trying to use my body weight to hold her down. Even drugged, she's strong; she works out every single day. That freaking Peloton. She writhes and slithers out from underneath me.

My hyper focus on her gun arm distracts me. She whips me around, and now she's on top, the gun pressed to my chest again. She's straddling me, sweating, face beet red and full of contempt.

I can't quit. The second I hold still, she's going to find a way to angle that gun and make it look like I did this to myself.

"Fuck you," I gasp, barely able to breathe. "You might kill me, but no way in hell are you making it look like I did this to myself."

I grab her hand and hit myself in the face with the gun. It's like getting punched with a hammer; my cheek goes numb, and I growl with satisfaction. I do it again, same cheek, determined to leave a mark.

It's throwing her off. She's trying to get the gun back, trying to wrench it away from me.

"Evidence of a struggle," I manage to grunt out, and then I roll, toppling her off me, and she loses her grip on the gun. It falls to the carpet, and I grab it.

I stand up, panting, my cheek burning.

She's on her hands and knees, holding onto the ground like it's rolling. After a few seconds, she heaves and throws up on the carpet.

DNA evidence.

I point the gun at her and back away. My eyes fly to the door, the only exit. That's not going to work. She has that man out there, standing guard.

I have to try.

I cross the room, undo the locks, and yank the door open. The mustached man is leaning on the wall like he's waiting for someone. I explode into the hallway, gun pointed at him, ready for him to fire back at me.

"I will shoot you," I swear, and I'm telling the truth. I will. I am not dying here today.

He looks up at me with moderate interest.

I point the gun right at his chest. "I'll do it," I promise, backing away down the hall.

"Right." He doesn't change his position.

He's not stopping me. He's not reaching for a weapon or anything.

He laughs at my confusion. "Hey, I'm not going to fight you. I'm paid to keep people from coming in, not getting out. She wants more from me, she has to pay more." He crosses his arms over his chest and purses his lips, like he's thinking about something else entirely.

I decide not to question it. I turn and run.

Forty-Six

I WALK OUT ONTO THE CASINO FLOOR AT KATIE'S SIDE. IT'S A cacophony of sound and a hurricane of smells: food, alcohol, cigarette smoke, perfume.

I feel ridiculous in the waitress uniform: a bustier, stretchy black hot pants, and fishnet stockings. We pulled the front of my hair back and put a bunch of makeup on me real quick. I wouldn't have recognized myself in a mirror.

At my side, Katie is smiling brightly. "Make sure to smile or we'll get yelled at," she says between her teeth.

I plaster on a grin. "So what's the plan?"

"We'll head for the bar and pick up a tray. I think we should carry drinks."

That makes sense. My eyes flit from person to person, searching the crowded room. "Why don't I see any cops?"

"I don't know." Beneath the smile, her eyes look tight.

We hurry past rows of slot machines. The carpet is patterned, red and gold. The whole decor is meant to be glamorous, over the top, but it just looks cheap to me, like everything has been spray-painted and the finish will soon flake off.

"Hey," a man calls out from a slot machine. "Hey, girls! Will you bring me a Jack and Coke?"

Katie flashes him a thousand-watt smile. "Of course!"

We're nearing the huge bar, which is manned by three bartenders. I keep my eyes glued to the exterior doors, waiting to see police. Katie leads me to the station where other waitresses are picking up drinks and carrying them off on trays. She goes to a computer and types in a code, then flashes through screens and hits Enter. She grabs me a small drink tray and gets one for herself.

"I was thinking we could try to get you out through the kitchen." She nods toward a hallway behind the bar. As we watch, an expediter with a tray full of appetizers hurries out to one of the tables.

"Wouldn't they think it was weird to see a cocktail waitress in the kitchen?" I ask.

"Not at all. We go in there constantly. They feed us, or we're picking up something for a guest."

"And that doesn't let you out into the same parking lot as the locker room?"

"No, this actually lets out onto the alley with the dumpsters. You can turn left and go onto the main strip, blend in with the crowd, and head away from the casino."

I nod. I glance back behind us, searching the huge room for any sign of impending danger. The main entrance doors are visible from here, and I examine everyone who comes in, searching for uniforms.

A brunette with short-cropped hair and tanned skin is standing kind of still, looking around like she's lost. She reminds me of Frankie, and as I watch her, my stomach turns over with grief. When I leave here, I'm abandoning all hope of being reunited with Frankie, essentially deserting her after committing most of the crimes myself. It feels wrong, running while she's being arrested, but what's my other choice? Stay behind and let them get me, too?

I don't want to start a new life. Not without her. Sadness ignites like a bomb in my chest, and I can't even cry. I'm dry, empty, and hollow. I can't leave her in Las Vegas. I can't.

The girl who looks like Frankie wanders toward the slot machines. She even walks like Frankie.

I start toward her. I can't resist.

"What are you doing?" Katie asks, but my steps pick up speed. I pass a bar table full of guys, and they say something that sounds like, "Hey, can we get some drinks?" I hurry on, through the empty space in front of the main doors. The girl who looks like Frankie is walking through the rows of slot machines, like she's searching for someone. I start jogging, my heart pounding. I realize I'm praying again. *Let it be her, let it be her.* I warn myself against hope. *Remember, Maude—God is not on your side. No one cares. The universe is empty, uncaring. You are alone.*

And now I'm right behind her. I say, "Frankie," in a voice that barely sounds like my own. She won't turn. It isn't her.

The girl turns.

It's Frankie.

I put a hand to my stomach like I've been punched. It's her. Her cheekbone is swollen and red, her hair is messy, and her eyes are dark and intense.

We stare at each other for a long moment, separated by six feet of space.

"What are you wearing?" she asks, exactly as I say, "What happened to your cheek?"

And then we're closing the distance, my arms around her neck. I'm hugging her so tight, I don't think I'll ever be able to let go. I realize I'm crying, clutching her like she's a life raft and I'm sinking into the ocean. "I thought they got you," I whisper into her neck. "How did you get away from them? Was it the FBI, the cops?"

She pulls back. She's cupping my cheeks, searching my eyes like she's hoping to read something secret written inside them. "It was Leah. She brought some guy and grabbed me, tried to kill me. She tried to shoot me and make it look like I did it myself. Can you believe it?"

"Leah? Your stepmom?"

She nods. "She took me to a motel down the Strip to kill me. When I escaped, I got a cab and had to run because I didn't have money to pay. It wasn't my dad who was trying to kill me. It was Leah."

She's shaking, I realize. What the hell? Leah? It wasn't the FBI who put Frankie in the car? Holy shit.

That reminds me. The casino—the police. "Frankie, there are cops in here looking for us. We have to go."

"What kind of cops?"

"I don't know. Come on." I take her hand and lead her back through the slot machines. She's warm and real, her hand clutched tight in mine. Katie waits impatiently at the bar. "Sorry," I say as we approach. "I found my friend."

"I have to get back to work, so let's do this." She leads us into the hallway, which has a white-tiled floor and smells like French fries. The large kitchen is standard issue, with a guy making salads at one station, a lady frying stuff at another, and servers and expediters waiting for their food, hollering instructions and jokes back and forth with the cooks. She leads us past all this, past the dishwashing station, through another hallway with an EXIT door at the end of it.

"This is as far as I go," she says.

I turn to look at her. "I'll call you from LA."

She gives me a quick hug. "Good luck." She rushes off, leaving us in the darkened hallway.

"What's the plan?" Frankie asks. "Are we going our separate ways? Do you want to leave Vegas together, at least?"

I step toward her, put my hands on her cheeks, and kiss her. It's everything. She's here.

I inhale the scent of her skin, taste the softness of her lips, feel myself melting into her. Our arms wrap around each other, and I don't care who I am. Dreams can change. They can grow and make room. We could go to Italy, Mexico, Russia, Bali. We could be nomadic, living on the road, making enough money to last awhile and then moving on. We could go on a motorcycle road trip. *Anywhere.*

When the kiss is over, we hold each other for a moment. In case she needs to hear me say it, I murmur, "I'm not going anywhere without you."

She fixes my lipstick, running a thumb along the side of my mouth where it must have smudged. Her lips are pink from it, and I can't wait to get to the next stage, where we've escaped Vegas and are figuring out our big, beautiful plans.

"Ready?" she asks.

"Ready."

She grins.

I push the door open. Bright sunlight stings my eyes. We slip out into the alley, and the door closes with a *thunk* behind us. Like Katie had said, there's a bank of dumpsters lined up against the concrete block wall. We turn left toward the street.

Two squad cars pull into the alley, one right after the other. Their lights flare to life, red and blue. From the other entrance to the alley, a third police car speeds toward us. They stop, doors flying open, cops spilling out onto the asphalt.

"Freeze!"

"Get down!"

Guns pointed at us.

"Hands up!" a police officer yells, approaching us with his gun drawn.

In unison, we lift our hands into the air.

And then we're surrounded. Police forcing us to our knees, handcuffs. We look at each other while it's happening, eyes locked.

It's over.

Forty-Seven

THEY TAKE US IN SEPARATE POLICE CARS. HANDS CUFFED BEHIND me, I look out the window at the Vegas Strip. All these people, here to have fun and gamble their lives away. I gambled my life, too, and I guess I lost.

I feel empty. The loss hasn't hit me yet. It's too many emotions for my body to handle: losing Frankie and finding her, running for so long, highs and lows. It's a strange relief, being caught, but then there's the threat of what's to come. I'll probably be sent to jail. That would be the ultimate punishment for me, wouldn't it? A cell. Four walls; a compound.

"Where are you taking me?" I ask the cops through the wire screen separator. They glance at each other like they're not sure what to say. They're both young men, and they keep sneaking fascinated looks at me. I wonder what they're thinking.

"Back to the station," the one in the passenger's seat replies.

"Here in Las Vegas?"

He nods.

I wonder how it will work. I don't think they have me on record as committing any crimes in Nevada. They'll have to extradite me to LA or Hawaii, or maybe the FBI will take over the case completely. I can't believe I never researched this end of it; I always felt so sure I'd get away to London safely.

Does it matter where I go to court or which agency ends up punishing me?

Not really. Either in Maude's old life or in a cell, prison is what awaits on the other end of this car ride.

So I take a few minutes to be this Maude, the one with brave, bold plans, the one who conned her way across an ocean and a desert. The one Frankie likes, the one I guess I've always been.

They park behind the station, but I can see the bank of reporters on the sidewalk with their telescopic lenses. There are at least twenty. This is news. *I'm* news.

Well-behaved women seldom make history. It's a phrase I used to think was coined by Eleanor Roosevelt, but not so, I learned one night when I had insomnia at my mom's house and fell down a Wikipedia hole. The quote came from Laurel Thatcher Ulrich, a writer and professor. She was saying how sad it is that so many women who make positive impacts on society aren't remembered. I always read it as a blessing to go big and be bad. Now I see: people crave the spectacle of a young woman trying and failing. They like the crash more than the plane.

The police lead me across the parking lot and up a set of steps, through the back door into a bustling police station. The cop who'd spoken to me in the car is apparently in charge of making sure I don't do anything stupid. He keeps a hand on my cuffed wrists behind me, guiding me firmly through a hallway and into a conference room. Inside, around an oval table, is a group of stone-faced, angry people.

My mother. Todd. Morticia. Frankie's dad, Chris. A pair of men, strangers to me. I'm led in by the uniformed cop, and then a detective in a suit, recognizable by the badge and gun clipped to his belt, joins us. They tell me to sit in one of the chairs, and I do, because what point is there in fighting? I realize with an almost hysterical laugh that I'm still wearing the cocktail waitress uniform. I notice because my mom is staring at it, her cheeks turning pink like I'm embarrassing her.

Good.

I lift my chin. She narrows her eyes at me, but I don't look away.

Finally, she has to face the real me. She's going to hate me. Spitefully, I smile. I hope my lipstick is smeared. I hope my butt is even bigger than she remembers it.

And then they bring in Frankie. She's pale except for her cheek, which is blossoming into a hideous bruise. She scans the room and rests her eyes on me. We communicate word-lessly for a minute, each of us wanting the other to know we're here, standing together.

They seat Frankie far away from me, at the other end of the table. Before the detectives and lawyer can get started, Frankie leans over and tells her dad, "It was Leah. All the near-death experiences. It was her."

The lawyer beside Morticia says, "Please don't say any-thing else, Francesca."

I chime in. "Leah just tried to kill Frankie. Do you see her face? Leah's been trying to kill Frankie for months."

I'm met with silence. My mom seems to be seething. The detective is clearly glad to let me speak. The door opens and another detective enters, joining the original one near the lawyers.

"Well?" I ask Morticia. "What are you going to do about it?"

"Maude," Chris begins, cautioning me to be quiet.

"No!" I turn on him. "She's your only daughter. Say something. Do something."

One of the lawyers glances around the room like he's remembering how many people are listening. He says, "Maude. Please let us do the talking. We'll resolve every-thing in due time."

"No," I protest. "Just— "

Chris speaks up. He looks livid, face beet red, eyes flam-ing. "Leah is in Napa with her friends. I spoke with her just a little while ago. You can drop it right now."

I stare at him for a few seconds, a little shocked, and then I laugh. It's not funny, but it is. How did Leah do it? Did she send her phone with her friends and managed to convince him she was calling from it? Did she clone her phone?

Frankie looks back and forth between Morticia and her dad, then at my mom and Todd, and at last she says, "You all are the worst. The actual worst."

I smile at her.

What a ride it's been, I think, remembering rainy Hawaiian nights and LA bus rides and her skin shining blue in clubs and the smell of blood in Hollywood. What a wild fucking ride.

She smiles back.

Forty-Eight

I STAND IN FRONT OF THE DOOR. IT'S NINE O'CLOCK, AND THE SUBUR-
ban street is quiet. I smell wet grass and flowers, and the
blue-lit circle around the doorbell is a bright, poisonous
little beacon. I lift my finger, but I don't want to press it. I
don't want to go inside.

The cop, a woman in her forties who obviously has
other places she'd rather be, clears her throat on the steps
behind me.

I sigh. Fine.

I push the button.

It rings inside the house, and there's an extended silence
during which I shiver in the cool night air and wonder if I
should ring it again. I hate this feeling of insecure trepida-
tion. I never wanted to feel it again.

Footsteps, soft and light. My mother. She was on an

earlier flight; we'd all spent three days in Vegas, sorting out the charges against us and letting the FBI figure out jurisdiction. We have upcoming court cases in both LA and Hawaii. There are charges related to the passport theft, to using a false identity on an airplane, a fun one called "body concealment," and another set of charges related to the guy I'd stabbed. We're not sure what that will be, but our lawyers think I'm looking at manslaughter. I'm grateful Frankie isn't getting charged with anything in that one. The lawyers all think she'll get off pretty easy. That's a huge relief. This was my plan; it's only fair that I should suffer the bigger consequences.

The door swings open, and my mother stands in front of me, tight-lipped. I don't say anything. What is there to say? "Sorry I faked my own death and am costing the family a kajillion dollars in legal fees"? I'm not sorry. I'm grieving the loss of the life I could have lived. I'm furious at her for finding me.

She stands back to let me in. I step over the threshold into the foyer, bumping my ankle bracelet against my other foot, and look around at the familiar tiled floor and white walls. I don't know how it can feel so strange and so familiar at the same time.

The cop tells my mom, "Home, school. That's it."

My mom nods. We've been over this. Until our court dates, which have yet to be set, Frankie and I are on house arrest. Our movements are being tracked by these ankle bracelets, since we're considered a flight risk. We can expect the rest of high school to be spent like this. We're lucky; other people in our situation would be thrown straight in jail. But we're rich white girls from Orange County, so we get the ankle bracelets and the expensive lawyers.

The cop retreats, and my mom closes the front door. She doesn't look at me.

I head for the stairs and have one foot on the bottom step when she says, "Unbelievable. You are unbelievable."

I turn, surprised. She wants to fight? I thought she wanted to ignore each other.

"Why?" I ask.

"How about a little gratitude? Do you know what you've put us all through?" She almost growls the words. "Your brothers—" she begins.

I step forward and put an angry hand up. "Do you know what you've put *me* through? Shuttled back and forth between you and my dad like an old couch no one wanted in the divorce? Living out of a suitcase for the last six years?"

"You're a spoiled brat." Her face is red with anger. "There's a college account waiting for you, two beautiful houses for you to live in. We've given you *everything*."

"I'd rather have nothing!" I cry, eyes burning. "I'd rather pay my own way through college than get shipped back and forth between two parents who don't love me. The only reason there's a college account is so you can be a hundred percent sure I'll go away to school and get out of your house for good, so you can move on with your new kids and live your new life. Look at Leah, trying to actually murder Frankie so she can have the money and the husband without the inconvenience of the stepkid. How do you think that feels?"

"Stop lying. It's exhausting."

Everyone is gaslighting us. They've treated us like we're pathological liars, and Leah is skipping around acting like an innocent bystander while the whole family kisses her ass and tries to make up for the horrible teenage sociopaths.

My mother steps forward, and I can tell what she's about to say is going to hurt.

"Did you ever think maybe there's a reason I don't feel the same way toward you that I feel toward your brothers? You've always been this way. Angry. Difficult."

"Unlovable," I supply.

"You give *nothing* back." Her lips are drained of color.

I walk away, up the stairs. I don't rush. I take my time. I won't let her see me sweat. I let my hips sway from side to side, sticking my butt out a little, hoping she can really see it through the sweats.

I turn down the hall and let myself into my usual room. It's exactly the same way I left it, like a furniture store showroom.

I shut the door behind me and lean against it, and then I notice the suitcase sitting at the foot of the bed.

It's my kitty suitcase, the one I've had for years.

I sink to the carpet in front of it.

I reach out a hand and touch it. It feels like home.

I lean forward, press my forehead to the plastic, and finally, after holding it in for days, I start to cry.

Forty-Nine
Frankie

THE DRIVER STOPS OUTSIDE THE SCHOOL'S FRONT gate. I stare out the tinted window at the groups of students, heart pounding. It's my first day back.

A few kids turn to look at the town car, curious. I slump down lower in the back seat, then remember to close my legs. Stupid skirt. But when I try to cross them, the ankle bracelet scrapes against my shinbone. I grit my teeth against the sting.

"Would you like me to open the door for you?" the driver asks.

"I got it," I grumble. I feel like I'm going to be sick. I don't want to face down the stares and cries of "Frank" that are waiting for me.

"Miss?" he prompts, and I groan. I open the door and get out, self-conscious about the skirt. I hate it so much, but of course it's the only thing my grandma will give me to wear to school, and I've been cut off from any money to buy pants. It's so unfair, so violent, to force me to wear this. I want to scream.

Instead, I close the door behind me, shoulder my backpack, and keep my eyes on the ground as I walk up the path to the front steps of the school. As I pass by students, they go quiet. Great.

"Frankie," cries a girl's voice. I keep my eyes on the ground and make my feet go faster. "Frankie!" A hand grabs my arm, and I whip around, ready for a fight.

It's Gia. She's breathless, clearly having run to catch me. "Just wanted to make sure you were all right. I saw you all over the news and stuff." She looks down at my ankle bracelet.

Jaw clenched, I say, "I'm fine."

Her cheerleader friends are closing in on us. I feel like I'm in danger. I start to back away. "Wait," Gia says. "I want to apologize. We all do."

I stare at her for a long moment, but I don't see deception or meanness in her face. "For what?"

"For everything." She gestures at her legs, and for the first time I notice they're all wearing loose-fitting khakis, which are the boys' uniform pants. "You were right about the uniform. It's sexist. We're with you on this."

I look around at the kids on the lawn, and I realize that every girl here is wearing the same khaki pants as the boys. I'm the only one in a plaid skirt. I look back at Gia, speechless.

She smiles. "I have an extra few pairs in my locker. You want to change in the bathroom?"

Silently, I nod.

"Come on." She winds her arm through mine and walks me up the path. The cheerleaders walk on either side. I feel like they're my bodyguards.

They are. That's exactly what this is. Gia organized this whole thing.

My eyes prick with tears. "What about Matt?" I ask her. "Won't he—"

"Screw that guy," she replies, and I laugh. It's the first time I've done that since being separated from Maude. She shoots me a smile that reminds me of eighth grade and the Gia she used to be.

I don't know how I'm going to do this, build my life back up without Maude. How many days were we on the road together—ten? Fourteen? How can she have changed my life so much in just a couple of weeks?

And now Maude and I will be separated for years. I can't imagine we'll end up in the same prison or juvie. With her possibly facing murder charges, she could be locked up for decades.

The grief of it is too heavy. But I'm in the hallway now. Gia is chattering happily as she gets the khakis out of her locker, and I'm grateful for this small moment, and any other moments of freedom I have left.

———————

The town car drops me off at my grandma's, and I wait on the front step for a while. I don't want to go inside.

I can't stand here forever.

On the other hand, maybe I can.

I'm stalling.

The door swings open, and my dad looks down at me. "What are you doing? They see you on the security camera."

I step over the threshold. "Sorry," I mumble. We stand there for a minute, both of us with our hands in our pockets. It's the first time we've been alone since I came back; I've been relocated to Grandma's house, and Dad has been keeping his distance.

"Your grandmother wants us to have dinner together," he says, thankfully ending the awkward silence.

"Oh." I clear my throat. "Does she want to discuss anything in particular?"

He shrugs. With his hands buried in his pockets like that, he looks like a teenager.

"Are you still with Leah?" The question bursts out of me against my will. I've been avoiding him because I'm afraid I know the answer.

Sure enough, he frowns. "Of course I'm with Leah. What you're doing is killing her."

Anger bubbles up inside me. "What I'm doing?"

"Using her as your scapegoat. Spreading rumors about her. Trying to get her in legal trouble. I don't know who you are anymore. I thought you welcomed her into our house, into our lives."

"I did," I retort fiercely. "I welcomed her every step of the way. I defended her."

He shakes his head. He looks disgusted, like I've done something shameful.

The tapping of heels sounds around the corner, and Leah appears. She's wearing a white dress—the heavy-handed symbolism is suffocating. She smiles at me meekly, like she's hoping I'll be nice to her. "Hi, Frankie. How are you?"

I meet her eyes, looking for the coldness I saw in the motel. My heart is pounding, memories of the gun pressed to my chest flooding my head. "Did you tell my dad what you did yet?" I ask. "Do you feel bad at all that the Jet Ski fire could have killed an innocent kid?"

She looks at my dad as though for help, and he draws her to him, wrapping an arm around her waist. "Frankie, that's enough," he says, authoritative.

This is goodbye, I realize. No matter what happens after this, he and I will never be the same. Gone are our irresponsible ditch days of eating In-N-Out on the beach. We won't come back from this.

I've never missed anyone as much as I miss Maude right now.

Fifty

THE BELL RINGS. I'VE BEEN READY FOR FIFTEEN MINUTES, BUT AS the kids around me erupt into talking, I'm frozen solid.

Is it nerves?

I can't take my eyes off the clock. Three oh two. They'll be waiting for me.

The class is emptying, and I feel the teacher's eyes on me. It's a familiar feeling after two weeks back—not a pleasant one.

I shoulder my backpack and stand. The ankle bracelet is a constant annoyance, clunky and awkward. I leave the classroom and turn left down the hallway.

Lucas is right there, talking to a few of his friends. I stop just short of bumping into him. We lock eyes. I walk faster, hoping he'll leave me alone.

"Maude, wait," he says, stepping toward me. Dammit.

"I have an appointment," I tell him, not slowing.

He keeps up with me, gesturing in frustration. "What the hell? Why are you treating me like a complete stranger? Every time I try to talk, you, like, disappear."

I stop walking. He's right.

I don't have to hide anymore. My mess is on the table for everyone to see.

I turn toward him. He's a few inches taller than I am, his face drawn with hurt. "I was so worried about you," he says. "I thought you were dead. And you were faking it? You went around killing people? Who are you? How could you do all this?"

I consider my response for a long moment. "I'm so sorry you were worried. But you're right. I am a stranger. You really don't know me."

He frowns. "What's that supposed to mean?"

I sigh, impatient. "Lucas, I'm gay. I'm a lesbian. Okay? I was dating you because I was afraid of people knowing."

His big brown eyes widen, and he takes a few seconds to process this. "But . . . what does this have to do with you, like, faking your own death or whatever?"

I laugh. "You know what, I'm not sure. But I thought I owed you the truth. You're a nice guy. Go find a nice girl."

I continue down the hall, and I feel lighter. I realize all the deception and energy it took to be someone else was a huge weight that's now been lifted. Whatever happens next, I guess I have that.

The thought makes me angry. Furious. So I'm settling

for this life I hate, but at least I've learned to be my authentic self? What kind of self-help seminar have I become?

I leave the building and turn left to cross the courtyard. Deanna is standing there with her group of friends. As always, she casts me a furtive glance, and I remember our secret make-out session at camp. I remember all the times I was afraid to meet her eyes afterward, afraid she'd out me, afraid, afraid, afraid. Not once did I consider that I might be hurting *her* feelings. I remember Frankie telling me, "*You left me in bed, Maude.*" I never considered that someone I wanted might want me back, and that I might be rejecting them in my moments of self-hatred.

My steps slow, and I turn toward Deanna. She's back to talking with her friends, but they notice me and nod in my direction. When Deanna looks at me, I smile. "Hey," I say.

She looks confused. "Hey . . . ?"

"How are you? How's life?"

"It's . . . good?"

"Good." I give her a last smile and walk away. I can feel the pressure of their eyes on my back, but I'm past caring.

One of Morticia's drivers is waiting for me in a town car. I get in and buckle up. Through the tinted window I watch the even, perfect streets pass by on the way to the law offices in Newport Beach, my stomach in knots. I'm going to see Frankie for the first time in two weeks, since we were caught in Vegas.

Rather than drop me off in front of the office building, the driver parks in the underground lot and personally escorts me through the marble lobby and up to the seventh floor. A receptionist leads us down a hallway to a large conference room, where a number of people are in conversation. This is a strategic planning session where the lawyers are going to go through our account of what happened in Hawaii, which is the only reason Frankie and I are being allowed in the same room. They need our stories to match, I guess.

My heart sinks when I walk in. She's not here.

I don't recognize anyone except the lawyers. Amanda Nazaryan, the lawyer I've been working with the most, gestures that I should come sit beside her.

Morticia walks in, Frankie trailing behind her. She's wearing her school uniform—khaki pants and a baggy polo shirt with the school logo embroidered on the chest. Her hair has grown a little longer, and she's gelled it to the side in a way that looks really cute. I watch her as she sits next to her grandma. I try to make eye contact, but Morticia is between us, blocking my view of Frankie's face.

"Let's go ahead and get started," the man at the head of the table says. He's the lawyer boss, the senior partner or whatever, the one who's in charge of this team trying to keep Frankie and me out of jail. "We're here today to prepare for your first hearing. There will be a few virtual sessions before we go to Hawaii, so let's prep for them one at a time but keep our long-term strategy in mind."

Frankie leans forward, and I lock eyes with her. I'm

suddenly vulnerable, worried she's mad at me, wondering if she regrets what we did.

She must see it in my face, because she tilts her head to the side and gives me a half-smile. It's such a Frankie expression, a little sad, a little careless. Everywhere she goes, she seems to take the temperature down ten degrees. I feel tears well up in my eyes. I miss her so much. I blink hard, willing them not to spill over.

She pushes her chair back and stands up. Everyone pauses and looks at her. "Keep talking, ignore me," she says. They return to their discussion; clearly she's going to the bathroom or something.

She walks around the table, but instead of heading for the door to the restrooms, she approaches my seat. She swivels my chair so I'm facing her, and she drops to a knee in front of me. I'm aware that the room has gone silent again.

"You okay?" she asks, taking my hands in hers, like we're alone and not surrounded by dissenting adults.

I look down at our hands. Hers are warm, and I feel the tears welling up again. When did I become so soft? Crying in front of Morticia? Who *am* I?

"I miss you," I whisper.

She pulls me into a hug, and I wrap my arms around her neck. We sit like that for a minute, and then Amanda says, "Excuse me, girls? We'd like to proceed."

"Get them off each other," Morticia demands.

I give Frankie a last squeeze, and she sits back on her

heels. I smile down at her and fix her hair. "Morticia's mad," I tell her.

"She is."

I lean down and kiss her lips, nothing risqué, just a sweet, soft kiss. I'm so full of happiness that she doesn't regret me, that I can't care about our audience. I'm just so grateful to have this one moment.

"Oh, for God's sake," Morticia says. "Someone stop this."

"We can't physically—" Amanda begins to protest.

I turn my chair around to look at Morticia. She's half-standing, beet red with rage. "Did you want to say something?" I ask.

"This is your fault," she tells me. "Francesca never would have done any of this without you." She gestures between us. I'm flattered. She thinks I'm an evil temptress.

I'm contemplating the right response when Frankie stands and puts a hand on my shoulder. "Grandma, everyone has known I was gay since preschool. Maude didn't do anything except try to save me from Leah." To the lawyers, Frankie says, "Leah actually did try to kill me. Four separate times. For my trust fund. Are you working on *that* case?"

No one answers her. I can see Amanda looking sideways at her colleagues, all unsure what they're supposed to say.

"I didn't think so." She walks back around the table. She's so different than she was when we first started on this journey. She's holding her back straight and has her chin up. She returns to her chair and says, "Since you won't help with the real crimes, let's at least try to keep Maude and me out of jail." She smiles at me across the table, and in this moment, I feel all the fight returning to my body. My hands clench in my lap and my brain whirs to life, my planning instincts rising from the dead.

I've been defeated since I returned, but no more. There's no way in hell I'm going to let these people have the last word.

I'm not done yet.

Fifty-One
Frankie

MY GRANDMA IS EATING BREAKFAST IN THE DESIG-
nated breakfast nook, which is not to be confused with the
dining room. A maid is bringing her a refill of coffee, and
she has half a grapefruit and a piece of toast in front of her.
This is the first time she's been here when I've come down
for breakfast; usually, she eats at six thirty and is already
at work by the time I make it downstairs.

She looks up from her newspaper, catching me in the act
of hovering awkwardly in the doorway. "Francesca. Good
morning. Sit down and eat." Her tone is formal. I've been
emotionally excommunicated.

"Morning," I reply, sliding into a chair. We haven't spoken since two weeks ago at the law offices. I'd ridden home

in the back seat of a town car while she'd gone back to her office and worked late. I got the feeling she was so disgusted she couldn't even be in the same room with me.

The maid brings me a cup of hot chocolate and a plate of eggs and toast. I stare down at it, not hungry.

"Your eggs are going to get cold," Grandma says.

I lift my chin and meet her eyes. I consider my words for a few minutes, and then I say, "I always knew it would be like this. There's a reason I never told you."

She takes off her reading glasses and sets her newspaper down. Leaning forward, she says, "Francesca, what you do in your private time is your business. I'll never involve myself in that. But the way you present to the world—that *is* my business. Do you understand?"

"So, as long as I look and act straight, you're fine with me?"

She makes a face. "I want you to look and act like the person you are. You're my oldest grandchild." She gestures to the house around us. "This is all going to be yours to manage. Do you think your cousins, the twin brats, will grow up to be shrewd businessmen? Come on, Frankie. You've met their mother."

I rest my elbows on the table and consider my words carefully. "Leah has been trying to kill me for months, and you think I'm lying about it. If you think I'd make something like that up, why would you even consider giving me the keys to the castle?"

"You're young and confused. I don't think you're lying; I think you're mistaken. You've had bad influences." Maude.

I keep my voice level. "Leah pointed a gun in my face and tried to kill me. How could I be mistaken about that? I'm either lying or I'm telling the truth."

"She was in Napa. I had a private investigator look into it thoroughly."

I look up at the clean white ceiling for a moment, and then I return my eyes to my grandma. "I want you to disinherit me."

"Excuse me?"

"I appreciate your help with the legal fees, the lawyers. I can't thank you enough for that. But I don't want to be the one who inherits all this. It was never going to be me. Give my trust fund to someone else, someone who wants it."

There's a moment of shocked silence. "Francesca—"

"No." I make a slashing motion with my hand. "Maude was right to try and escape this family. This is toxic. And once I'm written out, Leah won't come after me. Give it to my dad, to Todd. Give it to the twins. Hell, give it to Maude. She'll do something great with it. She's smarter than any of your actual blood relatives." Grandma makes a snorting noise in the back of her throat. "I don't want it," I tell her, being as direct and clear as I can.

She's opening her mouth to speak when footsteps ring out on the marble floors around the corner. They're heavy and clunky, a man's. The swinging door opens, and Todd bursts through, face red, shirt untucked. "Mom, here you are."

She rises, alarmed. "Todd, what is it?"

"It's Maude." He glances down at me.

Now I'm alarmed. I can't stand up, though, like my grandma, who's walking around the table toward him. I'm stuck in my chair, terrified. I don't think Maude would ever hurt herself, but suddenly I can't help but think—

"She's gone," Todd says to Grandma, who's got her hand on his arm and is looking at him with great intensity.

"Gone?" she repeats. "What do you mean, gone?"

"Gone! Like, gone!" He looks at me. "You know, don't you? You know!"

I hold my hands up in protest. "I have no idea what you're talking about. What do you mean, she's gone?"

Like we're idiots, he says, "She—is—gone."

"Like, dead?" I ask.

"Not dead! Gone! She's not in her room, the house, nowhere."

Grandma says, "Well, she has the ankle bracelet. Did you call the attorneys? The police can trace her."

He's already shaking his head. "Something's wrong with the ankle bracelet. I already called, and they have her location as our house. She either hid it somewhere in the house, or she did something to it. But we've searched everywhere and she's not there."

I think I'm beginning to understand. My heart is pounding, my head light. Is it possible?

His phone rings in his pocket, and he fumbles it out. "Hello?" He listens, eyes wide, and then his face darkens, wrinkles creeping in between his eyebrows.

"Who is it?" my grandma asks.

"It's Anne." Maude's mom. "It seems like…" He pauses. "Hang on, honey." To Grandma, he says, "It looks like we're missing some money."

"As in, cash?"

"No, Mom, like major money out of the bank." He pauses, clearly listening to Maude's mom. Then to my grandma he says, "One of the accounts has been cleaned out."

"How much?" I ask, finally rising out of my chair.

"A hundred and fifty thousand."

I sit back down with a plop.

Oh my god.

My grandma says, "You called the attorneys already? Are they notifying the police?"

As he nods confirmation, the doorbell rings. Seconds later, three uniformed cops and a detective are in the room with us, and Grandma is yelling at them to wait for the lawyer to be present before they ask me anything. They protest in loud voices, demanding that I answer them. Do I know where Maude is? Do I have any information?

I stare out the window at the rose garden, ignoring the commotion.

She did it.

She got out of her ankle bracelet.

She's gone.

I'm so proud of her I think my heart is going to explode.

She won't make any mistakes this time. She's probably halfway to London already.

I know in every inch of my body that I will never meet another girl like Maude. Never in my life.

Fifty-Two
Frankie

"FRANK," THE GUY BEHIND ME WHISPERS AS MR. HENderson drones on about some war or other, flipping through a PowerPoint. "Fraaaank."

I'm a wall. I'm a rock.

My refusal to engage just makes him giggle in wispy, hysterical little breaths. "Frannnnk," he tries again.

I feel someone watching me and glance to my right. I catch Gia with her eyes on me. She makes a fist and punches it into her other hand, and I smile. We used to make that gesture in middle school. It means, "You want me to fight him?" I shake my head and she shrugs as if to say she will fight him if I change my mind.

The wall clock's minute hand jumps forward. Three minutes left of class. I grab my water bottle and take a sip.

"Fraaaaaaank," the guy whispers again.

I can't believe I'm trapped here while Maude is out in the world. Las Vegas was a month ago now. I try not to think about it; it makes me too sad, picturing her liberated while I'm stuck waiting for the school year to end so I can wait for the summer to end so I can wait for senior year to end, and then what? Where will I go? London was Maude's dream, not mine. When I let myself think about her, I picture her there, getting on the Tube toward the British Museum. Sometimes I marathon shows set in London so I can imagine her wrapped up in a jacket, strolling through a light rain or sunning herself on the grass in Regent's Park. That's what I hope her life is like.

I've never had any dreams for myself, have I? It's always been a matter of survival; my life was laid out for me by my grandmother. Until Maude, it never occurred to me that I could walk away. Grandma is like a black hole; her gravity is too strong.

The bell rings. My stuff is already packed—I wasn't taking notes—and I stand up first. I turn to leave through the back door of the classroom, and the guy behind me gives me a wide, excited grin. "Frank!"

In a swift, fluid motion, I uncap my water and dump it onto his crotch. He gasps, shocked. The people around us freeze.

I cap the water, smile at him and his soaked pants, and head for the door. Behind me, I hear Gia laugh.

"Francesca!" calls Mr. Henderson, but I'm already in the hallway, navigating the after-school chaos.

I smile to myself as I walk. Maude would be proud.

I exit the main school building; Grandma's driver always picks me up out front. I spot his town car down the street in the line of cars waiting. The lawn is already scattered with kids standing in clusters, laughing and talking. A few of them spot me and point, turning to say things to their friends. This is my life now: everyone watching all the freaking time.

Ignoring them, I walk across the grass toward the sidewalk, and then I notice a car parked right in front of the school, in the loading zone. A girl is standing by it, leaning against the passenger's door, waiting.

My steps slow.

She has chin-length brown hair and is wearing a black T-shirt and jeans. Her face is partly covered by big sunglasses, but I'd know her anywhere.

She gives me a little wave.

It's Maude.

My steps falter. I stop.

We face each other across fifty feet of grass. My heart isn't beating right. I'm suddenly trembling.

And then I'm walking fast, almost running, closing the distance between us. She's right in front of me, real, in the flesh. She laughs—I must look like I'm seeing a ghost. "Hi," she says, smug and playful.

I throw my arms around her waist and squeeze, almost lifting her off the ground. She's real, warm, soft. My backpack drops, and we're kissing, my hands tangled in her hair.

I pull back and examine her. She's so glowy and happy, like a new version of herself. "I thought you'd be in London by now. How did you get out of your ankle bracelet?"

She grins. "I had to duplicate the signal and then disable it. I had to buy a laptop to do it. I got one on Amazon by using my mom's wireless-enabled refrigerator."

I blink at her briefly and then say, "And you stole a bunch of money?"

She nods, eyes sparkling. "I bought a bunch of unmarked gemstones I can sell in Europe. Found a guy in the Downtown LA jewelry district who wanted a nice cash deal. But don't feel bad for my mom and Todd; I took my own college fund. Nothing more."

Suddenly, I remember where we are. I grip her elbow, protective and paranoid. Kids all over the lawn are watching us. The town car is inching closer to the school as the line of cars advances.

"You shouldn't have come, though. You're going to get caught." But I know why she's here. She didn't feel right leaving without saying goodbye.

God, it hurts. It's pain in my chest.

She pushes her sunglasses up onto her head. I love her brown eyes. She starts to answer, and the pain in my chest spreads to the rest of my torso.

"Don't say it," I tell her. I draw her into another hug. "I'm going to miss you so, so much." I smooth her hair after messing it up. "But I'm happy for you. Don't feel guilty. You can go."

She's staring at me like she's memorizing my face. She traces a hand down my cheek, thumb on my upper lip. I understand. I'm memorizing her, too.

"Can I ask you something?" she says. "You don't have to say yes. Or no. Just answer truthfully. Okay?"

I nod.

"Do you want to come with me?"

I freeze, blood cold. "I—"

"It's okay to say no. You're not going to end up in jail. You're not the one who stabbed that guy. You have your whole life ahead of you. I just need to hear you say it."

I feel tears well up, and I push them aside with shaky, impatient fingertips. "Maude, I—" I choke on the words. "You always wished I hadn't come along. You always wanted to go alone. So no. I want you to be free."

She's shaking her head halfway through what I'm saying. "You're not understanding me. I'm here because I don't want to go without you. I want you to come with me. I'm asking if *you* want to."

I can't breathe. How can I answer if I can't breathe? I shake my head, then nod, then shake my head again. "I want to come," I manage at last.

"You do?" She looks uncertain. "Are you sure?"

I kiss her. She's real. She's here. "Let's go."

She opens the passenger's side door for me. "Then let's get going."

I throw my backpack into the back seat, next to a suitcase with cartoon kitties printed on it that I recognize from her luggage in Hawaii. "What car is this?"

"I stole it."

"Oh." I laugh.

"Not to worry, I switched the license plates for ones no one will be looking for. And the owner will get it back in a few days."

"Of course." I get inside and she shuts the door behind me. A horrible realization hits me. I look down at my feet. "But wait. I have my ankle bracelet."

"I'll get you out of that the old-fashioned way. I have bolt cutters in the back. The alarm will go off, but we'll be gone by the time they respond to it."

My mind is spinning. "How will we get out of the country without our passports?"

"Oh, we have them. They're safe; they're in Vegas. Don't worry. I've thought of everything."

She pulls away from the curb and into traffic. Across the street, the town car waits for a Frankie who will never come.

Maude turns left onto the wide, six-lane street, and she hits the gas. We shoot forward, into the bright, sunny afternoon, into the future.

Fifty-Three

THE LONDON UNDERGROUND IS MAGICAL. I'M STILL NOT USED TO IT. I sit here with a newspaper that someone discarded, reading the sensationalized account of a politician's affair, and I sneak peeks at my fellow passengers. It's ten o'clock at night, so the train isn't as packed as it would have been a few hours ago, but it's half full of people dressed for a night out. I smile a little and force my eyes back onto the newspaper.

"London Victoria Station," the calm announcer voice says over the loudspeaker. The train shudders and squeaks, slowing as it approaches. I stand, leaving the newspaper for someone else, and make my way toward the doors as the train comes to a final halt.

The doors slide open, letting me out onto the crowded platform. It's warm here by the tracks, and I love how British people queue up so nicely for everything; they don't push or shove, but work together off some silent agreement that I'm starting to get the hang of. Of course, there are tourists lugging giant suitcases and messing up the whole flow, eliciting a wave of silent British disapproval.

Past all this, up into a tunnel and onto an escalator-sidewalk, I keep my steps quick. My whole body feels like it's smiling. My chest is full of light. Here, I'm both Sherlock Holmes and Moriarty, both the hero and the villain.

The tunnel leads to another escalator, and at last I'm out on the main floor, a magnificent, cavernous place built in the 1800s. This is a perfect example of what I love about London: an old, ornate building filled with bright, ultra-modern shops and restaurants. They border the perimeter of the massive structure, and the floor has colorful lines all over it, directing you to various places so you don't get lost. Through the glass ceiling, a purple twilight sky shines pale light down into the station; in the summer, it doesn't get dark until eleven o'clock. Magical.

I find Frankie on our usual bench, drinking tea out of a paper cup and reading a book they've been working their way through. I watch them for a minute, enjoying the voyeurism of pretending they're a stranger. Their hair is very short and a little longer on top, parted on the side and combed neatly into place. They're coming from work, so they're wearing black pants and a white T-shirt with black Converse. One foot is crossed over their knee, and they're slouched back on the bench, one arm slung casually across the back of it, occasionally bringing the cup to their lips while the other hand holds the book.

I could stand here and watch them all day. I remember back to the Frankie I knew in California, to their defensive slouch and blank-faced apathy, and it makes me feel all misty and emotional looking at them here, so confident and relaxed.

I shake it off. God, I've gotten soft.

I weave through the people to Frankie and drop onto the bench beside them. They look up from the book and smile at me. "Hey."

I lean in and kiss their cheek. They smell like French fries. Excuse me, chips.

"Hello, darling. How was work?" My accent has gotten pretty good, if I do say so myself.

They shrug, closing their book and stretching. "Fine. Made a lot of sandwiches." They work in a commuter sandwich shop in Central London. I work in a pizza restaurant a little farther north. "So what's this mysterious thing you wanted to show me?"

I grin. I'm so excited. "It's kind of a surprise."

They examine me. "You're really, really proud of whatever this is."

I'm all but bouncing on the bench. "I really am."

They laugh. "Go ahead then. Tell me."

I get my phone out of my purse and scoot closer. Now I'm nervous. "I hope you're not mad."

"I thought this was a good surprise?"

"Yeah, but..." I can't quite figure out what to say next. They wait.

I unlock my phone and navigate around, finally coming up with what I wanted to show them. I hesitate, suddenly realizing this might make them want to go back home to Orange County. Maybe I've made a huge mistake.

"Maude?" Frankie prompts, clearly trying to understand the expressions flying across my face.

"Sorry. I'm just... Okay, fine." I turn my phone toward them. It's a news story. The headline reads: "Woman Charged for Attempted Murder in Case of Missing Orange County Teenager." Below the headline is a photo of Leah being walked, handcuffed, out of a restaurant. Her face is turned toward the camera. She looks shocked.

Frankie skims the article. "I don't understand."

"I've been working on a little project."

They look up from the phone. "What project?"

"When Leah fooled everyone into thinking she was in Napa, I got curious. How did she do it?"

They nod slowly. "Okay."

"She clearly planned everything out. She's smart. What if she sent her phone off to Napa, but she was actually answering texts and calls and stuff from Vegas? Remotely accessing her phone, get it?"

"I guess."

"That gave me the idea to clone her phone and try to find something that might implicate her. I was thinking, she had to have gotten those drugs you overdosed on from somewhere. She needed money to pay off that guy in Vegas. And what about how she sabotaged your car? There had to be some evidence somewhere in her search or accounts history, in her bank statements, something."

"But that would all be password-protected," they protest.

"Yeah, it's taken me, like, a month. It's been a huge pain in the ass."

They raise their eyebrows. "Remind me never to piss you off."

I nod gravely. "If you cheat on me, it will not go well for you."

"Noted."

"So...I found stuff. Large withdrawals from her personal bank accounts, the app that she used to shadow her own phone, all kinds of things. And I sent them to your grandma using a VPN."

They stare at me with huge eyes. "You didn't."

"And to the police. From an anonymous email," I add hastily. "It's completely untraceable."

"Oh my god," they breathe.

"I wasn't sure if it would do any good, but I had to at least try. I couldn't let her just skip around after nearly killing you."

"Maude," they say, but then they don't say anything else. They just stare at the phone, reading the article.

"She even searched some things without using Private mode about a year ago. Rookie move."

"What kinds of things?"

"About sabotaging brakes."

They sit there for a few seconds, eyes on the middle distance, and then hand me the phone back. "My family made me feel so..." They swallow. "Worthless."

"I know." I shove the phone into my purse and lean into their warm side. They wrap their arm around my shoulder, and we sit there, watching the people come and go. Old and young, couples and colleagues, individuals rushing here and there, big families from all over the world. I swallow. It's not easy for me to say the direct truth, but Frankie deserves it. "I want you to know how much I love you," I say. "I will literally do anything for you."

They press their face to my cheek and speak quietly into the side of my neck. "I feel like you didn't just give me my own life back. You gave me the whole world."

I remember driving down a dark country road in Hawaii, fleeing the scene of a crime, feeling like I was alive for the first time. I was wrong. I wasn't alive then. I thought I was running toward Elizabeth, but I was just escaping Maude.

Not anymore. I'm Elizabeth, I'm Maude, and it's Friday night in London.

I stow my phone in my purse and stand up. "Come on. Let's go get lost."

They shove their book in their backpack and sling it over one shoulder. Standing, they grin at me. We're eye to eye.

"We did it," they say.

"We did."

They take my hand, and we move through the busy, noisy station out into the cool night with the periwinkle sky. "You want to head that way?" Frankie asks, nodding to the right. "I've been wanting to walk across the Chelsea Bridge."

"Sure." We turn our steps south and join the bustling crowds of pedestrians. No one looks at us twice. We all have our own places to go.

Acknowledgments

I wrote this book in 2020. What a year to make art. It was fascinating, actually, examining what this (gestures at world) did to my creative process. I found it affected the type of art I wanted to make, and I shelved a rather claustrophobic project in favor of this more adventurous premise. I had always wanted to write an on-the-road book; since childhood, I've been fascinated with stories where the main character must undertake some arduous journey. So, while the world burned around me and I hid inside my house, I wrote about two girls abandoning their lives in favor of the great unknown.

Maude was a character I'd considered for years. I've always imagined what would happen if one of these brilliant, high-achieving high school girls turned her brain to crime; she'd be an uncatchable criminal of the first degree. I'd like to thank all the girls who inspired Maude, every girl who decides she's tired of playing nice with a world that doesn't play nice with her.

I would not have been able to write this book without

my core writer friendships, those brainstorming partners, creative powerhouses, and ride-or-die encouragers who help me when I get to rough patches in the road. Layne Fargo, my work wife; Halley Sutton, my Angeleno crime sister; Mike Chen and Diana Urban, my wonderful sounding boards; Ray Stoeve, whose notes and thoughts have proved absolutely invaluable to this project; Dea Poirier, who always helps when I need a new way to kill someone; Aiden Thomas; Kit Rosewater; Wanda Morris; Andrea Hannah; and all the others I wish I had space to list here.

This book wouldn't exist without the dual commitment of Lauren Spieller, superagent, and Jessica Anderson, editor extraordinaire. I cannot overstate how much I have enjoyed working with these incredibly gifted professionals. I'm eternally grateful for all the exhaustive work they have done to move these stories toward the vision we share for them. Thank you to the Little, Brown Books for Young Readers team for welcoming my dark little book to your inimitable roster.

Of course, I must thank my family members for tolerating me during yet another cycle of drafting/revising/publishing/agonizing. I thank you for your continued tolerance, even if it's rooted in fear after having read so many of my books, and I love you more than I can say.

Wendy Heard

WENDY HEARD

is the author of the acclaimed young adult novel *She's Too Pretty to Burn*, which *Kirkus Reviews* praised as "a wild and satisfying romp" in a starred review, as well as two adult thrillers: *The Kill Club* and *Hunting Annabelle*. Wendy lives in Los Angeles, California, and she invites you to visit her online at wendyheard.com.